A Texas Hill Country Christmas

William W. Johnstone
with J. A. Johnstone

THORNDIKE PRESS

A part of Gale, Cengage Learning

GALE
CENGAGE Learning·

Farmington Hills, Mich • San Francisco • New York • Waterville, Maine
Meriden, Conn • Mason, Ohio • Chicago

GALE
CENGAGE Learning®

Copyright © 2015 by J. A. Johnstone.
WWJ steer head logo is a Reg. U.S. Pat. & TM Off.
Thorndike Press, a part of Gale, Cengage Learning.

Thorndike Press® Large Print Western.
The text of this Large Print edition is unabridged.
Other aspects of the book may vary from the original edition.
Set in 16 pt. Plantin.
Library of Congress Cataloging-in-Publication Data

LIBRARY OF CONGRESS CATALOGING-IN-PUBLICATION DATA

Names: Johnstone, William W. | Johnstone, J. A.
Title: A Texas Hill country Christmas / William W. Johnstone with J. A. Johnstone.
Description: Large print edition. | Waterville, Maine : Thorndike Press Large Print, 2016. | ?2015 | Series: Thorndike Press large print western
Identifiers: LCCN 2015036668| ISBN 9781410482044 (hardback) | ISBN 1410482049 (hardcover)
Subjects: LCSH: Large type books. | Christmas stories. | BISAC: FICTION / Action & Adventure. | GSAFD: Western stories.
Classification: LCC PS3560.O415 T48 2016 | DDC 813/.54—dc23
LC record available at http://lccn.loc.gov/2015036668

Published in 2015 by arrangement with Pinnacle Books, an imprint of Kensington Publishing Corp.

Printed in the United States of America
1 2 3 4 5 6 7 19 18 17 16 15

A Texas Hill Country Christmas

PROLOGUE

Fredericksburg, Texas, Christmas Eve, 1975
It was a rare day for this part of Texas. Snow covered the Hill Country. Only a couple of inches, true, but it was enough to lay a white mantle over the rugged countryside. The snow and the thick growth of evergreens made it look more like a picturesque scene from New England or some old Currier & Ives print than central Texas. Having a white Christmas in these parts wasn't unheard of, but it *was* uncommon.

Helen Sievers thought it was beautiful as she stood at the picture window in the living room of the rambling ranch house and looked out. In the distance she saw the dark, looming, humped shape of Enchanted Rock. A lot of people thought of it as gloomy and forbidding but not Helen.

She had been born in Fredericksburg seventy years earlier and raised on various ranches in the area, so to her Enchanted

Rock was just part of her home. She remembered climbing to the top of it many, many times over the years. To a wild tomboy like her, who could rope and ride as well as any of the boys she grew up with, exploring it had been as natural as breathing.

The first time she had stood atop Enchanted Rock and looked around at the magnificent scenery, her last name had been Jensen. She had been born a Jensen and would always be one, no matter how much she had loved her late husband Gerald.

Christmas carols played softly on the radio in the big mahogany home entertainment center that sat on one side of the living room. The sound was nice, especially blended as it was with the voices of Helen's children and grandchildren, laughing and talking as they always did at these family get-togethers. Luckily, the snow hadn't been bad enough to make travel dangerous, so the kids had been able to come in from Austin, Brownwood, Fort Worth, and Tyler. Once again the ranch house was full, and Helen liked it that way.

She turned away from the window as the sunlight faded outside. It got dark early this time of year.

Helen's daughter-in-law Jenny came in from the kitchen, wiping her hands on the apron she wore, and said, "Dinner will be ready soon, Mom."

Helen was glad Jenny called her that. But then, most folks tended to call her Mom, whether she was related to them or not. That was just the sort of woman she was. She smiled and said, "I wouldn't have minded helping, you know."

"Oh, I know that," Jenny said with a wave of her hand. "But you deserve to take one day off from taking care of everybody, don't you? One day a year?"

"I suppose so. I was raised to work, though." That was true of just about everyone in her generation.

"You've worked plenty and you will again. Why don't you sit down and take it easy?"

Helen managed not to say, "Hmmph." Taking it easy *didn't* come natural to her.

But as she sat down in her recliner, six of her grandchildren came running into the living room. Ranging in age from seven to twelve, they were a veritable stampede. Helen motioned for them to slow down and then sit down, and they settled cross-legged on the carpeted floor in a semicircle around her.

"Tell us a story," one of the girls said.

"About the old days," one of the boys added.

"You mean when I was a little girl?" Helen asked with a smile.

The boy shook his head and said, "No, before that. The old, *old* days. When there were still gunfighters and outlaws and Indians in Texas."

"There are still Indians in Texas," Helen pointed out. "Many of them. And they're fine people."

"What about gunfighters and outlaws?" another girl asked. "Are they still around, too?"

"I suppose there will always be outlaws," Helen said. "Not so many gunfighters, though. Not like Smoke Jensen."

"Was he our grandfather?" the boy asked.

"No, he was my great-grand-uncle . . . I think. I get mixed up about those things. Smoke Jensen's brother Luke was my great-grandfather. That would make Smoke your . . . great-great-grand-uncle?"

"But he was a gunfighter, right?"

Helen nodded and said, "One of the most famous gunfighters who ever lived. His brother Luke was good with a gun, too, and their adopted brother Matt was very fast. They were men to stand aside from in those days, let me tell you. Like your great-grandfather Ace."

"He was named after a card?"

"Well, not really. His real name was William. Ace was just his nickname. His twin brother was named Benjamin, but everyone knew him as Chance. Those were the names they were called by the man who raised them, and they used those names all their lives."

"I like Ace and Chance," another of the girls said. "Did they look just alike, since they were twins?"

"Did they dress alike?" the first girl asked.

Helen laughed and shook her head.

"Oh, my, no. They were what's called fraternal twins, not identical, so it was easy to tell them apart even though they resembled each other, of course. And they dressed very differently, judging by the pictures I've seen. Chance liked to be well-dressed, usually in a suit, while Ace looked more like a cowboy."

"Our great-grandfather was a cowboy?" the oldest boy asked.

"Sometimes. Sometimes he did other things. He drove a stagecoach, worked for the railroad, even wore a lawman's badge a few times."

"What did Chance do?"

Helen hesitated. Chance Jensen was a gambler, not really a shady character but definitely someone who spent a lot of his

11

time in, well, disreputable places like saloons. That probably wasn't the best thing to tell a bunch of impressionable children.

"He did a lot of different things, too," she answered, being deliberately vague. To keep the youngsters from pressing the issue, she went on, "You know, Ace and Chance traveled all over the West, but I remember hearing about one Christmas when they were right here in this neck of the woods. They were spending some time in Austin."

The capital city of Texas was about eighty miles from Fredericksburg.

"Was it snowing that Christmas?"

Helen thought back on the story as she had heard it. She shook her head and said, "No, but it was raining a lot that year. In fact, that was probably the rainiest Christmas season this part of the country has ever seen . . ."

CHAPTER ONE

Austin

Ace Jensen looked out through the saloon window at the steady drizzle falling from the gray sky and wondered what had gone wrong with the plan. He and his brother Chance had drifted down here to Texas to spend the winter, thinking that it would be warmer, the weather more pleasant, than in Wyoming or Colorado.

Maybe it wasn't as cold here as it would have been up north — although the dank air was pretty chilly — but nobody in his right mind could call this climate pleasant.

It had been raining off and on for days as Ace and Chance rode across Texas. The roads were muddy, and they had to be careful not to let their horses get bogged down. The legs of Ace's big chestnut and Chance's cream-colored gelding were covered with mud and the horses looked downright bedraggled.

The same could have been said of Ace and Chance when they reached Austin. Despite their slickers and hats, they were soaked to the bone. They had resembled nothing so much as a pair of wet rats, Ace figured.

At least their situation had improved somewhat since they'd ridden into town. The horses were in a nice warm livery stable getting cleaned up by a friendly hostler who had introduced himself as Enrique. Ace and Chance had used some of their dwindling poke to rent themselves a hotel room and have a tub of hot water brought up. They had flipped a silver dollar to see who got to soak away the chill first. Chance won, as he usually did when it was anything involving pure luck.

Unless his brother had slickered him somehow, Ace had thought at the time. Chance was, to put it mildly, crafty.

But they had both gotten washed up, dressed in dry clothes, and during a spell when the rain stopped had walked across Congress Avenue to the saloon, where Chance hoped to find a game and maybe improve their finances.

Ace had contented himself with nursing a beer and snacking on the crackers and chunks of ham and cheese sitting out on the bar on a silver tray. When the bartender

14

started glaring at him, he ordered a refill and stopped eating, picking up the mug instead and wandering over to one of the saloon's front windows to look out at the broad avenue and the steady *drip-drip-drip* from the heavens.

When the rain had stopped earlier, Ace had hoped that meant it was over for a while. Obviously, he'd been wrong.

"Full house, gentlemen," Chance said from the table where he was playing poker. "I believe that means the pot is mine."

Ace looked over his shoulder. He had warned his brother in the past about gloating too much when he won. That got on the other players' nerves, and an annoyed card player was liable to turn into an angry card player. From there it was just one step to accusations of cheating, shouted curses, and hands reaching for guns.

Chance wasn't smirking in triumph, though, as he raked in the pile of coins and greenbacks in the center of the table. He was very matter-of-fact about it, and the other players didn't appear to be upset.

In fact, one of them was smiling. In a voice that had a hint of a southern drawl, he said, "Well played, my friend. I honestly thought you were bluffing."

"Oh, I never bluff," Chance said. "Too

15

hard on the nerves."

That brought chuckles from several of the men at the table. Chance didn't look like the sort of hombre whose nerves would ever give him trouble. In his neat brown suit, white shirt, vest, and expertly tied cravat, he looked cool and collected. He was a handsome young man with close-cropped brown hair, compactly built, and athletic.

Ace was a couple of inches taller and more rugged, with broader shoulders and features that were roughhewn in comparison to Chance's. His thick, slightly tousled hair was a darker shade of brown. He wore boots, jeans, and a buckskin shirt. A broad-brimmed black hat was thumbed to the back of his head.

Anybody could look at the two of them and guess they were related, and most folks would take them for brothers. Not many would guess that they were twins, however.

The young man who had complimented Chance on the hand that just ended gestured at Chance's winnings and said, "You're going to give us the opportunity to reclaim some of that bountiful harvest, aren't you?" His face was rather thin under curly black hair, and he sported a handlebar mustache with waxed tips.

"I don't know," Chance said. "It might be

time for me to cash in."

"You don't want to do that." The young man waved at the windows, where the rain was dripping off the awning over the board-walk in the rapidly fading light. "It's miser-able out there. It's warm and dry in here, with a convivial atmosphere to boot."

Chance grinned and said, "Well, when you put it that way . . ." He gathered up the cards and began to shuffle for the next hand, since this was a friendly game with no professional dealer at the table.

The saloon's front door opened. The man who came in pushed the door hard enough to make it swing back and bang against the wall. The saloon was about half full, and most of the customers turned to look at the newcomer.

"Porter!" the man said in a loud, angry voice. "I figured I'd find you here, you grin-ning jackanapes!"

He was short and broad, built like a stump, with a face like an angry bulldog. Dark hair grew down to a point on his forehead. His hands clenched into fists as he stomped across the room toward the table where Chance was sitting. The man had been out in the rain without a hat or slicker. His clothes were soaked, and water dripped off his face. He was so angry and

17

intent he didn't seem to notice or care.

The young man with the handlebar mustache pushed his chair back a little. He was worried, Ace thought, but he was trying not to show it.

"Why, Dale," he said, "what brings you here?"

"You know good and well why I'm here, Porter," the newcomer declared as he came to a stop beside the table. "You've been pitching woo at my girl Clarissa."

"Nonsense," Porter said. "I'm barely acquainted with the young lady."

"Then what were you doing singing outside her window last night?" The question was phrased in a furious shout.

Porter didn't flinch. He said, "I won't deny serenading Miss Jenkins, but I wasn't alone, you know. There were three other lads with me. That's why they call us the Hill City Quartet. There are four of us."

"Yeah, but you were the one standing out front, strumming on that guitar of yours. You were the ringleader!"

"Not a word you often hear applied musically," Porter murmured. He straightened in his chair and went on briskly, "Listen, Dale, I assure you I have no romantic interest in Miss Clarissa Jenkins. My friends and I serenade young ladies simply to hone our vocal talents. We've found that it's easier to put our hearts and souls into the songs if we're singing them *to* someone. But it doesn't really mean anything."

Dale's eyes narrowed. He said, "So you're not smitten with Clarissa?"

"No, I'm not." A rather dreamy look came into Porter's eyes. "Truth be told, I have my sights set on a certain other young lady —"

Dale's hand shot out. He grabbed the front of Porter's shirt and jerked the young man to his feet.

"Are you saying Clarissa's not *good* enough for you, you fancy-pants little scribbler?"

Chance pushed his chair back, stood up, and said, "That's about enough, mister."

Dale didn't look at Chance. He just leaned forward a little and shot out his left fist. Chance wasn't expecting the punch and couldn't get out of the way. It caught him on the jaw and knocked him backward. He tripped over the chair he had just vacated and crashed to the floor.

Ace was moving before his brother even hit the sawdust-littered planks. He crossed the room swiftly, clamped his left hand on Dale's shoulder and hauled the man around. Dale tried to hang on to Porter's coat, but Ace jerked him loose.

19

Ace's right came up in a looping punch that landed cleanly on Dale's nose, flattening it. Blood spurted over Ace's knuckles. Dale fell onto the baize-covered table, scattering money and cards. He rolled off and fell on the floor, moaning as he fumbled at his bleeding nose.

Somebody yelled from the still-open doorway. Several men crowded through it and came toward the table. They were wet from the rain, too, and looked almost as angry as Dale had when he burst into the saloon.

"Well, this is unfortunate," Porter muttered.

"What is?" Chance asked. He had climbed back to his feet and was rubbing his jaw where Dale had punched him.

"Those men are friends with this lout," Porter said with a nod toward Dale. "And they just saw you knock him down."

"They're not gonna let me get away with that, are they?" Ace said. "Even though he started it."

"I'm afraid not," Porter said. "Prepare yourselves, my friends. We're about to come under attack."

CHAPTER TWO

There were four men in the group that had just come into the saloon. Bellowing curses, they charged Ace, Chance, and Porter. Customers leaped to get out of their way, as did the girls working in the saloon.

Ace didn't reach for the gun on his hip, although he considered it for a second. Firing a shot into the ceiling might shock the men into stopping their attack. But the saloon had a second floor, and Ace wasn't willing to endanger anyone up there.

So it would be hand-to-hand combat. *Mano a mano.*

Not the first brawl the Jensen boys had been mixed up in, that was for sure.

Ace stepped up to meet the charge. The closest man swung a wild, looping punch at his head. Ace ducked under it and hooked a left into the man's belly. The man bent forward as the breath *whooshed* out of him. Ace straightened him up with a hard right to the jaw.

Meanwhile, another man lunged at Chance and tried to wrap him up in a bear hug. Chance twisted away and peppered a left-right combination to the man's face. That slowed the attacker down but didn't stop him. The man barreled into Chance and carried him backward. Chance slammed into the wall behind him.

The third man yelled, "There's that blasted gee-tar player! It's all his fault! Get him!"

He and the fourth man grabbed Porter by the arms and dragged him away from the table. Porter tried to writhe out of their grip but wasn't able to. He exclaimed, "Gentlemen, please! This is all a misunderstanding! I'm an intellectual, not a roughneck!"

"Shut him up," one of the men growled.

"With pleasure," the other said, and an instant later he sunk a fist into Porter's midsection.

Ace saw that from the corner of his eye, but there was nothing he could do about it. He was too busy blocking the punches his opponent threw at him and trying to launch a few of his own. One of the blows got through and caught Ace in the chest, rocking him back against a chair. He almost stumbled and fell, and as he did, the man crowded in to try to take advantage.

Ace turned that against him, grabbing the man's arm and letting himself fall. As he went down, he hauled the man with him, planting a foot in his belly and levering him up and over. The man flew through the air and landed on his back hard enough to make the floor shake a little under Ace.

Chance's opponent had pinned the young man's left arm to his side, but Chance's right arm was still free. He hammered that fist into the man's ears as arms like young tree trunks closed around him and started squeezing. Chance's feet came up off the floor and his ribs seemed to creak under the inexorable pressure. He hit the man again and again, seemingly without any effect.

Then one of the punches landed on the man's jaw, and his grip loosened. Chance hit him there again, then a third time. The arms fell away from him as the man's eyes started to look a little glassy.

Panting for breath, Chance stepped back and said, "Glass . . . jaw . . . eh?"

He began to use his speed and agility, dancing around his opponent as the man swiped at him with those apelike arms. Chance snapped punch after punch to the man's jaw, lefts and rights that flew with blurring speed to strike home.

It wasn't long before the man's eyes rolled up in their sockets and his knees buckled. He went down with a heavy thud and didn't move again.

With their foes disposed of, Ace and Chance turned toward Porter, who was still being thrashed by the other two men. Each held an arm with one hand and used the other hand to take turns punching Porter.

Ace and Chance tackled them, knocking them loose from the slender, mustachioed Porter. The battling men staggered back and forth, upsetting chairs and tables as they traded punches. Some of the people in the saloon had fled into the rain. The others had pulled back to give the combatants in the wild melee plenty of room.

Porter leaned on a table and shook his head, evidently trying to get the cobwebs out of it. Then he straightened, grabbed a spittoon from the floor, and swung it like a club. With a resounding *bong!,* the spittoon landed on the head of the man who was slugging away at Chance. The man went down, splattered by the spittoon's reeking contents.

That distracted the final troublemaker enough for Ace to finish him off with a powerhouse right and left that lifted him from his feet and dumped him across the sprawled bodies of his companions. Ace stood there with his chest heaving a little from the exertion.

"You . . . all right . . . brother?" Chance asked.

Ace dragged the back of his hand across his mouth to wipe away some blood and said, "Yeah. How about you?"

"I'll live," Chance replied.

Porter moved between them and rested his hands on their shoulders, either in a gesture of comradeship or to help hold himself up . . . or both. He said, "I can't thank you fellows enough for coming to my aid. I hate to say it, but we should probably depart. These barbarians won't take long to come to their senses, and when the local gendarmerie hear about this altercation, they might bestir themselves enough to venture out into the rain to investigate."

"You mean the law might haul us off to the hoosegow?" Ace said.

"And those polecats will come to and want to fight some more?" Chance added.

"Indubitably, on both counts," Porter agreed.

Ace stooped to pick up his hat, which had fallen off during the fight, and slapped it against his leg to get the sawdust off of it. Chance found his hat as well, and Porter clapped a straw boater on his head.

"Let's light a shuck out of here," Ace said.

The rain had tapered off to a mist that didn't get the three young men too damp as they strolled along Congress Avenue a short time later. Up at the top of a slight hill, about half a mile north, loomed the Texas Capitol Building.

"What set those fellas off?" Ace asked. "Something about a girl?"

Porter sighed and said, "Yes, but like I tried to tell them, it was a complete misunderstanding. Miss Clarissa Jenkins is a perfectly fine young woman, if a bit . . . dull. But my affections are centered on another lady." He sighed again. "Unfortunately, she hasn't proven receptive to my suit, at least not yet. I'm nothing if not determined, though. Sooner or later, I'll win the heart of Miss Evelyn Channing."

"I hope you do," Ace said. "By the way, we never got the chance to introduce ourselves." He stuck his hand out. "I'm Ace Jensen."

Porter clasped it and said, "William Sydney Porter, at your service, sir."

"And I'm Chance Jensen," Chance said as he shook hands with Porter.

"Brothers, I take it. I thought I saw a

distinct resemblance."

"Twin brothers, actually," Ace said. "We just don't look exactly alike."

"And your names are Ace and Chance," Porter murmured. "No wonder you're so good with the galloping pasteboards, Chance. How could you be otherwise with a name like that? But why weren't you sitting in the game, Ace? You're even more aptly dubbed."

"Most of the time I leave the card-playing to my brother," Ace said. "He's more cut out for it than I am."

"Our stepfather, the fella who raised us, was a gambler," Chance explained. "You might have heard of him. Ennis Monday. Doc Monday, some called him."

Porter shook his head and said, "I'm afraid not. I came to this region fairly recently from North Carolina."

"What do you do?" Ace asked. It wasn't considered polite to inquire too much into a man's background or business, but he didn't think Porter would take offense.

"Oh, a bit of this and that. I've been a pharmacist, but at the moment I'm working as a clerk in one of the banks here in town. My real interest is the arts, though. As I mentioned to Dale, I'm a member of a local quartet, and I play the guitar and mandolin as well. I've also been playing around with the idea of writing. You know, stories and sketches and essays."

"You should write dime novels," Ace said. "Folks read 'em by the bushel basketful."

"Oh, I've read them myself," Porter said with a smile. "Say! I thought the name Jensen was familiar. Are you any relation to the famous gunfighter Smoke Jensen? Dime novels have been written about him, you know."

"Yeah, I've seen them. And we've actually met Smoke Jensen, haven't we, Chance?"

"That's right," Chance said. "We're no relation, though, as far as we know." He chuckled. "Ace here likes to think that maybe we're some sort of long-lost relatives, but that's just a little hero worship, I reckon."

"You could do worse than to be related to a man like Smoke Jensen," Ace said.

"No doubt," Porter agreed. "If what's in the dime novels is even half of the truth, he's quite the stalwart individual." He stopped short and pointed across the street at a café where the windows glowed yellow with lamplight in the mist. "Would you gentlemen care for a cup of coffee to warm up on this rather raw evening? I'm buying."

"I won't argue with that," Chance said.

As they started across the street, Porter went on, "I confess I have an ulterior motive in paying a visit to this establishment. Miss Channing works here."

"The gal you're sweet on?" Ace asked.

"One and the same."

"It would be an honor to meet her."

Just before they reached the café's front door, it swung open and a man stepped out. In the light that came from inside the building, Ace saw that the man was somewhat older, probably around thirty. He wore a dark suit and a black, flat-crowned hat. He had a handlebar mustache like Porter, but his face was beefier. He stopped short at the sight of the three young men, and his hand moved to his coat, sweeping it back so that the butt of a revolver with ivory grips was revealed.

"Porter," the man grated coldly, and Ace wondered just how many enemies William Sydney Porter had in Austin.

CHAPTER THREE

"Hudson," Porter said. His tone was just as curt and chilly as the other man's had been, but Ace could tell that Porter was nervous. That was understandable. Hudson had the look of a gunman about him. Porter went on, "What are you doing here?"

"I think you know," Hudson said. "Just as I know why you're here." He smiled, but the expression did little to relieve the grim lines of his face. "But it's not going to do you any good. Miss Channing has just consented to be my wife."

Porter took a sharp step back and looked like someone had just slugged him in the gut. He said, "No! That can't be."

"It's the truth. Surely you can't be that surprised. Evelyn's never given you any encouragement, after all."

"I don't believe it," Porter said stubbornly as he shook his head.

"You might as well. She's going to meet

me in Fredericksburg a few days from now, and we'll be married. And there's not a thing you can do about it."

Porter's hands clenched into fists. Ace could tell that he wanted to take a swing at Hudson, but natural caution held him back. Hudson was older, bigger, and no doubt stronger. Plus he had that ivory-handled gun on his hip. Ace didn't know for sure if Porter was armed, and he hadn't caught sight of any weapon so far.

Hudson's cold gaze took in Ace and Chance. His hand shifted a little and rested on the gun butt.

"Who are your friends?" he asked.

"They're not part of this," Porter snapped. "This is between you and me."

"You're wrong about that, too." A bark of laughter came from Hudson. "There's nothing between you and me. Less than nothing. You're completely insignificant to me, Porter. And to Evelyn as well."

He was trying to goad Porter into taking a swing at him, Ace realized. If that happened, he and Chance might have to step in, and that would give Hudson an excuse to draw his gun. The man must have figured he was pretty good, to be willing, even eager, apparently, to take on odds like that.

And maybe he was. Ace didn't know. But

31

he was certain he didn't want to get mixed up in a shooting on their first night in Austin. He and Chance had been on the drift for quite some time and hoped to stay here for a while.

Ace put his left hand on Porter's right shoulder and said, "Listen, why don't we go on inside? That cup of coffee we were talking about sounds better all the time."

"I'm not afraid —" Porter began.

"Nobody said you were," Chance told him. "Come on in. We'll talk about it."

Hudson said, "There's nothing to talk about. It's all settled."

"If there's nothing to talk about, why don't you move on, mister?" Ace suggested.

"Maybe I don't like being told what to do," Hudson replied, thin-lipped with anger.

Slowly, Ace shook his head. His hand tightened on Porter's shoulder. Chance took hold of Porter's other shoulder. Together, they started to steer him around Hudson toward the door of the café.

"We're not looking for any trouble," Ace said.

Hudson laughed, and the smugness of the sound made Ace's jaw tighten. It was almost enough to cause him to throw caution to the wind and find out just how slick on the draw Hudson really was.

There was only so much prodding he could take.

But then Porter shook loose and said, "It's all right, fellows. Come on." He took a deep breath. "Let's go inside."

Narrow-eyed, Ace told Hudson, "Things might be different, happen we cross trails again."

"Sure, kid." Hudson smirked. "Whatever you say."

He turned and strolled off through the mist.

"That son-of-a —" Chance began.

He didn't finish because the café door opened and a woman said, "Mr. Porter, is that you? I thought I saw you out here. Please, come in out of the weather."

She didn't step out into the mist, but she extended a slim hand and smiled. Her blond hair was put up on her head. She wore a crisp gingham dress with a white apron tied over it. From the looks of the outfit, she worked as a waitress in the café.

"Miss Channing," Porter said. "I . . . I . . ."

He couldn't go on. Instead he turned and started walking along the street in the opposite direction from the way Hudson had gone. His head was down.

"Oh, dear," Miss Channing said. She looked at Ace and Chance.

"Don't worry about him, ma'am, we'll go after him," Ace said as he lifted a hand and pinched the brim of his hat. He wasn't sure why he had just volunteered himself and Chance to look after Porter, unless it was because somebody needed to.

"Ma'am," Chance said as he touched the brim of his hat as well. Then he and Ace took off after Porter. They were taller than the man from North Carolina, and their longer legs allowed them to catch up fairly quickly.

As they came up on either side of Porter, Ace said, "What was that all about? I think you may have insulted the young lady."

"She's worried about you, anyway," Chance said. "You could tell that by the look on her face."

Porter shook his head and muttered, "She doesn't care about me. If she did, she wouldn't have agreed to go to Fredericksburg and marry that . . . that Oliver Hudson!"

He made the name sound like a curse.

"Let's find some place to get in out of the weather, and you can tell us all about it," Ace said.

"Why would you do that? Why do you care?"

"We've been through a fight together,"

Chance reminded him. "I took a poke in the jaw because of you, remember? That makes us brothers in arms, I guess."

"All right," Porter said. "But I warn you, it's not a pretty story."

"You said you were thinking about being a writer," Ace told him. "Make it better."

They wound up in a smaller, quieter saloon. The bartender had a pot of coffee on the stove, so Ace and Chance got cups of the potent black brew while Porter nursed a glass of whiskey as they sat at one of the tables.

"I think I fell in love with Evelyn Channing the first time I went in that café and laid eyes on her," Porter mused. "I began going there almost every day, and we became friends. I wanted it to be more than that. You saw how beautiful she is. You can understand why I felt that way."

"She's a mighty pretty young woman," Ace agreed.

"But it's not just that," Porter said. "She's smart and charming and has a wonderful sense of humor. And a lovely singing voice! You should hear her."

"So you started trying to court her," Chance said.

Porter nodded.

"Every time I began to approach the subject, she turned it aside," he said. "It wasn't long before I found out why. I had a rival for her affections."

"That fella Hudson," Ace said.

"And she liked him better," Chance said.

Porter buried his face in his hands.

"Yes," he said, his voice muffled. He lifted his head and laughed. "Can you imagine that? Just because he's big and handsome and tough, she prefers him to me!"

Porter laughed again. Ace edged the glass of whiskey away from him and said, "Maybe you'd better lay off this stuff for a spell."

"I never dreamed she'd actually agree to marry him, though. I thought for certain that eventually she would see through him." Porter lowered his voice to a confidential tone. "I don't trust the man, and it's not just because Evelyn likes him. He's dangerous, you can tell that by looking at him. I think he's a gunman. It wouldn't surprise me if he had several killings in his past."

"But you don't know for sure," Ace said.

Porter shook his head and said, "No, I tried to look into his background, but I couldn't find out anything about him. He's only been in Austin a few months."

"What's his connection to Fredericksburg?" Chance asked. "That's a settlement west of here, right?"

"Yes, out in the Hill Country. The town was settled by German colonists. Excellent food, from what I hear. But I have no idea why Hudson is going there or why that's where he and Evelyn plan to be married, instead of here in Austin."

Ace leaned back in his chair, thumbed his hat to the back of his head, and said, "Well, there are some things in life we have to just accept without understanding them, I reckon. Chance and I, we never knew our ma. She died when we were born. Nobody knew why. That's just the way it was."

"It was meant to be," Chance said. "Maybe it's meant to be that you and this gal Evelyn won't wind up together."

Porter doubled his hand into a fist and thumped it on the table with unexpected vehemence.

"No," he said. "No, I won't accept it. I know destiny when it's staring me in the face, gentlemen. I'm going to Fredericksburg, and I'm going to put a stop to this ill-fated wedding!" He looked back and forth between Ace and Chance. "And you two, my newfound friends, are going with me!"

CHAPTER FOUR

San Antonio

That same night, the rain that was widespread over central Texas moved south into San Antonio and dumped a brief downpour on the city before moving on. Puddles covered the cobblestone street in front of the Menger Hotel as Luke Jensen stepped out of the entrance that led into the hotel bar. He glanced to his right. A block away stood the hulking building that had once been known as Mission San Antonio de Valera. The pediment at the top of its front wall was crumbling. Luke had heard that it was being used these days as a warehouse where grain was stored.

People had once known it by another name: the Alamo.

Luke's eyes narrowed as he thought he spotted movement in the shadows next to the old mission. He didn't see anything else, though, and decided it could have been anything — a drunk stumbling along, a tomcat on the prowl, a stray dog looking for food. It didn't have to be anything to do with him.

He left his black coat unbuttoned, though, so he could reach the twin Remington revolvers in their cross-draw rigs. He hadn't lived this long in a dangerous profession by getting careless.

Luke Jensen was a bounty hunter. He had made his living that way since the end of the Civil War. It was a bloody business, and he had long since accepted the fact that it would probably be the death of him, sooner or later.

Later, if he had anything to say about it, he thought as he began to stride along the street.

He was a tall man dressed in black from head to foot, the darkness relieved only by a silver concho on his hat band and the long-barreled, silver-plated, pearl-handled revolvers he wore at his waist. He was far from handsome. His features looked like they had been hacked out with a dull ax, in fact, but there was something compelling about them that women found attractive. A neatly trimmed mustache adorned his upper lip above a wide, expressive mouth.

He had been in the Menger talking to a

man who tended bar there. Clancy was a burly, gray-haired Irishman with an extraordinary memory for faces. If the man Luke was looking for had passed through San Antonio and spent the night at the Menger or even just had a drink at the bar, Clancy would remember him.

Because of that, this had been Luke's first stop. If he didn't find out anything, he would move on to the Buckhorn and then to all the other saloons, gambling dens, and whorehouses in town.

Sam Brant had been headed this way, and Luke didn't think the outlaw would have gone around San Antonio without stopping. Brant had expensive taste, too, which meant it was more likely he would have stopped at the Menger. That tendency toward extravagance meant Brant needed a lot of money, which explained why he had turned to robbing banks and holding up trains. Because of that he had a five thousand dollar bounty on his head, and Luke intended to collect it.

Luck was with him. Clancy had remembered the man Luke was looking for.

"Aye," Clancy had said as he wiped the polished mahogany of the bar with a rag. "Sandy-haired fella with a little scar over his left eye. Bit of a lantern jaw. He was here, all right."

"How long ago?" Luke had asked.

"Oh, 'tis nigh on to six months ago, I'd say. No, wait . . . Bless me, 'twas more like eight or nine."

"That long?"

"Oh, my, yes. But I can see him plain as day, as if 'twas yesterday."

Luke had known that Brant's trail was cold, but he hadn't expected it to be *that* cold. Still, he had run into a man over in Refugio who had told him that Brant was headed in this direction, and now he had proof of that, so he asked Clancy, "I don't suppose he said where he was going from here."

"No, I'm afraid not." Clancy frowned. "But I believe he mentioned something about Enchanted Rock."

"What's that?"

"Big mounded heap of stone up in the Hill Country north of Fredericksburg. Never seen it meself, mind you, but I've heard tell of it. Sounds like a place where the old Druids would have one o' their pagan ceremonies, if ye ask me."

That was interesting, Luke had thought, but he couldn't think of any reason why an outlaw like Sam Brant would be headed there. Still, it was a starting place, a trail for

41

him to follow, and he had never asked for anything more.

He didn't have the money to stay at the Menger, so he would have to find some place cheaper. He had left his horse at a stable on the other side of the old mission. He was walking in front of that building with its blood-soaked heritage when three men stepped out of the shadows to block his path.

Luke wasn't surprised. The hint of movement he had seen in the gloom had alerted him to the possibility of trouble. He stopped short but didn't reach for his guns just yet. He wanted to find out who these men were and what they wanted with him before any gunplay broke out.

Luke didn't care to kill someone if there was no profit in it.

"You just hold it right there, mister," the middle one of the trio said. "We got some business with you."

"I doubt that," Luke said. "I'm not looking for any business this evening, or any trouble, either."

"You're Luke Jensen," the man on Luke's left declared. "I recognized you through the front window of the Menger."

"You've got the advantage on me, then." Luke's keen eyes had adjusted to the darkness, and he could make out the faces of the three hombres in the faint light that came from nearby buildings. They were all cut from the same cloth, men with hard-planed, beard-stubbled faces. Men much like him, Luke mused, but he was convinced they were on the opposite side of the law.

"I'm Dewey Dunham," the man in the middle said. He angled his head toward the man on Luke's left. "Thad Barnes." Then the one on Luke's right. "Ned Godfrey. I'll bet you know the names, don't you . . . *bounty hunter*?"

Dunham's voice was full of contempt and scorn. Luke was accustomed to that attitude. Most folks didn't have much use for his kind, even the law-abiding ones.

As a matter of fact, Luke did recognize all three names. He had seen them on various wanted posters. None of them had a particularly large bounty on his head, but together they would add up to a not-bad payoff. They were wanted for rustling, stagecoach robbery, attempted murder, and assorted other crimes.

"Yeah, I know who you boys are," Luke said, "but I haven't been looking for you. Wouldn't be worth my while to go out of my way to do so. Since you've been kind enough to turn yourselves in to me, though —"

Barnes cursed bitterly, interrupting him. Dunham said, "We're not turnin' ourselves in, you fool, and you know it. We're here to kill you, Jensen. You killed Henry Stockard out in El Paso a few months ago. Henry was a friend of ours. We rode with him for nigh on to a year."

"You're here to settle the score for Stockard, eh? Well, he had a chance to surrender. I called on him to put down his gun. It was his choice not to do it."

"So you killed him!" Godfrey yelled. "You son-of-a —"

He broke off and clawed at the gun on his hip.

The three outlaws had called the tune, and there had never been any doubt in Luke's mind what it would be. So he was ready, and as soon as Godfrey made his move and the other two hardcases followed suit, Luke went for his guns, too.

He was twice as fast as any of them. Both of his Remingtons were out before any of the trio cleared leather. The guns roared at the same time. The one in Luke's left hand was aimed at Barnes, the one in his right at Godfrey. Both shots found their target. Barnes staggered back as a slug drove into his chest.

The hit on Godfrey wasn't quite as clean. He was moving a little when the bullet struck him in the right shoulder and spun him halfway around.

Dewey Dunham had his gun out by now. Flame lanced from the muzzle. Luke heard the shot whip past his ear as he pulled both triggers again. The lead hammered into Dunham's body and knocked him backward off his feet. His revolver went off a second time as his finger jerked the trigger in a dying spasm, but the weapon was pointed skyward by then.

Barnes caught himself as he stumbled backward but couldn't stay on his feet. He pitched forward on his face. Godfrey was the only one still upright. His right arm hung limp at his side as streams of blood rolled down it from his bullet-shattered shoulder. He had dropped his gun. It lay on the dirt at his feet.

"Don't do it," Luke warned as Godfrey started to lean over and reach for the fallen Colt with his left hand. Luke held the Remingtons at waist level and pointed both guns at him. "You won't have a chance, you blasted fool."

"You . . . you done killed Thad and Dewey," Godfrey panted. Pain drew his face into gaunt lines. "Just like you killed Henry."

"But you don't have to die," Luke said. "That gun arm's never going to be any good again, mister. Your days as an outlaw are over no matter what you do. Might as well serve a stretch in prison and try to make something out of the life you've got left." Luke shrugged. "Doesn't make any difference to me. The reward's good dead or alive."

Godfrey licked his lips, said, "Prison?" He laughed harshly. "Go to —"

He lunged for the gun without finishing the epithet. Luke waited for him to grab it before squeezing both triggers. The slugs knocked Godfrey into a limp sprawl next to his dead comrades. He kicked once and then lay still.

Luke holstered one of the Remingtons and started reloading the other. As he carried out that task with practiced ease, he glanced from the dead men to the stone and adobe wall looming over them. These three were hardly the first to die in front of the Alamo, but they were a lot more craven than the men who had given up their lives fighting for Texas's independence.

Somebody shouted nearby. Footsteps pounded on the street as they came toward Luke. The law would be on hand soon, and

46

he'd have to go to the trouble of explaining who he was and why he had killed the three men. He would put in a claim for the rewards he had coming, too. The whole thing might delay him here in San Antonio for a day or two.

But that shouldn't matter, since he was already months behind Sam Brant. As soon as everything was taken care of, he would head north into the Hill Country and see if he could pick up the outlaw's trail.

Enchanted Rock might be the best place to start.

CHAPTER FIVE

Fort Worth

The man and woman who got off the train in Fort Worth the next morning drew admiring looks from everyone who saw them. The man was only slightly above medium height but was so muscular and well-built he appeared bigger. His shoulders were especially impressive. They seemed to be as wide as an ax handle. He wore a brown tweed suit but looked like he would be more at home in range garb. The tan, broad-brimmed hat on his ash-blond hair just reinforced that image.

The woman with him was also dressed well. She possessed the sort of classic beauty that made men sigh and other women scowl if they were the jealous sort. Her thick, dark hair was arranged in an elaborate pile of curls under the neat little hat pinned on it.

Together they made a mighty attractive couple. A perceptive observer might have taken the man for the owner of a successful ranch and the woman as his wife. And that was exactly what they were . . . as far as it went.

As a porter took the couple's bags from a baggage car, he asked, "You want me to have those taken to one of the hotels, Mr. Jensen?"

"No," Smoke Jensen said. "We're not staying overnight in Fort Worth. We're supposed to catch a stagecoach later today."

"A stagecoach?" the porter repeated. "Not many of those runnin' anymore, since the railroad's come to Texas."

Smoke smiled and said, "The railroad still doesn't go everywhere."

"Where are you and the missus bound, if you don't mind my askin'?"

"We're going to spend Christmas on a ranch owned by a man named Chester Fielding, down on the Llano River south of Mason," Smoke explained. "I've come down here to do a little business with him."

Sally Jensen's arm was linked with her husband's. She smiled and tightened her grip a little as she added, "And since it's almost Christmas, I certainly wasn't going to be separated from Smoke at this time of year if I could help it. So we're making an excursion of it."

The porter shook his head and said, "Well, you folks sure didn't pick a very good time for a trip. I hear it's a mess down that way, what with all the rain."

The sun was shining here in Fort Worth at the moment. Smoke frowned and said, "I hadn't heard about that."

"Word's come in over the telegraph from Austin and San Antonio that it's been rainin' off and on for days down south of here. You're liable to run into some high water on that stagecoach."

"Well, I hope not," Smoke said. "I want to get to Fielding's spread and see about this prize bull he's got that I want to buy. Ought to be a good deal for both of us."

"So your bags need to go to the stagecoach station?"

Smoke nodded and said, "That's right. The Cross Timbers Stage Line, over on Belknap Street."

"Know right where it is," the porter said. "I'll see that the bags are delivered there. When does your stage pull out?"

"Twelve thirty this afternoon."

"You've got some time to kill, then."

Sally frowned slightly, and Smoke knew why.

She didn't care for the phrase the man had used. Too many times in the past, for

50

Smoke "time to kill" had to be taken literally.

In the years since young Kirby Jensen had headed west with his father, right after the Civil War, violence had dogged his trail. A chance meeting with an old mountain man known as Preacher, an attack by Indians, a desperate fight for life . . . and Preacher had dubbed Kirby "Smoke," since he was that fast and accurate with a gun. The lethal skill was something that came natural to the young man, and over time it had been honed to the point that many people considered Smoke Jensen to be the fastest, deadliest gunfighter the West had ever seen.

The fact that Smoke had married, settled down, and become a successful rancher in Colorado had done nothing to lessen his reputation. Trouble still seemed to seek him out and follow him wherever he went.

Smoke knew Sally was hoping this trip would be different. So did he, but experience had taught him to have a more fatalistic attitude. Whatever happened would happen, and he would deal with it to the best of his ability . . . which was considerable.

He and Sally left the depot while the porter was supervising the loading of the bags onto a cart that would carry them to the stage station at the other end of Fort

Worth's business district. They strolled along Calhoun Street and cut over to Throckmorton. It was a beautiful winter day in Texas, with crisp, cool temperatures and an achingly blue sky overhead. The weather might be bad farther south, but nobody here could say that.

They passed the Panther City Saloon. Sally smiled at the sign and commented, "That's an odd name."

"Some folks call Fort Worth Panther City because they used to say it was so sleepy the panthers would come in from the hills and doze in the middle of Main Street at high noon," Smoke said with a smile of his own. "That all changed when the cattle drives started and there were hundreds of cowboys coming through here all the time, and then when the railroad arrived the place got even busier."

They stopped at a restaurant and lingered over a late breakfast that became lunch before they were finished. Smoke enjoyed a last cup of coffee, and as he did so he reflected that this was one of the most peaceful spells he had experienced in quite a while.

That realization was enough to make his nerves tighten a bit. When things were too peaceful for too long, he began to worry. It always seemed like hell was saving itself up and sooner or later would break loose.

They left the restaurant and walked on to Belknap Street, which followed a bluff overlooking the winding course of the Trinity River. The old army fort that had given the town its name had been erected here many years earlier. It was long since abandoned and gone, but the settlement that had grown up around it remained.

The headquarters of the Cross Timbers Stage Line consisted of a building that housed the office, plus a barn and a large corral next to it. A Concord stagecoach, painted a faded red with yellow trim and brass fittings, was pulled up in front of the office with a six-horse team hitched to it. The canvas covering over the boot at the back of the coach was thrown to the side so a man could load baggage into it, including the bags belonging to Smoke and Sally. Several trunks were already on top of the stage, lashed in place by ropes attached to the brass rail that ran around the vehicle's roof.

A lanky, brown-haired man with a ragged mustache came out of the office and approached Smoke and Sally. He smiled and stuck out his hand as he said, "Mr. Jensen? I'm Jed Ferguson, the manager of the line."

Smoke shook hands and said, "Pleased to meet you, Mr. Ferguson. I reckon you got my wire booking passage to Mason?"

"Yes, sir, I sure did, and we're mighty happy to have you traveling with us. The stage is almost loaded and ready to go. It'll be pulling out in ten or fifteen minutes, I'd say."

"We've heard that the weather is bad south of here," Sally said. "Is that going to affect our trip?"

"It shouldn't," Ferguson said. "There are some low-water crossings along the route, but I haven't heard anything about the streams being too high for a coach to get through. We have excellent drivers and the best teams that can be found. We'll take good care of you, you have my word on that, Mrs. Jensen."

"How long will it take to get there?" Smoke asked.

"Barring any delays, you ought to roll into Mason late in the afternoon a couple of days from now. You'll spend two nights at stops between here and there. The accommodations may not be exactly what you're used to . . ."

"They'll be fine," Smoke said, smiling faintly as he recalled some of the nights he had spent sleeping on cold, hard ground, back in the days when he had followed the owlhoot trail. The accusations of him being an outlaw were unjust, but he'd had to live like one anyway. Sally had known her share of hardships, too.

"Well, if you folks want to go ahead and get aboard," Ferguson said, "we'll finish up and be ready to roll."

Smoke opened the door on one side of the coach and helped Sally into the vehicle. He followed, settling himself on the forward-facing bench seat beside her.

Five other people were already in the coach. A middle-aged woman sat on Sally's other side. Across from them in the seat facing backward were a young couple and a fat, balding man who appeared to be some sort of traveling salesman. A young cowboy in his late teens perched on the bench in the middle of the coach with his saddle beside him. He reminded Smoke of Calvin Woods, one of his most trusted hands back on the Sugarloaf, the ranch Smoke owned in Colorado.

The youngster, who had a shock of red hair trying to escape from under his hat and fall forward across his forehead, looked wide-eyed at Smoke and exclaimed, "Say, I know you, mister! I've seen your pictures in the illustrated papers. You're Smoke Jensen!"

Smoke smiled, nodded, and said, "That's right."

"Arley Hicks," the cowboy said. He stuck out his hand. "It's a pure-dee honor to meet you, sir."

Smoke clasped the young man's hand and said, "Pleasure to meet you, too, Arley."

The other couple looked puzzled. From their clothes and general demeanor, Smoke pegged both of them as Easterners. It was likely they had never heard of him, which was just fine with him. The drummer recognized his name, though, when Arley blurted it out, and so did the middle-aged lady.

The young husband said, "Are you supposed to be someone famous, sir? I'd like to know if we're traveling with a celebrated personage."

"Famous?" Arley repeated before Smoke could answer. "Mister, this here is Smoke Jensen. He's just the fastest, slickest gunhand there's ever been."

The young woman frowned and said, "We're traveling with a gunman? Isn't that dangerous?"

"Don't worry, dear," her husband told her. "I won't let anything happen to you."

"There's nothing to worry about," Smoke

said, "because there's not going to be any trouble." He inclined his head toward Sally. "This is my wife Sally. We're just making a little Christmas trip, combining business with pleasure. Hope to spend a pleasant couple of days with you folks, that's all."

"My name is Donald Purcell," the young man said stiffly. "My wife Mildred."

Mildred Purcell didn't say anything, but her lips thinned in obvious disapproval.

"I'm Herman Langston," the salesman said. "Patent medicines is my line."

"And I'm Mrs. Genevieve Carter," the middle-aged woman said. "Going to live with my sister in Kerrville."

Grinning, Arley said, "You can tell by lookin' at me that I'm a cowboy. Got a ridin' job lined up down close to Bandera. Mighty lucky, findin' a place to sign on this time o' year, and I know it. I was afraid I might pert near starve 'fore spring rolls around." He looked at Donald Purcell. "You didn't say what line of work you're in, Mr. Purcell."

"That's right, I didn't," Purcell replied. His tone was a little curt. But he shrugged and went on, "I'm going to take a teaching position. The previous schoolmaster passed away unexpectedly."

"Now we all know each other," Sally said,

"and I'm sure we'll get along splendidly."

Smoke wasn't so certain of that, but time would tell.

A minute later, the stagecoach shifted on the broad leather thoroughbraces that ran underneath it as the driver and guard climbed to the box. A whip cracked and the coach lurched into motion as the horses strained against their harness.

The pilgrims were on their way.

CHAPTER SIX

Palo Pinto Mountains

Major Patrick Macmillan raised his right hand in a signal for the cavalry patrol following him to halt. The soldiers reined in and so did the civilian riding beside Macmillan.

Matt Jensen rested his hands on the saddle horn and leaned forward to ease muscles grown stiff from long hours of riding. His black Stetson was cocked back on fair hair. Under an open sheepskin jacket, he wore a faded blue bib-front shirt similar to what the troopers wore, although Matt wasn't a soldier and never had been.

He had done a considerable amount of scouting for the army, though, now and then over the past several years while he'd been drifting around the frontier, always eager to see what was over the next horizon. He was Smoke Jensen's adopted brother, a respected gunhandler in his own right, and a young man with an adventuresome streak in his personality.

This expedition had started out as a bit of a lark for Matt. He had been at Fort Griffin, a good distance west of here, when word came that a group of renegade Comanches had left the reservation in Indian Territory and were raiding across the north central region of Texas. The fort's commanding officer had sent out a patrol right away, putting his second-in-command in charge, and Matt had signed on as a civilian scout. He was acquainted with Major Macmillan and liked the veteran officer. He and Macmillan had worked together before, so the whole thing seemed like a promising adventure to Matt.

But the task had turned deadly grim over the past few days, as the patrol had come across two isolated ranches that had been attacked by the renegades. The places were burned out, and the people who lived there had all been tortured, killed, and mutilated.

Families. Women and children. It was hard not to feel hate burning inside when you saw what had been done to those innocents and then had to bury what was left of them.

No, Matt reflected as he sat his horse next to Macmillan and looked down into the thickly wooded valley in front of them. This wasn't a lark anymore. It was a mission of vengeance now.

"This is marked on our maps as Dark Valley," Macmillan said. "It's easy to see why."

"Yeah," Matt agreed. Even though the sun was shining, an air of gloom hung over the narrow, steep-sided valley. It seemed almost like something kept the light from penetrating all the way to the bottom of the valley.

The slopes were covered with live oaks, which retained their leaves all year long. That gave the valley a dark green, almost black cast.

From behind Matt and Macmillan, Sergeant Houlihan said, "Why would anybody want to live in a place like this? 'Tis more of a fittin' home for demons, I'm thinkin'."

The sergeant, a wizened, birdlike, but extremely tough little Irishman with a bushy mustache, was just expressing what Matt felt.

Major Macmillan took off his hat and ran his fingers through his graying hair. He said, "According to what we've been told, there are several ranches in the valley. We have to warn the settlers about Black Moon and his band and encourage them to leave. They'll be safer going into the nearest town for a while."

"You'll get some arguments," Matt said. "Folks don't want to leave their homes, especially when they know they might come back to find everything burned down and in ruins."

Macmillan put his hat back on and said, "They may change their minds when they hear about what we've found so far. At the very least, all the women and children should be sent to safety."

"I agree with you, Major. I just know how stubborn some of these Texans can be."

"Stubborn is one thing," Macmillan said as he hitched his horse into motion and started down the slope into the valley. "Foolhardy is another."

Matt rode after the major. His eyes never stopped moving as he cast his gaze back and forth over the rugged landscape around them. Behind him came Sergeant Houlihan and the twenty troopers who made up the patrol.

After a few minutes, Matt nudged his horse up alongside Macmillan's mount and said, "Better let me ride on ahead, Major. That's what a scout's supposed to do, after all."

"I don't like sending out a man alone when there are hostiles in the area," Macmillan said with a frown. "Take one man with you. Your choice."

Matt thought about it for a second and

then nodded. He knew why Macmillan didn't want him scouting alone. If anything happened to Matt, a second man could gallop back to the others with a warning.

"I'll take Private Brenham," he said.

"Very well." Macmillan hipped around in the saddle. "Sergeant . . ."

"I heard, sir," Houlihan said. He turned his head and called, "Brenham, front and center!"

One of the young troopers pulled his horse out of the line and trotted forward to join the sergeant, Matt, and Major Macmillan as the three of them reined in again.

"Yes, Sergeant?" Brenham asked in a southern drawl. He was a Georgia boy, Matt knew from talking to him, who had been able to knock a squirrel out of a tree with a bullet from an old single-shot rifle almost before he could walk. Matt figured it would be good to have such a sharp-eyed marksman with him.

"You're goin' with Mr. Jensen," Houlihan said as he nodded toward Matt. "That is, if you're up for a wee bit o' scoutin'."

A quick grin appeared on Brenham's face before he made his expression solemn again.

"Sure, Sergeant."

"Keep your eyes open, trooper," Macmillan said. "And listen to Matt. You'll find that he knows what he's talking about."

Matt was only a couple of years older than Brenham, but he had been making his way on the frontier for a long time and had the added advantage of having spent several years when he was just a kid in the company of Smoke and the old mountain man called Preacher. Living with those two had been an extensive education in survival.

Matt lifted a hand to his hat brim in farewell to Macmillan and Houlihan as he turned his horse. Brenham fell in alongside him as they rode toward the valley floor. Live oaks grew thickly around them, mixed with post oaks that had lost their leaves during the autumn. That brown and tan carpet crackled a little under their horses' hooves.

The foliage was so thick it wasn't long before the two young men were out of sight of the rest of the patrol. Once that happened, they might as well have been the only humans for miles around. This valley was a lonely, desolate place, apparently without even much animal life.

Matt buttoned up his sheepskin jacket as he rode. The sun didn't have any warmth down here.

Brenham asked, "How long you reckon it's gonna be before we catch up to them renegades, Mr. Jensen?"

"Call me Matt. I'm not an officer."

"My name's Taw, then. It's a plumb honor to be ridin' with you. I've heard a heap about you and your brother." Brenham paused. "But about them hostiles . . ."

"I don't know," Matt answered honestly. His jaw tightened as he thought about the last ranch they had found in the aftermath of a raid. "They were less than a day ahead of us last time, so there's a good chance they're pretty close."

"I'd give a lot to catch one o' them varmints over the sights o' my rifle. I swear, the things they done . . ." Brenham seemed to choke on the words for a moment. "One of the gals at the last place, she reminded me of my own little sister."

"Best not to think too much about that," Matt advised, even though he knew that was easier said than done. The things he had seen would continue to haunt him for a long time, too.

"That Injun Black Moon, he's supposed to be the ringleader o' the bunch, ain't he? Some sort of Comanche war chief?"

"That's what the wire that came to Fort Griffin said."

"How did he come to jump the reservation right now, so close to Christmas? I could understand it more if he'd waited until spring to go raidin'. Thought most of those Injuns like to sit on the reservation durin' the winter when the weather's bad."

"Something happened to set him off, I reckon," Matt said. "We may never know what it was. But he was able to talk some of the other warriors into going with him, and that's all that really matters. We need to round them up and get them back where they belong."

"After what they done?" Brenham sounded surprised. "To tell you the truth, Matt, I didn't figure we'd be takin' any prisoners."

"More than likely it won't come to that," Matt said. "I don't expect them to give up without a fight."

"I hope they don't," Brenham said fervently. "I really do."

They rode on, watching and listening intently for anything out of the ordinary. Matt had studied Major Macmillan's maps of the area, but he had never been to Dark Valley before and wasn't sure exactly what they were going to encounter. About an hour after he and Brenham had parted company from the rest of the patrol, he brought his horse to a halt and pointed.

"Smoke on the other side of that ridge," he said.

"I see it," Brenham said. "Don't look like a house or a barn on fire, though. More like chimney smoke."

"I think so, too," Matt agreed. "That must be one of those ranches we're supposed to be looking for. I'll go ahead and ride on in so I can warn the folks living there. Think you can backtrack to the patrol and bring them here?"

"Sure I can," Brenham declared. "I been a backwoodsman all my life, Matt. Was runnin' around them Georgia hills when I was just knee-high to a possum."

Matt grinned and said, "All right, then, head on out —"

He stopped short as a volley of gunfire erupted somewhere not far away. The shots came from the direction of the chimney smoke they had spotted a few moments earlier, and there were too many of them to think it was somebody shooting at an animal or anything like that.

No, that was a real life-or-death fight they were hearing, and Matt knew what it had to mean.

They had caught up to Black Moon and the other renegades at last.

CHAPTER SEVEN

Matt jerked his Winchester out of the saddle boot.

"Taw, get back to the patrol!" he said. "Bring them back here as fast as you can."

"Dadblast it, Matt!" the young trooper protested. "I can't go off and leave you —"

"That's an order, soldier!"

Brenham pulled his horse half around and said, "You told me you weren't no officer, so I don't have to do what you say!"

Matt bit back an impatient curse.

"Listen, we both know what's happening on the other side of that ridge. There's at least a dozen renegades in Black Moon's war party. Two men can't stop them any more than one man can. The whole patrol needs to be here if we're going to have any chance of saving those settlers."

Matt's words made sense, but he could tell Brenham was torn by the logic anyway. Finally the soldier grimaced, hauled his horse the rest of the way around, and called over his shoulder, "Don't kill too many of the rascals 'fore I get back!"

He jammed his heels into the horse's flanks and sent it leaping into a gallop. The cavalry mount's hooves drummed against the ground as Taw Brenham raced back the way he and Matt had come.

Matt headed the other way, toward the ridge beyond where the fighting continued.

He rode most of the way up the slope, winding his way rapidly through the trees, but he reined in and swung down from the saddle just before he reached the crest. Charging blindly into the middle of a Comanche raid wouldn't accomplish anything except to get him killed. His long legs carried him quickly to the top of the ridge, where he stopped and stood with the rifle in his hands as he surveyed the scene below him.

The ranch house was about three hundred yards away, a double log cabin with a covered, open space known as a dogtrot between the two halves of the structure. A barn with an attached corral and a smaller outbuilding that was probably a smokehouse stood not far off. There was a vegetable garden, bare at this time of year, behind the cabin. It was a nice-looking spread, nothing fancy about it, but a place where a family could live and work and build something worthwhile.

Whoever had built the cabin had cleared all the trees for about fifty yards around it, leaving only short stumps. That was a wise move, because it meant attackers had to cross that open ground to reach the cabin. A sprawled, unmoving figure in a buckskin shirt and wool trousers showed that one of the renegades had tried and failed to do just that.

Puffs of powdersmoke came from loop-holes cut into the cabin's thick walls, as well as from gaps between heavy wooden shutters that had been pulled mostly closed over the windows. The settlers were putting up a good fight. Matt wasn't sure how many defenders were in there. Five or six, he estimated.

They were outnumbered, though. At least a dozen raiders were scattered around the place, some crouched behind trees, others firing from the barn as they poured lead at the cabin. Black Moon and his renegades were well armed with stolen Winchesters and Henry rifles. It wouldn't be easy to root out the defenders, but if the Comanche warriors had plenty of ammunition they could lay siege to the cabin and eventually force the settlers to come out and die.

Or maybe they would try to hurry things along by setting fire to the place, Matt thought. If they could get a torch onto the wooden shingles on top of the cabin, the defenders wouldn't have any choice other than staying inside and burning to death — if they didn't choke on the smoke first — or fleeing right into the bullets of the enemy.

From where Matt stood, he could see several of the renegades. They didn't know he was up here, so he was confident he could pick off two or three of them before they were aware of what was going on.

If he did that, however, he would lose the advantage of surprise.

It might be more effective to go right down there among them and try to kill as many as he could, hand to hand, before they realized he was there. That was what Preacher would have done. . . .

Then the decision was taken out of his hands as one of the raiders did something Matt never would have expected. The man stepped out into the open where the people in the cabin could see him.

They didn't fill him full of lead, though. In fact, their guns fell silent, because the renegade stood there with a prisoner held tightly in front of him. A boy, probably around twelve, skinny and ungainly, with a shock of fair hair that stood out sharply against the Indian's dark buckskins.

Someone inside the cabin screamed. A woman, Matt thought grimly. Probably the boy's mother.

Sunlight flashed on the heavy blade of the knife the renegade held at the captive's throat.

"Come out or the boy dies!" the warrior called in good English he had probably learned on the reservation.

One of the shutters flew open. A woman looked out in bug-eyed horror and cried, "Tommy!"

Somebody inside the cabin grabbed her and dragged her away from the window as rifles blasted outside. A man's arm came in sight as he tried to reach out and pull the shutter closed again. Blood flew as a bullet hammered through the back of his hand and made him howl in pain. Even wounded, though, he managed to grab the short piece of rope attached to the shutter as a handle and jerk it. The shutter thumped back into place.

A second later, guns roared from inside the house as the defenders opened fire again. None of their bullets came close to the renegade with the hostage, however.

They couldn't shoot at him without risking the boy's life.

That might not have made any difference, because the Comanche let out a shrill war cry and raised the knife. Matt knew he was about to either plunge it into the boy's chest or cut his throat.

Matt brought the rifle up, socketed the butt firmly against his shoulder, and took half a second to aim. That was all the time he had.

He pressed the trigger.

The boom of the shot was pretty well lost in the racket from all the other gunfire, but the results were obvious. The bullet took the renegade in the side of the head just as the knife started to fall, bored through his brain, and exploded out the other side of his skull in a pink spray of blood and bone. He dropped like a stone, letting go of both the boy and the knife.

It was a near-miraculous shot, and Matt knew he might not have been able to make it again.

But he had made it this time and that was what counted.

The results were instant. As soon as the renegade let go of him and collapsed, the boy took off running. He had the presence of mind not to try to make it to the cabin.

He never would have survived a dash across that open ground. The Indians would have shot him in the back if he'd attempted it.

Instead he turned and sprinted back into the trees, which were a lot closer. Matt lost sight of him right away.

At the same time, a couple of the renegades must have realized where the fatal shot had come from, because they turned and started up the ridge toward Matt's position.

He didn't give them a chance to reach him. The Winchester's lever flashed down and then back up as he worked it. The rifle cracked as it bucked against his shoulder. The slug tore through one renegade's torso and knocked him off his feet. He started tumbling back down the hill.

Almost before that man hit the ground, Matt had worked the rifle's lever again and shifted his aim. Once more the Winchester barked its deadly message. This time the target stumbled from the slug's impact but stayed on his feet until Matt drilled him a second time. That put the renegade down for good.

By now the rest of the raiders were beginning to realize they were caught in a crossfire. They went to the ground, hunting better cover, and within a matter of seconds

Matt couldn't see them anymore.

He knew they were still there, though, because bullets began to crackle through the brush and trees around him. He ducked behind a tree as a slug whined past his ear.

Now it was a question of whether the renegades would break off their attack on the ranch to come after him. He hoped they would, even though that would increase his personal danger. He wanted to draw them away from the cabin and give those settlers a better chance to survive.

He continued throwing lead at the raiders, although he had to aim by sound now that he could no longer see them. The longer he could keep them occupied and concentrating on him, the better.

A faint whisper of sound in the brush to his left was all the warning he had. As instinct made him turn in that direction, one of the Comanche lunged into the open and flew at him in a diving tackle.

Matt swung the Winchester and clipped the renegade on the jaw with the barrel, but the man's momentum carried him into Matt anyway. The collision's impact knocked Matt over backward.

He rolled and threw the attacker off him. Matt was up instantly on one knee and drove the rifle's butt down at the man's head. It landed in the middle of the renegade's face with a crunch of gristle and bone.

Another branch crackled, this time to Matt's right. He twisted in that direction and fired the Winchester from the hip as he caught sight of a face twisted in a hate-filled snarl. The slug caught the raider under the chin and angled on up into his brain. He toppled as blood fountained from the wound.

Matt surged to his feet and glanced at the man he had struck with the rifle. The renegade was dead with blood leaking out of his ears. In a matter of moments, Matt had killed five of the Comanche, cutting their force almost in half.

But there were still more than half a dozen of them on the loose, so he wasn't out of the woods yet — literally.

More crashing in the brush made him lift the Winchester. He saw movement and almost fired, but he held off on the trigger at the last second.

The boy who had been taken prisoner by the Indians burst into view, stopped short, and stared at Matt over the barrel of the rifle. His face was pale to start with and dusted with freckles, but it got even more washed out as he must have realized how close he had just come to dying.

"Gosh, mister!" he said. "Don't shoot!"

Matt started to lower the Winchester, then whipped it up again and squeezed the trigger. The boy yelped in terror, then looked over his shoulder as he realized that Matt had targeted something behind him.

Another of the renegades lay there, staring sightlessly at the live oak branches above them. Matt's bullet had left a neat hole between his eyes.

More of the raiders were on their way, though. Matt heard them coming. He glanced around, spotted a deadfall several yards away, and grabbed the boy's arm.

"Come on, kid," he said. "We've got to hunt cover."

They ran for the log and vaulted over it. As they did so, shots rang out and slugs exploded splinters from the rotten wood. Matt pushed the boy down on the ground and thrust the rifle barrel over the log.

The odds were against them, but he would make a fight of it. He saw shapes flitting through the trees and said under his breath, "Here they come."

CHAPTER EIGHT

Matt opened fire as several of the renegades burst into sight. He didn't have time to see if any of his shots hit their targets because the enemy sent a volley of hot lead scream- ing back at him. He had to duck as the slugs struck the log and showered him with bits of rotten wood.

An Indian vaulted over the log and fired his rifle at close range. The shot pounded Matt's ears like a fist. He felt the fiery lick of the bullet as it passed close to his cheek and dug into the ground next to his head. Holding his Winchester one-handed, he shoved the muzzle under the renegade's chin and pulled the trigger. The man's head blew apart in large chunks. A sticky mix of blood and brains showered down on Matt.

He rolled and threw himself on top of the boy to shield the slender form with his own body. Dropping the Winchester, he snatched his Colt from its holster. The revolver was better for close work like this. It boomed and bucked in his hand as he triggered a couple of shots and saw another of the attackers spin away with blood flying from his wounds.

Then another volley roared nearby. Bullets scythed through the trees, cutting down several of the renegades. A familiar voice shouted, "Come on, men!"

Major Macmillan and the rest of the patrol had arrived and not a moment too soon.

The renegades who were still on their feet turned to flee. Matt pushed himself up on his left hand and fired the Colt in his right. His slugs drove into the back of one raider, made the man cry out and stumble, then pitch forward onto his face.

Normally Matt preferred his fights face to face, but after seeing what these savages had done in earlier raids, he knew he wouldn't lose one second of sleep over shooting the man in the back like that. Any of the renegades who got away meant that the settlers in this region were still in danger.

The fight didn't last long once the troopers rushed down the ridge and plunged into the thick of the melee. The Comanche were outnumbered now, and in a matter of moments, all of them had been cut down.

As the shooting died away, Matt looked down at the boy and asked, "Are you all right, son?"

The boy swallowed hard and nodded.

"Yeah, I . . . I think so, mister," he said. "I figured I was a goner for sure, though, when that Injun grabbed me."

"What were you doing?"

"Tryin' to get a squirrel for my ma's stew pot." The boy swallowed again. "That blasted squirrel was dang near the death of me."

Matt chuckled and got to his feet. He reloaded the Colt, pouched the iron, and then reached down to give the youngster a hand. While he was doing that, Major Macmillan, Sergeant Houlihan, and Private Brenham came over to them.

"Looks like we got here just in time, Matt," Macmillan said.

"Yeah, another couple of minutes would've been too late, Major," Matt agreed. "Those varmints were about to overrun us."

Macmillan nodded toward Brenham and said, "You can thank the private for that. He rode hard to find us, and then pushed us to get back here as fast as we could."

Matt smiled at the Southerner and said, "I'm obliged to you, Taw, and so is . . ." He looked over at the boy and asked, "What's your name, son?"

"Tommy Chadwick, sir. That ranch down yonder belongs to my pa."

"I'm Matt Jensen," Matt introduced himself. "This is Major Macmillan."

"Son," Macmillan said as he nodded. "We'd better get down there and make sure the rest of your family came through this fracas all right."

"I hope they did," Tommy said. "They ought to be fine if they all got in the house quick enough. Pa built it sturdy. He said we might have to fight off Injuns now and then. Never had no trouble until now, though."

Macmillan turned to Houlihan and said, "Sergeant, check on the enemy and see if there are any captives to deal with."

"Yes, sir," Houlihan said. Matt caught the glint in the man's eyes. He was pretty sure Houlihan would report that all the renegades were dead, even if he had to help some of them along into the next world.

Houlihan wasn't likely to forget what had happened at those other ranches, either.

Matt, Macmillan, and Tommy walked down the slope toward the double cabin. The doors opened before they got there. A stout woman with graying brown hair rushed out and cried, "Tommy!", then hurried to meet them and threw her arms around the boy in a hug.

"Aw, Ma!" Tommy said. Now that the danger was over he was embarrassed by such a show of affection, as any boy his age would have been.

A middle-aged man who was probably Tommy's father trailed the woman. He had a bloody rag wrapped around his hand as a bandage, indicating that he was the one who had reached out to close the shutter on the window.

He was followed by a pair of boys in their late teens, a girl about fifteen, and a girl a little younger than Tommy. Matt saw smears of powder smoke grime on the faces of the older boys and the older girl and knew they had taken part in the fighting. Youngsters sometimes had to grow up quickly out here on the frontier.

The man patted Tommy awkwardly on the shoulder, then turned to Matt and the major. As he stuck out his hand, he said, "I'm John Chadwick. I reckon my boy owes his life to you fellas. Probably the rest of us do, too. I'm obliged to you more than I could ever say."

"We're here to protect the settlers from renegades," Macmillan said as he shook hands with Chadwick. "I'm Major Patrick

Macmillan, in command of this patrol from Fort Griffin. This is our scout, Matt Jensen."

Chadwick clasped Matt's hand and said, "I think I've heard of you, Mr. Jensen. Sure was our good fortune that you came along today."

"I'm glad we did," Matt said. "We were on our way here to warn you that there might be trouble."

"You know, when we settled here, I expected a raid from time to time, but it's been so peaceful in these parts I guess we all sort of let our guards down. These Indians are the first ones we've seen except for some old-timers passing through once in a while. They never seemed like they wanted any trouble."

"Since Colonel Mackenzie broke the back of the Comanche resistance a few years ago up at Palo Duro Canyon, most of them have moved onto the reservation in Indian Territory," Macmillan explained. "But there are always a few firebrands who can't stand to be tamed. They jump the reservation and go raiding now and then." He paused, then added grimly, "This bunch won't do that again."

"I hope you'll stay a spell," Chadwick said. "We'd like to put on a feast and show you men just how much we appreciate what you've done."

Macmillan smiled and said, "That might could be arranged, although we can't delay too long in returning to the fort —"

He stopped as Houlihan approached them. The little Irish non-com was frowning.

"What's wrong, Sergeant?" Macmillan asked.

Houlihan jerked a thumb over his shoulder and said, "We got fourteen dead Comanch' here, Major."

"That's about how many we expected, isn't it?"

"Problem is, ain't none of 'em got that half-moon mark."

Matt knew what Houlihan was talking about. He had seen the report that had been sent out to the different forts in Texas, listing the names and descriptions of the men who had left the reservation. The leader of the group, Black Moon, had gotten that name because of a black, half-moon-shaped mark on the left side of his face. The stain had been left there when someone had fired a gun practically in his face during a battle when he was a young man. The burning powder had pitted and blackened his skin permanently.

"Are you sure, Sergeant?" Macmillan

asked. "Perhaps you should check again."

"Already checked twice, sir. That devil ain't here."

"Maybe he was killed in one of those earlier raids," Macmillan suggested. "The people at those ranches fought back, after all, before they were massacred."

Houlihan shrugged and said, "Could be." It was obvious, though, that he didn't really believe it.

Neither did Matt. Black Moon was the ringleader of the group that had jumped the reservation. It was likely none of the other warriors would have turned renegade without his urging. Maybe they would have continued their rampage anyway if Black Moon had been killed, but Matt thought it more likely they would have tried to head back to Indian Territory and sneak onto the reservation, hoping to escape punishment for what they had done.

No, his gut told him that Black Moon was still alive and out there somewhere, having slipped away from this ranch when it became obvious to him that his followers were about to be wiped out.

John Chadwick frowned and asked, "Do you think we need to worry about this Indian you're talking about, Major?"

Macmillan shook his head without hesitation and said, "No, he's just one man. I don't think he represents any real threat. Local authorities can handle him from here on out. We'll spread the word that he may be in the vicinity so the Rangers and other lawmen can keep an eye out for him."

"I'm not sure that's good enough, Major," Matt said.

Macmillan sounded a little annoyed as he asked, "What do you mean?"

"You're going back to Fort Griffin, aren't you?"

"That's right. I can't justify keeping an entire patrol out just to hunt for one man."

"You shouldn't need me anymore, though. I think I'll see if I can pick up Black Moon's trail."

"You're going after him by yourself?"

Matt smiled.

"Like you said, he's only one man."

Matt could tell that the major didn't like the decision he had made, but Macmillan had no way of stopping him. Matt was a civilian and subject to the officer's orders only as long as he was riding with the patrol. He hadn't signed a contract, so if he went off on his own it was none of the army's business.

Chadwick said, "You'll wait and let us feed you a good meal before you set out, won't you, Mr. Jensen?"

"I reckon I can do that," Matt replied with a smile. "And I'm obliged to you for it."

"Not as much as we are to you." Chadwick put a hand on Tommy's shoulder again. "You saved my son's life."

"Sergeant, have the men bring in their horses," Macmillan ordered. "We'll be stopped here for a while."

"Yes, sir," Houlihan said. He hurried off to carry out the order.

Matt gazed at the wooded slopes of Dark Valley. He didn't like the gloomy place any more than he had when he'd first laid eyes on it.

In fact, he liked it even less . . . because he knew there was a good chance that somewhere out there was a crazed killer named Black Moon.

CHAPTER NINE

The Texas Hill Country

Seth Barrett put his shoulder against the back end of the wagon and heaved. Beside him, a short, stocky boy of ten grunted as he threw all his strength into the effort as well. Charlie couldn't help much, Seth knew, but the youngster thought of himself as the man of the family because his father was dead. It was important for him to try to do as much as he could.

The wagon didn't budge, though. Its wheels remained stuck in the mud.

The blasted mud was the result of more than a week of intermittent, unseasonal downpours. Folks around here talked about how it never rained like this in December, nearing Christmastime. But it was raining this year, and that was all that mattered.

Seth stopped pushing and straightened up to catch his breath. He leaned to the side to call to the woman who stood at the heads of the mule team hitched to the wagon, "We'll try again in a minute, Mrs. Kennedy."

"I don't believe this wagon is going anywhere, Mr. Barrett," she replied in a despairing tone. "I'm afraid Charlie and I are just going to have to leave it here." She sighed. "I should have paid more attention to where I was going and stayed on the drier parts of the road."

Seth put a weary smile on his face and said, "The Lord tells us to persevere. I'm prepared to take Him at His word . . . at least a few more times before I give up."

Charlie leaned over, put his hands on his knees and puffed for breath. He looked up and said, "No offense, Preacher, but I don't reckon even the Good Lord His own self could get this danged ol' wagon outta the mud."

"Charlie," his mother scolded. "That's no way to talk to Mr. Barrett. You shouldn't be doubting the Lord, either."

"I just know how sticky this stuff is," Charlie muttered.

Charlie was right about that, thought Seth. The rain had turned all the roads in these parts into gumbo. It wasn't raining now, but it had poured again earlier in the day and a thick overcast still covered the sky. Even if it didn't rain any more for a while, it would take days, maybe even weeks, for the ground to dry out.

Seth didn't figure that would happen anytime soon. The clouds were still ominous as they roiled and scudded through the sky overhead.

While he took a break from trying to free the wagon, he put his gaze on something a lot more appealing than the threatening sky.

Delta Kennedy's lovely face.

It was heart-shaped, framed by thick wings of dark brown hair that escaped from under the bonnet she wore. She had a small beauty mark on her right cheek and a tiny scar on her upper lip that just made her attractiveness distinctive rather than distracting from it. Her eyes, Seth happened to know, were a rich brown and could kindle a warm glow inside a man just by looking at him.

He knew that because he had experienced just such a glow more than once while talking to Mrs. Kennedy. On such occasions, just being near her had a tendency to make him a little tongue-tied. That was a definite drawback for a man who had always considered himself to be a little on the glib side.

Today she wasn't making quite as strong an impression on him because of the circumstances. He was concentrating on getting her wagon out of the mud, instead of thinking about how pretty she was. There was nothing flirtatious about her attitude, either. Naturally, she was worried about this dilemma. The wagon was loaded with supplies she had bought at Mr. Truesdale's crossroads store, and she had to get them back to her farm somehow.

Seth's saddle mount was standing nearby, reins dangling. He had been riding back to the Enchanted Rock Baptist Church, where he was the pastor, after visiting one of the congregation who was ill, when he spotted the stranded wagon. He would have stopped to help no matter who the wagon belonged to, since he liked to think of himself as a Good Samaritan, but he recognized the wagon's passengers right away and that made him even more eager to be of assistance.

"All right, Charlie," Seth said as he clapped a hand on the boy's shoulder. "Are you ready to try again?"

"Any time you are, Mr. Barrett," Charlie affirmed.

"Mrs. Kennedy, if you'll take hold of the harness and urge the team forward while we push . . ."

"Of course," she said.

91

"If we don't get it loose this time, I'll tie my horse to the wagon as well and see if that will help."

Seth and Charlie bent to the task, but before they could heave against the stubborn wagon, Seth heard riders coming along the road toward them. Horses' hooves splashed loudly in the puddles. Seth looked over his shoulder and saw four men approaching. He straightened up as he recognized the barrel-chested rider in the lead.

Felix Dugan reined his horse to a stop about twenty feet behind the wagon. The burly rancher was older than Seth, around forty. His face was round and sported what seemed to be a permanent sunburn year 'round. A mustache like a graying brush adorned his upper lip. His jaw was like a slab of Hill Country granite.

As a preacher, Seth was supposed to like everybody, but he didn't like Felix Dugan. The man had a hard, ruthless arrogance about him. His ranch was the largest in the area, and he tended to run roughshod over his neighbors anytime they clashed with him. Naturally enough, the men who rode for him weren't any better. They smirked at Seth's mud-splattered clothes.

Even if Dugan had been a prince among men, though, Seth wouldn't have liked him for one simple reason.

Dugan was sweet on Delta Kennedy.

A widower for quite a few years, Dugan had been heard to express his admiration for Delta on more than one occasion and voiced the opinion that she would make a fine wife for some man. He left no doubt that he was talking about himself.

Now Dugan took off his hat, forced a smile onto his normally dour face, and greeted Delta by saying, "Good day to you, Mrs. Kennedy. You appear to have a bit of trouble on your hands."

He didn't say anything to Seth. In fact, he acted like Seth wasn't even there.

"My wagon is stuck," Delta said unnecessarily.

"Well, we'll take care of that right away," Dugan said. "Won't we, boys?"

The ranch hands riding with him grinned and nodded. One man said, "Sure thing, boss."

"Mr. Barrett is helping us —" Delta began.

"Preacher," Dugan said curtly, acknowledging Seth's presence for the first time. "You'll never get that wagon out of the mud that way."

Seth thought the rancher probably was right, which certainly didn't improve matters. But stubbornly, he said, "Charlie and I don't need any help."

"I reckon we do," the boy piped up. "This ol' wagon's a whole heap stuck."

"Get out of the way," Dugan snapped at Seth. "Boys."

The ranch hands rode around Seth. A couple of them dismounted and tied ropes to the wagon while the third man went to the head of the team and said, "Let me have 'em, ma'am." Delta relinquished her hold on the harness and moved aside.

The two cowboys tied the other ends of the ropes to their saddle horns. One man was on each side of the vehicle. They moved their horses forward until the ropes were taut. They pulled steadily while the man leading the mules urged them on.

"I'll give you a hand," Dugan called. He swung down from the saddle and slogged through the mud to the back of the wagon.

"Step back, Charlie," Seth told the boy. He wasn't going to let Dugan do this alone.

"I don't need any help, preacher," Dugan said with a sneer.

"Neither did I, but you insisted anyway," Seth shot back. He bent over and braced his shoulder against the wagon as he set his feet. Dugan did likewise. Both of them heaved against the weight and the grip that the mud had on the wheels.

Slowly but surely, the wagon began to move. Just an inch or two at first, then another and another and then with a loud squelching sound, the mud let go of the wheels and the wagon jolted forward.

The sudden movement threw Seth off-balance and made him stumble. He caught himself before he fell.

Felix Dugan wasn't as fortunate. His feet slipped out from under him, and he sprawled face-first in the mud, landing with a wet slapping sound.

A laugh burst from Seth's throat. He couldn't stop it. That pompous windbag wallowing around in the mud like a hog was the funniest thing he had seen in a long time. Charlie joined in the laughter, too, until his mother said his name sharply to silence him.

The three ranch hands kept the wagon moving until it reached a stretch of road that wasn't so muddy. Then the man who had been leading the team let go of the harness and hurried back to where Seth was standing. A few feet away, Dugan sputtered and spit as he tried to push himself up out of the mud.

The cowboy grated, "Think it's funny, do you?" as he snatched his coiled lasso off the loop where it was attached to his saddle. He crowded the horse toward Seth and slashed at him with the rope.

Seth darted out of the way, reached up, and caught hold of the man's arm. Taken by surprise, the cowboy couldn't stay in the saddle as Seth heaved on him. He let out a startled yell, turned over in the air, and splashed down into the mud.

He got up faster than his boss had managed to, and as he came to his feet, rage twisted his features and he clawed at the gun on his hip.

Delta cried, "Charlie, get away from there!" as she ran toward her son.

Seth crouched as instinct made his hand move toward his hip. There was nothing there for him to grab, though.

Dugan had made it to his knees. He yelled, "Andrews! Hold it!"

The cowboy stopped with his revolver half clear of the holster. He shook with anger and the urge to complete the draw. He said, "Boss, this varmint needs to be taught a lesson! He needs to know he can't laugh at his betters like that!"

"I agree," Dugan said as he finished clambering to his feet. "But I'll be the one to teach him!"

He clenched his big hands into rock-hard

fists, let out a bellow like a maddened bull, and charged toward Seth.

CHAPTER TEN

Dugan's men shouted encouragement to their boss. Seth tried to dart out of the way of the attack, but the mud sucking at his boots slowed him. Normally he would have been quicker on his feet than the lumbering, heavyset rancher, but the weather conditions took away that advantage.

Seth was able to move enough that the looping punch Dugan aimed at his jaw clipped him on the shoulder instead. Even though it was a glancing blow, it packed enough power to stagger him. He caught himself and jabbed a swift left at Dugan's face. It landed on the man's nose with a satisfying pop and rocked Dugan's head back.

Dugan was about to learn that just because Seth was a man of God, that didn't mean he was a pushover in a fight.

Delta had grabbed Charlie and pulled him away from the battle. She held on to him and called to the two men, "Please stop! Don't do this!"

Dugan was too angry to pay any attention to her, and Seth was determined to defend himself. If Dugan wanted a fight, Seth would give him one.

Grunting with the effort, Dugan swung wild, roundhouse punches at Seth, who managed to avoid them despite being slowed down by the mud. The burly rancher had no technique at all, Seth noted. Either Dugan was used to winning his fights by sheer power, or else his opponents held back because he was a wealthy, influential man.

Seth didn't care how much money Dugan had or about his standing in the community. The old wild streak had welled up inside him when he was attacked, and as Dugan flailed away at him, he began to take pleasure in the way he blocked the punches or weaved aside from them, then stepped in to pepper Dugan with hard lefts and rights of his own.

The thud of fists against flesh and bone felt good, mighty good.

Dugan's nose was swollen and blood leaked from it. His mouth was puffy, too, and one of his eyes had started to turn black. Seth didn't waste time and energy pounding away at Dugan's torso, sheathed as it was in thick slabs of muscle. Instead he turned his efforts to the rancher's face and steadily, methodically, chopped it into something resembling raw meat.

One of the cowboys shouted a curse and said, "He's handin' the boss a lickin'! We gotta do somethin' about this!"

Another agreed eagerly and profanely with that sentiment.

Andrews, the man Seth had jerked off his horse and thrown in the mud, held his companions back.

"Mr. Dugan said to let him handle this," Andrews pointed out grimly. "That's what we got to do." He paused, then added, "But if he goes down, we'll hand that preacher man a thrashin' he'll never forget!"

Seth heard that and knew he faced bigger odds than just Dugan. Chances were, this confrontation would end with him taking a whipping from the cowhands, but he didn't care. In the time he had been in this part of the country, he had seen how Dugan had most folks cowed, and it was past due for somebody to stand up to him.

Dugan was halfway out on his feet by now. He was still throwing punches, but they were even slower and more clumsy than they had been at first. He didn't come close to making contact with Seth, who was punching him at will. Finally, with a bit of a shock, Seth realized that both of Dugan's eyes were swollen nearly closed. The rancher probably couldn't even see him anymore and was striking out blindly, unable to defend himself.

Suddenly, a wave of shame washed through Seth. This wasn't the sort of man he was, or at least the sort he was trying to be. He lowered his fists and stepped back.

"That's enough, Dugan," he said. He was breathing hard. The air rasped a little in his throat. "We don't need to fight anymore."

"Come on!" Dugan mumbled. "Come on, you blasted coward!" His speech was thick because of his puffy, bloody lips.

"No. It's over."

Dugan roared furiously and somehow found the strength for one more charge. Seth didn't hit him this time. He just stepped out of the way. Dugan lost his balance and fell, plowing the mud with his face again.

"That's it," Andrews barked. "Get him!"

The three cowboys had just started toward Seth when a loud boom froze them in their tracks.

It wasn't thunder, although there had been some of that with the storms over the past few weeks. This blast came from a shotgun. Delta Kennedy held it in her hands with the twin barrels pointed toward the overcast sky. She lowered the weapon and said in a ragged voice, "That's enough! No more fighting!"

The shotgun was aimed mostly at the three cowboys, but where Seth was he found himself staring down the barrels, too. He said, "Uh, Mrs. Kennedy, you might want to be careful —"

"This gun won't go off unless I want it to," Delta snapped. "I've had to shoot enough rattlesnakes and run off enough coyotes to know what I'm doing. Now somebody roll Mr. Dugan over before he drowns in that mud."

Seth was the closest, so he bent down and grasped Dugan's shoulder with both hands. He rolled the man onto his back. Dugan gasped for air. Seth wiped some of the mud away from his mouth and nose so he could breathe easier.

"You're gonna be sorry you jumped the boss like that, preacher man," Andrews said coldly.

"He went after me first," Seth said as he straightened. "I just defended myself."

"And I'll back up Mr. Barrett's story to anyone who cares to ask," Delta said. She frowned at Seth and added, "Although you didn't have to defend yourself quite so . . . ruthlessly."

Seth understood what she meant, but a part of him disagreed with her. When a man was attacked, surviving was all that mattered. If that meant fighting back as hard and brutally as he could, then so be it.

He tamped those impulses down and forced himself to nod.

"I'm sorry," he said. "I guess I just got carried away."

"Carried away, nothin'!" Charlie exclaimed, wide-eyed with excitement. "You whipped him good!"

"Charlie, get in the wagon," Delta said.

"Aw, Ma —"

"In the wagon."

As Charlie obeyed, his mother went on to the cowboys, "You'd better pick up Mr. Dugan, get him on his horse, and take him home. He'll need to be cleaned up and have any injuries attended to. I think his nose may be broken."

If it wasn't, thought Seth, it wasn't from lack of trying on his part.

Delta finally lowered the shotgun as the three ranch hands went to help Dugan, but she didn't put it back in the wagon where she had gotten it. Seth wasn't surprised she had brought the weapon with her when she went to Truesdale's store. The Hill Country was still wild enough that a person could run into trouble here and needed to be prepared.

The men got Dugan on his feet and half-dragged, half-carried him over to the big black horse he had ridden up on. With much grunting and straining, they lifted him into the saddle. Dugan was still in a stupor, but when Andrews wrapped his hands around the saddle horn, he hung on and kept from falling, although he still swayed some.

The cowboys mounted up. Andrews took Dugan's reins to lead the horse. He glared at Seth and said, "This ain't over, preacher man."

"You know where to find me," Seth said coolly.

"Yeah. Hidin' in that church."

"I'm a little surprised you know where it is. I haven't seen you there." Seth smiled faintly. "But I'll come out anytime you want to talk to me."

"It ain't talkin' I got in mind."

Andrews jerked his horse to the side. He and his companions rode around the wagon and plodded on in the direction they had been going before the fight.

Seth watched them until they had disappeared around a bend. Then he turned to Delta, who was putting the shotgun back into the wagon bed behind the seat.

"I'm sorry about that —" he began.

"You ought to be," she interrupted him. "It was your fault."

"My fault?" Seth stared at her. Even though he liked her, he felt a flash of anger at the accusation she had leveled at him. "How in the world was it my fault? You saw the way he came after me. You told Andrews you'd say as much."

"I saw what happened, yes, but I also know it's unlikely Mr. Dugan would have attacked you if you hadn't laughed at him."

"You didn't think it was funny when that stuffed shirt fell in the mud?"

Delta didn't say anything for a moment, then replied, "Maybe it was, but you had to know it would provoke him. A man like Mr. Dugan can't stand to have his pride wounded."

"A man like Dugan needs to have some of the hot air let out of him now and then. That's all I did."

Delta shook her head and said, "No. What you did was make an enemy. A bad enemy."

"Some say you can tell a lot about a man by the quality of his enemies. And I don't believe in running scared from a bully.

That's all Felix Dugan is."

"I don't have any interest in arguing with you, Mr. Barrett." Delta started to climb to the wagon seat. Seth moved to take her arm and help her, but she pulled away before he could. As she settled herself and took up the reins, she went on, "You should be careful."

"I always am," he said. That had been a habit of his for a long time, and he hadn't put it aside just because he had felt the calling and taken up preaching. As Delta clucked to her team and flicked the reins, he added, "I'll see you and Charlie Sunday morning?"

"We'll be there, like always," she promised.

Seth watched as the wagon rolled on down the road toward the Kennedy farm. Delta was being careful now to stay in the middle of the path where the mud wasn't as bad. With any luck she and Charlie would get home with no more trouble.

As Seth turned toward his horse, he felt a drop of rain strike his cheek. He glanced up at the clouds and said, "More, Lord? Really?"

Then he felt bad for doubting the Lord's intentions, swung up into the saddle, and headed for the church, hoping he would get there before another downpour started.

CHAPTER ELEVEN

Austin

Ace and Chance were in the hotel dining room, just finishing up an enjoyable breakfast, when William Sydney Porter came in, spotted them, and started toward their table.

"Uh-oh," Ace said under his breath. "Here he comes. I was sort of hoping he'd forgotten about what happened last night."

"I don't think he's the kind of fella who forgets things," Chance said. "Claimed he wants to be a writer, didn't he? I'd think a gent like that would have to have a good memory."

"I don't see why, just to make up a bunch of nonsense."

Porter reached the table, grinned, and said loudly, "Good morning, amigos. It's a beautiful day, isn't it?"

"Well, it's not pouring down rain right now," Ace said. "I reckon that's an improvement."

107

"I think I even saw a sliver or two of sunshine," Chance added. "Didn't look like it was going to last, though."

Without waiting for an invitation, Porter pulled out one of the empty chairs at the table and sat down. A waitress in a starched white apron started toward him. He turned to smile at her and said, "Just coffee, my dear."

Narrow-eyed, Ace looked at Porter and said, "You don't look much the worse for wear."

"Why would I be?" Porter asked, sounding genuinely puzzled.

"Well, you put away a considerable amount of whiskey last night," Chance pointed out.

After the confrontation with Oliver Hudson and the brief meeting with Evelyn Channing, Porter, Ace, and Chance had spent some time in one of Austin's saloons, Porter knocking back glasses of whiskey while the Jensen brothers stuck to coffee. Under the circumstances, they had figured it might be a good idea to keep an eye on Porter. They had just met the hombre and had no responsibility for him, of course, but Ace felt sorry for him and knew that Chance did, too.

There was nothing like love to make a

man act like a full-blown idiot. Unrequited love, which was apparently the case with Porter, was even worse.

He had kept raving about how he was going to follow Evelyn to Fredericksburg and stop her from marrying Oliver Hudson. It would be a grand, romantic gesture, he proclaimed, and when he did, she would see how much he loved her and realize that she should have been with him all along.

As gently as possible, Ace and Chance had tried to talk him out of that crazy idea, but they weren't able to get through to him. Finally, in sheer frustration, Ace had said bluntly, "You show up at the wedding and try that speak-now-or-forever-hold-your-peace business, Hudson's liable to put a bullet in you."

"I know that," Porter had said as he poured another drink. "That's why you two young cavaliers will be accompanying me."

"You want us to come along and protect you?" Chance had asked. "Sort of like body-guards?"

"Both of you wear revolvers. And I suspect you're quite capable with them, because I know from the earlier altercation that you're no strangers to violence."

"We've run into our share of trouble," Ace

had said with a frown, "but we're not hired guns."

"Anyway," Chance had added, "you don't appear to be all that flush. You couldn't afford to hire us."

"I thought I would prevail upon you to come with me as friends." A thoughtful expression had appeared on Porter's thin face. "Although . . . I *do* work in a bank and have access to a considerable amount of funds . . ."

"Stop that," Ace had said sharply. "You start talking like that and we'll just leave you right here."

"We've run across some shady characters before," Chance had said. "We throw in with an embezzler and we're liable to wind up behind bars."

A shudder had run through both brothers at the thought of that prospect.

"We don't intend to be locked up," Ace had said in a tone of finality.

Porter hadn't said anything more about getting money from the bank where he worked, but he hadn't backed off from his determination to win Evelyn away from Hudson. That was the way it had been left when Ace and Chance walked him back to the house where he was living. Ace had hoped that when Porter woke up this morning, he would be hungover and would have forgotten the events of the previous evening.

Obviously, that wasn't the case. From the looks of it, Porter was one of those fellows who could get staggering drunk and then be bright-eyed and bushy-tailed the next morning.

Porter sipped the coffee the waitress brought him and said, "It's lucky I remembered you mentioning the hotel where you're staying, or else I might not have been able to find you in a place the size of Austin."

"Yeah," Ace said dryly. "Lucky."

"I've already been out and about this morning, doing some investigating. Evelyn has tendered her resignation at the café where she works. She's taking the stage to Fredericksburg this afternoon, so we've no time to waste."

"How do you know that?" Chance asked.

"I talked to the clerk at the stage line office," Porter explained.

"I didn't think they were supposed to give out information like that," Ace said.

Porter smiled and said, "Well . . . when I told him that I was searching for my dear, sweet, innocent sister who had fallen under the spell of a dastardly, conniving, evil man who wished to lure her away and besmirch

111

her honor, I was able to convince him to assist me. When I described Evelyn, he admitted that he had sold her a ticket for the Fredericksburg stage."

"You don't need to be writing stories and essays," Ace said. "You ought to write melodramas instead."

"Melodramas are the stuff of life, exaggerated for effect," Porter responded with a smile.

"What about Hudson?" Chance asked. "Is he going on the stage, too?"

Porter shook his head.

"Apparently not. I described him for the clerk as well, and the man claimed never to have seen him, let alone sold him a ticket. I believe the gentleman. He was eager to help. Most men live small, quiet lives and are happy to take part in grand, exciting adventures, even though it be vicariously."

"Hudson must have a horse and plan to ride to Fredericksburg," Ace mused. "Could be he's left town already."

Porter made a fist and thumped it on the table.

"That's exactly what I fear has happened," he said. "He's stolen a march on us, gentlemen, and we must act quickly to forestall him!"

"What?" Ace said with a frown. "You can't

stop him from riding to Fredericksburg if he wants to. It's a free country."

"And neither can he stop us. You have horses, I take it?"

"Yeah, we have horses," Chance said. "Do you?"

"As a matter of fact, I have a saddle mount I sometimes take for rides in the country. The animal is stabled near here. I can go back to my boarding house, pack a few things, and be ready to ride in, say, half an hour?"

Ace leaned forward, clasped his hands together on the table, and said, "Listen to me, Will. This is a bad idea you've got. You're just going to get yourself in trouble. I didn't like Hudson, either, but if Miss Channing wants to marry him, that's her decision to make."

"And he's not going to put up with you making a pest of yourself," Chance added. "You'll be better off if you just forget about both of them and get on with your life."

Porter looked back and forth between the brothers as if he couldn't believe what he was hearing. After a moment he said, "Have you no passion in your souls, my friends? Have you never been in love? Have you never had your heart broken?"

"I've had my heart broken plenty of

times," Chance said. "It's sort of like when a red ant bites you. Stings for a while, but then it gets better."

"Ace, surely you understand," Porter said as he turned to the other Jensen brother. "I sense that you and I, we're kindred spirits."

"I don't hardly see how you get that," Ace said. "We didn't come to Austin to get mixed up in any trouble. We figured to just spend some time here taking life easy. Besides, it's going to be Christmas in less than a week. It's a time for celebrating, not fighting."

"Christmas!" Porter slapped the table. "The holiest time of the year. You'd allow a poor man to be emotionally devastated at Christmas?" He heaved a sigh. "What a bitter present the wise men doth deliver!"

"Now, dadgum it —"

Porter held up both hands, palms out, to stop anything else Ace and Chance had to say.

"Never mind," he said. "I understand. We barely know each other. I have no right to ask you to inconvenience yourselves by helping me." He scraped back his chair and stood up. "I'll deal with this matter myself."

"Hold on a minute," Chance said. "You're still going to try to stop Miss Channing from marrying that fella Hudson?"

"I have no choice in the matter," Porter declared. "A man must follow the dictates of his heart."

He turned and walked out of the hotel dining room, head held high.

Chance looked across the table at his brother and said, "Ace, you know he's going charging off to get himself killed, don't you?"

Ace sighed and said, "Hudson didn't strike me as the sort of hombre to put up with anybody interfering with his plans."

"He's a gun wolf, and you know it. We've seen plenty like him."

"We have," Ace agreed soberly.

"And Will, there, he's just hopeless. He wouldn't stand a chance against Hudson."

"Not a chance in the world. But he's not our responsibility, either."

"We can't let a poor fool go off and get shot to pieces at Christmastime."

"A man's not any deader from getting shot at Christmas than he is any other time of the year." Ace put his hands flat on the table and pushed himself to his feet. "But you're right. Let's go after him."

Chance grinned as he stood up.

"You heard what he said about Fredericksburg. Place is full of Germans. I'll bet they celebrate Christmas mighty fine up there in the Hill Country!"

CHAPTER TWELVE

When Ace and Chance hurried out of the hotel a moment later, they saw Porter leaning casually against a lamppost a few yards away with a smile on his face.

"Blast it, you knew we were gonna come after you, didn't you?" Ace said.

"I had high hopes," Porter replied. "As I mentioned previously, we're kindred spirits. I couldn't bring myself to believe that you wouldn't embrace this romantic adventure."

"Yeah, well, let's hope it doesn't get us all killed. Our horses are in the corral back of the hotel. Get your mount and meet us there as soon as you can."

"We'll settle up our bill and gather our gear," Chance added.

"Success awaits us, gentlemen!" Porter said. "I can feel it in my bones!"

"Best hope you don't feel a .45 slug in your bones before this is over," Ace warned him.

Porter wagged a finger at the brothers as he started along the street. He said over his shoulder, "You can't fool me. You're looking forward to this!"

Once Porter was gone, Chance said, "We didn't really want to just sit around Austin for the rest of the winter, did we?"

Ace chuckled and shook his head.

"No, I reckon not. We would have gotten bored. But it might have been nice to enjoy some peace and quiet for just a little bit longer!"

Chance waved a hand in dismissal and said, "Peace and quiet are overrated."

It didn't take long to get their belongings from their room, pay what they owed, and head out to the corral to saddle their horses. They tightened the cinches and led the animals out of the enclosure. Ace shut the gate behind them. They waited for Porter to show up.

As Chance had mentioned in the dining room, the thick clouds had parted in a few places to reveal narrow stretches of blue sky. Sunlight slanted through those gaps. However, darker clouds loomed on the western horizon, and Ace cast a worried glance toward them.

"Looks like more storms moving in," he commented. "And we'll be heading that way, I reckon."

"Maybe it won't be too bad," Chance said. "And we've been rained on before and will be again." He sniffed. "Have to admit I don't much like being soaked to the bone, though. How long do you think it'll take us to get to Fredericksburg?"

"Never made the trip, but a couple of days, I'd guess."

"If the stagecoach Miss Channing is on leaves this afternoon, we might beat it there."

"So Will can be waiting for her when she steps off the stage."

"Yeah, but Hudson likely will be, too."

Ace nodded solemnly and said, "I know." He pointed. "Here he comes."

Porter was walking toward the corral leading a skittish-looking mare. The horse didn't strike Ace as being very strong, but Porter didn't weigh a whole lot, either. That might slow them down a little, since Porter wouldn't be able to push his mount as hard as Ace and Chance could with theirs.

But the whole trip was a bit of a fool's errand anyway, Ace reminded himself. If they weren't in time to stop Evelyn from marrying Oliver Hudson, maybe Porter would finally have to face facts.

Porter had traded his suit for working-man's clothes, although he still wore the straw boater that was more suitable for serenading young ladies than riding across central Texas in what might be building up to a gully washer. He had a carpetbag tied behind his saddle.

"Hope you've got a slicker in there," Ace told him. "From the looks of those clouds, you're liable to need it before the day's over."

"I do," Porter said. "I have something else, too." He opened the carpetbag, reached inside, and brought out a gun.

"Good Lord, Will!" Chance exclaimed. "Where'd you get that smoke wagon?"

The gun was a Colt dragoon revolver, probably more than thirty years old, a heavy, long-barreled weapon that packed quite a punch. Porter had to hold it with both hands to keep it from sagging toward the ground.

"It's a beauty, isn't it?" he asked with a grin. "I bought it a few days ago when I realized that I might have to fight for Evelyn's honor."

"How are you gonna fight with it?" Chance asked. "You can barely lift it!"

"In fact," Ace said as he put a hand on the dragoon's barrel and pushed it down, "why don't you point that cannon at the

120

ground? We wouldn't want it to go off accidentally. That is, if it's loaded."

"Oh, it's loaded, I assure you," Porter said. "The fellow who sold it to me took care of that. I have a full six rounds."

"You don't have any other ammunition for it?"

"No, I thought that would probably be enough."

Ace tried not to roll his eyes. He said, "First of all, give me that thing."

"It's mine," Porter protested. "I bought and paid for it."

"Yeah, but if you carry it around with the hammer resting on a full chamber, all it would take for you to shoot your foot off is a little bump."

"And you'd be lucky if it was just your foot you shot off," Chance added.

Reluctantly, Porter surrendered the revolver. Ace unloaded one of the chambers and carefully lowered the hammer on it.

"That's safer," he said. "Put it back in your bag."

"What if I need it in a hurry?"

Chance said, "That's too much gun for you to get out in a hurry, Will, no matter where you carry it. Might as well be where it's the safest."

"I suppose," Porter said with a shrug.

"That's a percussion revolver," Ace said. "Not as easy to find ammunition for it as it used to be, I imagine. But we'll stop at a store on the way out of town and see if we can buy some. That way you can get some practice with it while we're on our way to Fredericksburg."

That made Porter grin again. He said, "You mean you'll teach me how to be a gunman?"

Chance said, "More likely we'll teach you how not to shoot yourself or anybody else you don't intend to . . . if we're lucky."

The rain still held off as the three young men rode out of Austin a short time later. The storm building in the west didn't seem to be in any hurry to move in. The wind was almost still, barely stirring the chilly air.

Austin perched at the edge of the Balcones Escarpment. The terrain immediately became more rugged just west of town. The road was a good one, though, running almost due west. Ace wasn't sure how many towns were between Austin and Fredericksburg, but if they needed to, they could camp out that night. It would probably be cold, wet, and miserable, but it wouldn't be the first such night he and Chance had spent on the trail.

The hills were covered with junipers. Out-croppings of limestone and granite broke up the vegetation here and there. Deep, nar-row canyons thickly choked with brush slashed through the landscape. The place had a wild beauty about it, and once Austin was a few miles behind them, the road was the only sign of civilization except for an occasional cabin clinging to the side of a hill. Now and then the land leveled out enough to support a small farm or ranch. The riders also passed what looked like some sort of fruit orchard, although the rows of trees were starkly bare at this time of year.

Ace told Porter, "You'd better start think-ing about what you're going to say to Miss Channing the next time you see her, Will."

"I've barely thought of anything else this morning," Porter replied. "I'm going to declare my deep and abiding love for her, of course. I plan to wax eloquent about her beauty and pledge that my affection for her will be eternal. I'll promise to make some-thing of myself and provide for her so splendidly that never again shall she know a single day of discomfort or doubt."

"You figure on doing that by clerking in a bank or a drugstore?" Chance asked. "Isn't that what you said you've been doing? Or maybe if you make a hand at writing, you'll get rich doing that?"

"Doesn't seem likely," Ace said with a dubious shake of his head.

"Whatever I do, all my efforts will be dedicated to making Evelyn happy," Porter insisted. "What more could any woman ask for?"

Chance laughed and said, "In my experience, women aren't much on the idea of giving a fella credit for trying. They're more interested in what he can actually *do.*"

"I'll convince her. You'll see."

"I hope you do," Ace said. "Otherwise we'll have made this trip for nothing more than some good German food."

"Not a bad reason in itself," Chance put in.

They rode on, trying to avoid the worst mud. The wind picked up a little, but it still wasn't raining. When the time came to rest the horses and the three of them had dismounted, Ace took the dragoon revolver out of Porter's carpetbag and handed it to the young man.

"Let's see what you can do with this," he suggested.

Porter took the gun eagerly. He wrapped both hands around the smooth walnut grips and asked, "What do you want me to shoot at?"

Chance pointed at a dead tree about fifteen feet from the edge of the road.

"That tree trunk's almost as wide as a man," he said. "See if you can hit it."

"That should be a simple task." Porter stretched both arms out in front of him as far as they would go and pointed the revolver at the tree. The barrel wobbled up and down and side to side, despite his efforts to hold it still.

"Pull your arms back in a little," Ace told him. "And that's a single-action revolver, Will. You've got to cock it before you can shoot it."

"Oh. Yes. Of course." Porter had to use both thumbs to pull the hammer back and lock it into place. He aimed again, and the gun was a little steadier this time. He still didn't squeeze the trigger. Instead he said, "I must admit, it's a bit unsettling to think about shooting at, well, a fellow human being. I mean, you said the tree is about the same size, Chance, and that made me reflect on what a deeply profound experience it must be to take aim at someone for the express purpose of doing them harm, nay, ending their very existence —"

"Just shoot the tree already," Ace said.

"Very well." Porter took a deep breath and squeezed the trigger.

The dragoon boomed like thunder and kicked up so hard that it flew out of Porter's hands as the recoil knocked him backward. Chance exclaimed, "Whoa!" and jumped forward to catch the revolver before it fell into the mud.

Nobody caught Porter. He wound up sitting in a puddle looking stunned and miserable. Ace managed not to laugh, but he couldn't keep from smiling and shaking his head.

Porter opened his mouth and then closed it again a couple of times. Chance grinned and said, "I reckon Will's been struck speechless for once in his life."

Ace stepped forward to offer Porter a hand, but as he did, something whipped past his ear and thudded into the road. Ace knew instantly what had just happened.

Somebody was shooting at them.

CHAPTER THIRTEEN

The crack of the shot came almost at the same time as Ace sensed the slug passing by his ear, with just enough delay to tell him that the bushwhacker was a little distance away. That meant a rifle. He had a split-second while the would-be killer levered the weapon, so he lunged forward, grabbed Porter's collar, and hauled the man to his feet.

"Run!" Ace snapped.

Chance was moving, too, grabbing the horses' reins and pulling them toward the far side of the road. The trees and brush there were thick enough to provide some cover.

Ace gave Porter a shove in the same direction. Porter stumbled but stayed on his feet and hurried toward the trees behind Chance and the horses.

Another bullet whined past Ace's head. This time the sound of the shot gave him an idea where the bushwhacker was, and he yanked out his Colt and triggered three fast rounds in that general direction. He didn't expect to hit anything, especially at long range, but he wanted to give the rifleman something to think about.

Chance and Porter vanished into the cedars. Ace's long legs carried him into the trees as well. A third shot ripped out from the hidden gunman. The bullet clipped a tree trunk and showered Ace with splinters as he darted past it.

Then he was in relative safety with a lot of those trunks between him and the rifleman. He stopped and pressed his back against a tree. Several yards away, Chance had stopped with the horses. Porter's mare was spooked, and Chance had to struggle to keep the animal under control. Porter, his clothes smeared with mud from his fall, stood nearby, wide-eyed with fear.

"Anybody hit?" Ace called to the other two.

"We're fine," Chance said, then he cursed and thrust the mare's reins into Porter's hands. "Hang on to her, blast it!"

The brothers' mounts were more ac-customed to gunfire, so they weren't caus-ing any trouble. Chance could drop their reins and be confident that they wouldn't go very far. He did that and started dragging out the Winchesters from their saddle boots.

The bushwhacker couldn't see them anymore, but that didn't stop him from spraying lead through the stretch of woods where they had taken cover. Bullets tore through tree trunks and rattled through branches. Just by sheer luck, a few of them came a little too close for comfort.

Chance tossed Ace's Winchester to him. Ace plucked the repeater out of the air and said, "We need to discourage that varmint."

"That's just what I was thinking," Chance agreed. "Will, stay here."

"I . . . I can assure you that's precisely what I intend to do!" Porter responded with a gulp.

Ace and Chance split up and began working their way back toward the edge of the trees. When Ace reached a spot where he could see the road again, he watched the slope on the other side and waited for some telltale sign of the rifleman.

After a few moments his keen eyes spotted movement in the brush at the mouth of a gully about two hundred yards away. Ace concentrated on that location and saw a muzzle flash.

"I see him!" he called to Chance. He

couldn't see his brother anymore but knew he wasn't far away.

"I do, too!" Chance said. "Want to make it hot for him?"

"Bet a hat I do," Ace replied. He brought the Winchester to his shoulder, braced its barrel against the trunk of the tree where he had taken cover, and opened fire.

The shots were like a long roll of thunder as the Jensen boys poured lead at their attacker. Ace fired seven times as fast as he could work the rifle's lever, and Chance loosed a similar number of rounds. Squinting through the haze of powder smoke, Ace saw the brush in the gully's mouth whipping around under the onslaught.

They held their fire. The gun-thunder echoed in the hills for several seconds before fading. As it did, Ace heard the faint sound of a horse crashing through brush in the distance.

Chance laughed and called, "He's lit out! Reckon we blistered him a little?"

"I hope so," Ace said.

From deeper in the woods, Porter called, "Is . . . is it safe to come out now?"

"Stay right where you are, Will," Ace told him. "We want to make sure he's gone and not just trying to pull some sort of trick."

They waited and listened for a good five

minutes before Ace was willing to accept that the bushwhacker had fled. He and Chance went to get their horses and told Porter to come with them.

As they emerged onto the road, Ace looked around warily. Everything seemed peaceful again.

Chance had shoved Porter's big revolver behind his belt. He pulled it out and put it in the carpetbag again.

"I think that's enough practicing for now," he said dryly. "I'd rather put some distance between us and this place. Will, this was the first time you'd ever been shot at, wasn't it?"

"How . . . how did you know that?"

Chance chuckled and pointed, said, "By the seat of your britches."

Porter flushed and said, "You know I sat down in the mud when I fired that gun. That's all this is."

"Sure it is."

"As a matter of fact, this was indeed my first experience at being under fire, but I think I acquitted myself rather well. I didn't lose my head, did I?"

"No, you didn't," Ace agreed. "You moved quick and did everything we told you. Keep that up and you might live through this."

"You make it sound almost as if you

expect us to come under attack again."

"There's a good chance of it," Ace said. "Who do you think was shooting at us?"

"Why . . . some highwayman out to kill us and rob our corpses, no doubt."

"What about Hudson?" Chance asked.

Porter's eyes got big again as he said, "Do you really think the man would stoop to murder?"

"Maybe he's worried about you and Evelyn," Ace said. "Could be he was keeping an eye on you and saw us leave Austin this morning, headed toward Fredericksburg. He could have gotten ahead of us and set up this ambush."

"He might not have been trying to kill you," Chance added. "Maybe he just wanted to scare you off, make you give up and turn back."

Ace said, "I don't know. Those bullets were coming mighty close for warning shots."

"Yeah, but at that range, it's hard to cut things too fine."

Ace shrugged and said, "It's possible."

Porter looked back and forth between them and exclaimed, "Good Lord, you're both so casual about someone nearly killing you!"

"It's not like this is the first time it's happened," Chance said.

"And he missed, so there's no point in getting worked up about it," Ace said. "No matter who that bushwhacker was or why he was shooting at us, the most important thing is that none of us were hit."

"Yes, I can see that," Porter said, nodding. "I'm not sure I'll ever be as blasé about a brush with death as you two are, though."

The three of them mounted up and rode on. Ace and Chance flanked Porter now, and their eyes never stopped moving as they watched the slopes around them. Ace didn't think it was likely the bushwhacker would make another try right away, but there was no guarantee of that. He hoped that one of the bullets he and Chance had thrown at the man might have tagged him, so he wouldn't be interested in any more ambushes, but there was no way of knowing that, either.

Late in the afternoon, they came to a settlement along the banks of a river that twisted through the hills. A sign at the edge of town announced that the place was called Johnson City. One of the first buildings Ace saw was a stage line office.

The stagecoach from Austin hadn't overtaken them during the day, but it probably wasn't very far behind them now. Ace pointed out the stage station to the other two and said, "The coach will probably stop there for the night."

Eagerly, Porter said, "So I'll have an opportunity to speak to Evelyn and persuade her to abandon her plan to marry Hudson. I might convince her to turn back before she even reaches Fredericksburg!"

"Yeah, if you think that'll do any good," Chance said.

"Hope springs eternal!" Porter cried.

A low rumble sounded. To the surprise of Ace and Chance, the storm had lurked in the west all day without moving in to drench the already soaked landscape any more. The thunder meant that respite might not last much longer, though, and so did a sudden gust of cold wind.

"Let's find a stable for these horses and a place to get in out of the rain if it starts to pour," Ace suggested.

There was a stable on the other side of the street from the stagecoach station. The garrulous old man who ran it introduced himself as Carlton. He gushed over what fine horses Ace's chestnut and Chance's cream-colored gelding were and told them that the Pedernales Hotel, named after the nearby river, was the best hotel in town.

"Of course, it's also the *only* hotel," he

added with a chuckle. "But they'll take good care of you there. One of my brothers runs the place. Got a fine barbecue pit, too, so you'll want to eat in the dining room."

"You happen to know what time the stage from Austin gets in?" Ace asked.

"I know when it's scheduled to come in, since my other brother manages the station. Ought to be close to on time, since the good weather's held today. I sure didn't expect it to. I been givin' some thought to how maybe I ought to start buildin' me a big boat."

"So what time does the stagecoach get here?" Chance asked.

"Oh, I didn't say, did I?" Carlton took a turnip watch out of his pocket, flipped it open, stared at it, and said, "Right about now. Fact is, I hear it comin'."

So did Ace and Chance. They turned toward the stable doors as the stagecoach came bumping and splashing along the street.

Porter hurried out, unable to contain his eagerness. The brothers trailed him. Across the street, the Concord coach had rocked to a halt in front of the stage line office. A couple of hostlers came out of the barn to tend to the team. A man in a white shirt, vest, string tie, and sleeve garters emerged from the office. He was probably the stable-man's brother, the station manager, thought Ace.

The driver and guard climbed down from the box. The driver grasped the door latch, twisted it, and swung the door open.

"Johnson City, folks," he announced. "We'll be overnightin' here. The roads ain't in good enough shape these days to risk travelin' in the dark."

Porter came to a stop a few yards away and waited with a look of breathless antici-pation on his face for the passengers to emerge. Ace and Chance came up behind him.

Two men in cheap suits got off the stage, both of them obviously traveling salesmen. Porter began to look worried.

But then Evelyn Channing appeared in the coach's door like a blond vision, and with a glad cry, Porter started toward her. She saw him coming and paused, a look of complete surprise on her face.

Suddenly a hard voice ordered, "Not another step, Porter!" and the command was punctuated by the unmistakable metal-lic sound of a revolver's hammer being eared back.

CHAPTER FOURTEEN

Oliver Hudson stalked around the back of the stagecoach, gun in hand. Ace fought down the impulse to draw his own Colt. If he reached for it, that would just give Hudson an excuse to shoot him. Legally, it wouldn't be self-defense, but close enough that most Texas juries would give Hudson the benefit of the doubt.

And Ace would still be dead, either way.

He glanced over at his brother, saw that the same thoughts were going through Chance's mind. Ace shook his head just enough for Chance to see it.

"Oliver!" Evelyn exclaimed. "I didn't expect to see you here. You said you were going on to Fredericksburg to take care of some business before our wedding."

"That was my intention," Hudson said as he kept Porter, Ace, and Chance covered. The sight of the gun in his hand had made the hostlers and the station manager back away. They didn't want to be caught in the line of fire if any shooting broke out. The two drummers who had gotten off the stagecoach before Evelyn were scurrying toward the Pedernales Hotel, eager to be well clear of any trouble.

Hudson went on, "I got worried about you making the trip by yourself, though, so I decided to join you here. It's a good thing I did. You don't need this fool annoying you."

He sneered at Porter as he spoke.

Porter's face flushed with anger. Ace said quietly, "Keep your wits about you, Will."

Porter's head jerked in a nod. Even though Hudson's gun was pointed at him, he ventured a step closer to the stagecoach, where Evelyn still stood on the iron step just below the open door.

"I'm not here to annoy you, Evelyn," he said. "I just want you to listen to reason."

Before the young woman could respond, Hudson said, "And I want *you* to turn around and get out of here, Porter. You're a pest. A fly just buzzing around and bothering folks. Isn't that right, Evelyn?"

There was some sympathy in her eyes as she looked at Porter, Ace thought, but her lips tightened firmly. She said, "William, we've talked about this. You're a fine man and a good friend and I'm sure you're going to be successful at whatever you do. But I'm simply not interested in being courted by you. I've agreed to marry Oliver, and that's the way things are going to be."

"You can't mean that," Porter said as a tone of misery crept into his voice. "Can't you see he's a gunman? A reprobate? He's probably an outlaw!"

"You little worm!" Hudson snarled. "I don't have to take that sort of talk."

He took a quick step forward and swung the pistol at Porter's head.

"Oliver, no!" Evelyn cried.

Hudson didn't stop, though, and Ace didn't think Porter was going to be nimble enough to get out of the way. If Hudson pistol-whipped him, he might wind up with a busted head.

Ace lunged forward and tackled Hudson before the blow could fall.

Momentum carried them toward the stagecoach. Ace rammed Hudson's back against the vehicle as hard as he could, in the hope of jarring the gun loose from Hudson's hand.

The impact jolted the coach enough to make it bounce on its thoroughbraces, and Evelyn lost her balance on the step. She screamed as she toppled forward.

Porter sprang to catch her, but the collision knocked both of them off their feet. They sprawled in the muddy street. Evelyn let out a cry of dismay.

Ace saw that from the corner of his eye but couldn't pay much attention to the happenings because he had his own hands full. Hudson hadn't dropped the gun. He slashed at Ace's head with the barrel.

Ace jerked aside so that the blow didn't stove in his skull, but it landed on his left shoulder and made pain shoot through that arm for a second before it suddenly went numb.

His right arm still worked, though. He slammed that fist into Hudson's midsection as hard as he could. The gunman grunted and bent forward as the blow drove the air out of his lungs.

Evidently, Hudson was an experienced brawler. He took advantage of his bent-over position to butt the top of his head into Ace's face. That knocked Ace backward and gave Hudson room to bring his gun to bear. His features were contorted with rage, and as Ace fell back a couple of steps, he realized that Hudson was about to shoot him.

Before Hudson could pull the trigger, Chance snatched the stage driver's whip from its socket on the side of the box and brought it down with a flicking motion that wrapped the leather around Hudson's wrist. Chance jerked the whip back, burning the skin on Hudson's wrist and making him let go of the gun. It sailed away and landed in the street.

Hudson bellowed furiously, caught the whip, and yanked Chance toward him. Taken by surprise, Chance didn't let go of the whip in time. As he stumbled forward, Hudson sprang at him and swung his left fist in a brutal blow that crashed into the younger man's jaw.

Driven back by the punch, Chance tripped over the fallen Porter and Evelyn and sprawled in the street, too. Hudson went after him, obviously intending to kick and stomp him.

As Hudson's booted foot swung at Chance's head, Porter reached up, caught hold of it, and heaved. That threw Hudson off-balance and caused him to lurch against the stagecoach. He grabbed the open door to keep from falling and pulled himself upright again.

By now some of the feeling was coming back into Ace's left arm. He could use it well enough to bore in on Hudson and snap a couple of left jabs into the man's face. Hudson moved to block a third such punch, but it was only a feint and left him open for the roundhouse right that Ace threw.

Ace packed all the strength he had into the punch. It landed cleanly on Hudson's jaw, snapped his head back, and bounced him off the stagecoach again. As Ace stepped back, Hudson fell to his knees, swayed for a second, and then toppled over on his side like a falling tree. Ace felt some satisfaction as Hudson's head hit the street. This had been a hard fight.

That sense of triumph was tempered almost instantly as Evelyn cried, "Oliver!" and scrambled on hands and knees toward him. Her dress was already wet and dirty from the muddy street, and it was in even worse shape by the time she reached him. She lifted him and pulled his upper body into her lap. He was out cold and his head lolled loosely on his neck.

"Oliver, darling, please be all right!" she begged as she cradled his head against her. She glared up at Ace, Chance, and Porter as the latter two climbed to their feet. "You brutes! You awful, terrible brutes!"

"Evelyn, please —" Porter began.

"Stop it, William! I don't want to hear anything you have to say to me."

Porter looked devastated by that rebuke, like a child whose favorite toy had been snatched away.

"I hope you're all proud of yourselves," Evelyn went on scathingly. "It took all three of you to overpower Oliver. How brave of you, to attack a man with three-against-one odds!"

"Miss Channing, he's the one who pulled a gun on us," Ace pointed out.

"Because he knew he was outnumbered and might have to defend himself from a vicious assault!"

Ace saw that talking to Evelyn wasn't going to do any good. Whatever she felt for Hudson blinded her to the reality of the situation.

And the way things had worked out, it was true that the fight *had* been three against one . . .

"Evelyn, you have to listen to me," Porter tried again. "Surely you can see what a dangerous man Hudson is and how you shouldn't be involved with him —"

"Just go away, William." She sobbed as she stroked Hudson's hair. "I never want to see you again!"

"You heard the lady," a hard voice said from behind Ace, Chance, and Porter.

Ace and Chance looked around and saw a stocky, gray-haired man standing there with a shotgun in his hands. A lawman's badge was visible under his coat, pinned to his vest.

"Sheriff —" Ace began.

"Marshal," the star-packer interrupted. "Tim Covington, marshal of Johnson City. Which means you're in my jurisdiction, mister, and I got the right to tell you to get the blazes outta town!"

"But we just got here," Chance protested. Thunder rumbled again, not far off, prompting him to add, "And it's about to storm again."

"Should've thought of that before you started a fight," Marshal Covington said.

"We didn't start it," Ace said. "Hudson pulled his gun —"

"Like the young lady just said, maybe he did that because of the odds. Anyway, I don't care all that much about who's right and who's wrong. I just don't want any more trouble, and since that fella's out cold and you three ain't, you're gonna be the ones to get out of town." Covington gestured with the scattergun's barrels. "Now."

Ace could tell that it wasn't going to do any good to argue with the marshal. The man's mind was made up, and the law badge he wore — along with the shotgun he carried — gave him the upper hand in any dispute.

Besides, Porter ought to be able to see by now that they were wasting their time. He was never going to convince Evelyn to choose him instead of Hudson.

Ace sighed and nodded, then said, "All right, Marshal, we're leaving."

"I'm not going anywhere!" Porter objected.

Covington squinted at him and said, "Your only other choice is sitting in my jail for the next thirty days, mister. I'm pretty sure the justice of the peace'll go along with that sentence."

Porter swallowed and said, "Jail?"

"That's right. Don't like the sound of it, do you?"

Porter had to shake his head. He said, "All right, we'll leave."

"Our horses are over at the stable," Ace said. "We'll have to get them."

"I'll go with you," Covington said, "just to make sure there ain't no delays."

Porter held out a hand toward Evelyn and said, "Please, my dear . . ."

She wouldn't even look at him. She just kept stroking Hudson's hair and talking softly to him. He was starting to stir a little.

"Move," Covington snapped.

Carlton must have seen them coming. He was saddling the horses when the men walked into the livery barn.

"Sorry to see you boys go," he said as Ace,

Chance, and Porter mounted up a few minutes later. "No refunds, though."

They rode out of the stable. Ace and Chance started to turn east, back toward Austin, but Porter surprised them by heading west.

The brothers fell in alongside him. Chance asked, "Where do you think you're going, Will?"

"Fredericksburg," Porter replied grimly. "Where I set out to go."

"Are you really that loco?" Ace asked him. "You haven't given up yet? Will, that girl doesn't want anything to do with you!"

"She's just mixed up," Porter insisted. "Blinded somehow by Hudson's charm, which I must admit I find totally lacking. I just have to get Evelyn to realize that, too."

Ace glanced toward the stage station as they rode past. Hudson was conscious and on his feet again, being helped by Evelyn toward the building. He paused to look at the three riders, though, and Ace saw the killing hatred in his eyes.

"Will, this is a bad idea," Ace said.

"A really bad idea," Chance added.

"If you believe that to be true, then you're free to return to Austin," Porter said. "I release you from whatever bonds of friendship exist between us. But as for me, I have no choice but to follow the dictates of my heart."

Ace and Chance reined in and looked at each other as Porter rode on. They both knew that Porter probably wouldn't last a week on his own. Considerably less than that, more than likely.

They didn't have to say anything. They just nudged their horses into motion and caught up with Porter.

The rain started falling just outside of town, big, fat, hard drops that promised another good soaking.

CHAPTER FIFTEEN

The stagecoach carrying Smoke and Sally Jensen left Fort Worth and went west to Weatherford, stopping once along the way at a station atop a mostly bare, windswept hill to change teams. In Weatherford, the coach stopped again and fresh horses were hitched to it. The passengers had lunch there at a café on the busy courthouse square.

Farther along the route, the driver explained to the passengers, the stops wouldn't be quite as close together so he would have to ask more of the horses, and because of that their pace wouldn't be quite as fast. They would still make it to Mason in approximately three days, however, barring unforeseen delays.

"Three days?" Sally said to Smoke as they set out again. "That's a long time."

"Texas is a big place," he replied with a smile. "Lots of ground to cover."

He understood why Sally sounded a little dubious about the trip. She had ridden stagecoaches before, but it wasn't easy to get used to the vehicle's swaying, jolting tempo. Not only that, it was drafty, and the weather was cool enough at this time of year to cause chills. The stage line provided blankets for the passengers to wrap up in, but they were thin and not very warm, plus there was the added worry of not knowing what sort of varmints previous users might have had.

At least the rains of the fall and early winter meant that there wasn't much dust. At the height of summer, folks in a stagecoach almost choked on the dust that swirled in endlessly.

West of Weatherford, the coach crossed the Brazos River at a low-water ford. Rugged hills loomed to the northwest. Smoke recalled hearing old-timers from Texas talk about the Comanches and knew it hadn't been all that many years since bold warriors had ridden all over those hills, making it dangerous for any settlers who dared to venture beyond the Brazos.

Not long after fording the river, the coach reached a crossroads and turned south. As the driver had warned, the going was a lot slower now. The roughness of the terrain contributed to that, too. They had to cross a long stretch of hills, so the coach was nearly always going either up or down a slope.

That made it easier for the group of men on horseback to follow the stagecoach without being seen. All they had to do was make sure they weren't skylighted against one of the ridge crests.

Six men were in the bunch. Riding slightly in the lead were rawboned, lantern-jawed Harlan Gunderson and his stockier brother Karl. Four abreast behind them were Jed Lavery, Simon Dawson, Grady Kirk, and a kid who called himself Tioga, after the Texas town a good ways north of here where he'd been born. He was the only one of the six who hadn't done time in the state penitentiary at Huntsville, but that didn't mean he was any better than them. He'd just gotten started on a life of crime later, that's all.

Between them, they had robbed banks, rustled cattle, burned down barns, and murdered sodbusters. They had shot men from ambush for pay. Harlan Gunderson had beaten a man to death because he had one blue eye and one brown eye and it would have been wrong to let such an abomination live. His brother Karl had strangled a whore in Gainesville because she'd tried to steal his poke. The others had similar sordid, violent pasts.

They had been riding together for seven months, and today they had their sights set on holding up a stagecoach.

"You sure there's gonna be enough money on that coach to make it worth riskin' our lives, Harlan?" Karl asked.

Harlan Gunderson tamped down the annoyance he felt. His brother had a whiny way about him, guaranteed to get on the nerves of anybody who had to spend much time around him. He asked the same questions over and over, too. This was at least the fourth time since they'd left Fort Worth that he had brought up the matter of how much loot they could expect to find on the coach.

But Karl was blood kin, so Gunderson couldn't just shoot him in the head the way he felt like doing sometimes.

"You know what that fella from the bank told us," Harlan Gunderson explained with greater patience than he really felt. "There's a shipment of greenbacks hidden in the boot, bound for the bank in Stephenville. The driver don't even know about it. He thinks that valise just belongs to one of the passengers. The bank manager worked out the deal with Ferguson at the stage line.

There's supposed to be ten thousand dollars in that bag, and that ain't even countin' what we'll take off the passengers and outta the mail pouch. You saw some of those people were dressed pretty fancy. They ought to have money."

"But what if that bank clerk was lyin'?" Karl persisted.

Harlan Gunderson laughed and asked, "Do you really think he was up to lyin', what with all the blood leakin' out of him from where we carved him up?"

Karl scratched his beard-stubbled jaw, frowned, and said, "No, I reckon not. I forgot about that. I forget a lot of things, don't I, Harlan?"

"Don't worry about it, little brother. You got me around to remember 'em for you."

Harlan Gunderson wasn't likely to forget torturing that bank clerk anytime soon. It had been grisly work, sort of like slaughtering hogs back on the farm in Arkansas where he and Karl had grown up. What had been left of the clerk had gone to the hogs, too, so nobody would ever find the remains and the clerk's disappearance would be just one of those unsolved mysteries.

"It's gettin' kind of late in the afternoon," Grady Kirk said from behind the Gundersons. "If we're gonna stop that stage, we

152

better find a place to do it."

Harlan Gunderson hipped around a little in the saddle as he rode and said, "I've been thinkin' about that. I'll bet they're gonna lay over for the night at the station in Morgan Mill and go on to Stephenville in the morning. Like I just reminded Karl, the driver don't know he's carryin' as much money as he is. He's got no reason to push on after dark just to get to Stephenville."

"So what're we gonna do?" asked Tioga. "Ambush 'em in the mornin'?"

"That's exactly right," Harlan Gunderson said. "We'll ride on around Morgan Mill and set up an ambush in the hills on the other side. They won't be expectin' a thing."

"I like the sound of that," Jed Lavery said. He was a dour man who seemed to find no joy in life, or any mercy, either. "Kill the driver and the guard first thing, then we can take our time with the passengers."

"We gonna kill 'em all, Harlan?" Karl asked.

"Best way not to hang is to never leave no witnesses behind," Harlan Gunderson said. "You don't want to hang, do you, Karl?"

Karl hesitated in answering, as if it were a trick question, then said, "Uh . . . no, I don't reckon I do."

The others all chuckled at that, except for

153

Lavery.

The road dipped down from a long ridge into a valley about a mile wide. A line of trees marking the course of a creek meandered along the valley's center. From the stagecoach's window, Smoke spotted a church steeple and knew they were coming to a settlement.

At this time of year the sun went down early, and some clouds that had thickened up during the afternoon meant that evening would come sooner rather than later. For that reason, Smoke wasn't surprised when the jehu brought the coach to a halt in front of a stone building and leaned over on the seat to announce through the windows, "We'll be stoppin' here overnight, folks. This is Morgan Mill."

Smoke saw a large building on the bank of the nearby creek and figured that was the sawmill that gave the place its name. The settlement also boasted a Baptist church, a Methodist church, their respective graveyards, a general store, and a blacksmith's shop, in addition to the stage station. Houses and cabins were scattered haphazardly in the trees along both sides of the creek.

Arley Hicks, the young, redheaded cowboy, was the first one out of the stagecoach. He swung open the door and jumped to the ground with an obvious eagerness to stretch his legs after the long ride from Weatherford.

Smoke knew how Arley felt. He could spend all day in the saddle without any ill effect, but riding a hard bench seat in a stagecoach for hours on end was a different story.

Smoke got out next and turned back to help Sally and then Mrs. Carter climb down from the coach. After that, though, he backed off to let Donald Purcell disembark and assist his wife Mildred. Mrs. Purcell might not want a notorious gunman giving her a hand, Smoke thought dryly.

The patent medicines salesman, Herman Langston, was the last one out of the coach. Smoke said, "You don't seem any the worse for wear, Mr. Langston."

The drummer grinned and said, "When you've ridden thousands of miles on these contraptions like I have, son, your hindquarters toughen up and get as hard as steel."

Mildred Purcell sniffed audibly at that comment.

Langston touched the brim of his bowler hat and added, "Beg your pardon, ma'am, for my crudity." He looked at Sally. "Yours, too, Mrs. Jensen."

"That's all right, Mr. Langston," she assured him. "I'm around rough and ready cowboys all the time, back on our ranch in Colorado. I promise you I've heard much worse."

Arley Hicks slapped a hand on his thigh, grinned, and said, "I'll just bet that you have, ma'am."

A short woman who seemed as wide as she was tall came out of the stone building, wiping her hands on the apron she wore. She had graying auburn hair and a broad face with a friendly smile on it.

"Come on in, folks," she invited. "Always got beans, stew, and a mess of cornbread ready for travelers. The accommodations ain't any fancier than the grub, but they're comfortable enough. Any bad weather up Fort Worth way, Floyd?"

"Nope," answered the driver. "Seems like it's all stayin' down south of here, Miss Bertha."

"Well, it can stay there as far as I'm concerned. We've had plenty of rain already this fall."

That might be wishful thinking, Smoke mused. The sun had vanished behind the clouds. Gloom was stealing over the hills. Like all Western men who spent most of

156

their lives outdoors, Smoke had an eye for the weather, and to him it looked like those clouds had rain in them.

They would find out before morning, he reckoned as he took Sally's arm and led her inside the stagecoach station with the others.

CHAPTER SIXTEEN

Bertha's beans, cornbread, and stew were as good as she claimed, and the strong, hot coffee Smoke used to wash down the food was top-notch. He felt revitalized by the time supper was over, but Sally was yawning and Smoke knew she was ready to turn in.

"Why don't you go ahead?" he told her. "I'll be along later."

"Do you want me to try to stay awake?"

"No, that's all right," Smoke said.

Sally smiled and said, "Normally I might argue with you, but I'm really tired tonight. Some sleep is going to feel good."

The stagecoach station had a large dining room in the middle, with three small bedrooms for passengers on each side and the kitchen and Bertha's quarters in the back. Bertha's son Ronald, who had a friendly smile like his mother but wasn't quite right in the head, worked as the station's hostler and had a small room of his own in the barn behind the station.

Sally, Mrs. Carter, and the Purcells retired for the evening, leaving Smoke, Arley Hicks, and Herman Langston in the main room, along with the driver, Floyd Horton, and the shotgun guard, Tom Burke.

Langston took a cigar from his vest pocket and set fire to the gasper. Arley rolled a cigarette while Horton packed a pipe and puffed it to life.

From behind the counter at the back of the room, Bertha asked, "You boys want a bottle?"

"I could do with a snort," Arley said.

"Kid, the sort of tonsil varnish Bertha sells will peel the hide off your innards all the way down to your toes," Burke warned with a grin.

"If you're tryin' to scare me off, Mr. Burke, it ain't workin'."

Burke waved the heavyset proprietor over, telling her, "All right, bring a bottle and glasses. I'll buy everybody a drink."

Smoke lifted his cup and said, "I'm fine with this coffee. Thanks anyway."

Burke frowned.

"Where I come from, it ain't hardly polite to turn it down when a man offers you a drink," he said.

"Pull in your horns, Tom," Horton advised him. "You forgotten this here is Smoke Jensen?"

Burke suddenly looked nervous. He said, "I didn't mean no insult, Mr. Jensen —"

"And I didn't take it that way, Mr. Burke," Smoke told him. "Don't worry. I'm not quite as proddy as most of those yellowbacks make me out to be."

A relieved smile appeared on Burke's weather-beaten face as he said, "That's good, 'cause I wouldn't want to get on Smoke Jensen's bad side."

"That's the side where you wind up dead," Arley put in.

Bertha brought over four glasses and a bottle with no label on it. The liquid in the bottle was clear. She said, "Fresh corn squeezin's, boys. It's so wild and raw you may have to sneak up on it to drink it."

She poured, then took a tin cup from her apron pocket and went on, "I'll just join you in a nip, if you fellas don't mind."

Langston waved her into a chair and said, "You're perfectly welcome, my dear."

"Don't go sweet-talkin' me, Herman," Bertha said. "As many times as you've stopped here, you oughta know by now it ain't gonna work."

"I don't know what you're talking about,"

Langston said. "I'm perfectly content to bask in your beauty."

Bertha grunted and said, "Keep it up and I'll heave you outta here on your keister."

Smoke leaned back in his chair and smiled as he sipped his coffee and enjoyed listening to the banter. He liked frontier folks, for the most part, and had ever since he and his pa had started west from Missouri right after the war.

After a while, though, he felt the need to stretch his legs. He finished the coffee, stood up, and said, "I think I'll take a look around outside."

"Morgan Mill's a mighty peaceful place, Mr. Jensen," Bertha said. "No Indians hereabouts since all the Lipan Apaches moved on years ago, and there's nothin' here to attract outlaws."

"I know. I'm just in the habit of checking on things before I turn in for the night."

"Well, that's not a bad habit, I suppose."

None of the other men offered to come with him. They were still drinking, smoking, and talking. That was all right with Smoke. In younger years, he had spent a lot of time alone in the high country, and he was perfectly content with his own company.

At least, he was as long as he knew that Sally was safe and somewhere close by.

He got his hat from the nail where it hung and put it on as he stepped outside. A cold drizzle had started to fall softly. As long as it didn't rain any harder than this, the roads ought to be all right for traveling the next day, he thought as he walked around the station building.

The barn doors were open about a foot. Lantern light spilled through the gap. Smoke started in that direction, figuring that he would check on the horses and say hello to Roland, whom he had met earlier while the young man was unhitching the team.

He was about halfway there when he realized that something was wrong.

Rainwater dripped from the floppy brim of Tioga's battered old hat as the outlaw made his way stealthily through the shadows toward the barn. His heart pounded so hard in his chest it felt like it was about to burst through his skin. All he could think about was the ten thousand dollars in greenbacks that was supposed to be in a valise in the stagecoach boot.

Since the coach was just staying in Morgan Mill overnight, it wasn't likely that the bags would be unloaded. Even if some of the passengers wanted their things, the valise with the money didn't belong to any of them and would have been left aboard the coach. The driver and the guard didn't know about the money, according to Harlan Gunderson, and so they wouldn't think twice about the bag being left in the boot.

That bank president and old Ferguson, the manager of the stage line, had out-smarted themselves by being so secretive, Tioga thought with a sly smile as he ap-proached the barn from the rear.

He was supposed to be back up in the hills a mile from here, where the rest of the gang was camped. He and Karl Gunderson were sharing a turn on guard duty, and Tioga had known good and well it wouldn't take Karl long to doze off.

Sure enough, within half an hour, Tioga had heard snores coming from the spot where Karl had settled down with his back against a rock. The other four men were sound asleep in their bedrolls as well, with slickers spread over them to keep out some of the rain.

As quietly as possible, Tioga had saddled his horse and led the animal away from the camp. Karl's snores were so loud the young outlaw figured they would drown out any little noises he made.

Everything was working out perfectly, he

thought now. The night was pitch black because of the clouds and the drizzle. Those pilgrims from the stage would be snug inside the station. And the rain would help obscure his trail, so it would be difficult, if not impossible, for anybody to track him after he snagged that valise full of cash and took off for the tall and uncut. He figured to be a rich man and thirty miles away from here come morning.

He had to hope Harlan Gunderson wouldn't be able to follow him, because if Harlan ever caught up to him, Tioga knew what would happen. Harlan would take that Bowie knife of his and peel Tioga's hide off a strip at a time. He was so mean he should've been a redskin instead of a Scandahoovian, thought Tioga.

But danged if ten thousand dollars wasn't worth the risk.

This would be the biggest payoff by far that Tioga had gotten his hands on since running away from his pa's farm up in northern Texas. He would make his way to Mexico and spend the rest of his days there, enjoying the warm weather and the warmer señoritas. Harlan and the others could go on robbing and killing and wind up at the end of a hangrope. Tioga was going to put all that behind him.

His horse was tied in the edge of the trees, where the creek looped around behind the stage station. Tioga hurried across the open ground between him and the barn, toward the rear door. He could see faint lines of light from inside through the cracks around the door.

That probably meant somebody was inside. Maybe the hostler who worked here. Whoever it was, the hombre better not get in his way, or he'd be sorry.

Tioga wasn't going to let anybody or anything stop him from getting that cash.

He stopped just outside the door and leaned forward to put his right eye to the crack at the side. Somebody was moving around in there, but that was all he could tell. He took hold of the latch string and slowly pulled it down. The door swung open a little more as the latch unfastened.

Through the larger gap, Tioga saw a man a few years older than him step out of one of the stalls and close the gate behind him. The fella wore a homespun shirt and canvas trousers. He had tousled brown hair. Tioga heard an odd sound and realized after a moment that the man was singing to himself. What sort of loco fool did that?

Then the man turned toward him. Tioga saw the rather vacant smile on his face. He was some sort of dummy, Tioga decided. Probably just smart enough to take care of horses and not much else. Not smart like him. Not smart enough to steal a march on his partners and wind up a rich man.

The hostler went in one of the other stalls. Tioga opened the door wider and stepped inside. Wind and rain swirled in with him. He pulled the door closed and then drew his gun.

The hostler came out of the stall and stopped short at the sight of the slicker-clad figure in front of him. His mouth hung open in surprise. Tioga pointed the gun at him and said, "Don't you make a sound, mister, or I'll blow your brains out."

Maybe that wasn't the best threat to make, Tioga thought a second later. The dummy might not understand he had any brains to lose. His mouth opened even wider, and Tioga knew he was working himself up to a yell.

The outlaw cursed bitterly as he realized he couldn't pull the trigger. The people inside the station would hear a shot and charge out here to see what was going on. The stagecoach driver and the guard would be armed, and some of the male passengers probably were, too. Tioga wouldn't stand much chance of winning a gun battle against five or six men.

So he jammed the gun back in its holster and leaped forward, reaching under the slicker to pluck a knife from a sheath at his waist as he did so. The dummy couldn't yell with his throat cut.

Tioga tried to clap his left hand over the hostler's mouth while his right swiped the blade at the man's throat. The hostler jumped back. He was obviously terrified, and instead of being paralyzed by fear, it made him move faster than usual. The slashing knife missed, and that threw Tioga off-balance. He stumbled forward. His foot hit a bucket that was sitting next to a stall door and sent it clattering across the aisle in the middle of the barn.

He caught himself as the hostler turned to run. Tioga leaped after him, caught him from behind, and drove him to the ground with a hard tackle. He planted his left knee in the small of the man's back, grabbed his hair, and jerked his head back. That drew his throat taut for the blade that Tioga swept toward it, ready to spill the man's blood.

CHAPTER SEVENTEEN

Smoke heard the racket in the barn. It sounded like somebody had thrown a bucket across the floor. That wasn't enough by itself to be alarming, but instincts honed by years of danger sent him moving forward swiftly.

A second later he heard grunts and a thud. Some sort of fight was going on in there, and nobody was supposed to be in the barn except Roland. Smoke's Colt was already in his right hand as his left gripped one of the doors and hauled it open.

Lantern light reflected from an upraised knife blade. Smoke's keen eyes took in the scene instantly: Roland lying belly down on the ground with a man in a slicker and high-crowned hat on top of him, holding his head back as he got ready to slash the hostler's throat.

Smoke fired as the blade streaked down on its deadly thrust.

The would-be killer's head was tipped

forward as he looked at his prey. The hat brim obscured his face. Smoke's bullet clipped through the brim, blew the hombre's chin off, and bored on into the hollow of his throat to smash his spinal column. All the muscles and nerves below that went dead. The knife flew out of his hand since his fingers could no longer grip it. He fell forward over Roland as blood gouted from the wound and splashed on the back of the young man's head.

Naturally enough, Roland howled like a banshee.

Smoke rushed forward, grabbed the dying man's slicker, and slung him to the side. He rolled over, all his muscles limp, and came to rest on his back. His hat had fallen off, revealing a young, beard-stubbled face and wide, staring eyes. He made gurgling sounds, but that was all he could manage through his ruined throat.

Then those fell silent as the bulging eyes began to turn glassy in death.

The man wasn't more than twenty years old, Smoke thought disgustedly. What a waste. But it had been his choice to try to murder Roland, so Smoke wasn't going to lose any sleep over shooting him. There hadn't been time to try to wound him, either, not if he wanted to save Roland's life.

Roland was still screaming. Smoke holstered his gun and bent to take hold of the young man and lift him to his feet.

"It's all right," Smoke assured him. "You're all right, Roland."

More people burst into the barn behind him. Bertha cried out, "Roland! Oh, dear God!"

"Mama!" he said pitifully.

Smoke got out of the way. Bertha swooped down on Roland and grabbed him like a mama bear with a cub. Smoke said, "I don't think he's hurt, ma'am. I believe all that blood came from the other fella."

Sobbing with relief, Bertha began using her apron to wipe away some of the blood splattered on her son's head and shoulders.

"Who in blazes is this?" Tom Burke asked as he pointed his shotgun at the dead man lying on the ground a few feet away. Floyd Horton was beside him, pistol in hand.

"Neither of you know him?" Smoke asked.

"Never saw him before," Horton said, and Burke shook his head.

Smoke took out his revolver again and reloaded the chamber he had fired. As he slid the gun into leather, he said, "I came in and found him about to cut Roland's throat.

Wasn't time to tell him to stop or do anything except kill him."

"Looks like you done a good job of that," Horton said.

Grimly, Burke added, "We'd better take a look around the place and make sure there ain't any more skunks lurkin' in the dark."

"That's a good idea," Smoke agreed.

He and the two stage line employees left Bertha and Roland in the barn and went out to scout the area around the stagecoach station. When they came back a short time later, they all reported that there was no sign of anybody else in the vicinity.

Horton studied the dead man in the lantern light and said, "If you ask me, that fella looks like an owlhoot. And I've seen enough road agents in my time to know one when I see him."

Smoke nodded and said, "I thought the same thing. But what was he after?"

"The mail pouch, maybe," Burke suggested. "There's usually some money in it."

"You're not carrying anything else valuable on this trip?" Smoke asked.

"Just whatever the passengers have on 'em," Horton said. "The mail pouch is the only thing in the strongbox."

Burke said, "If a fella's desperate enough to commit murder, he might be willin' to take anything he can get, no matter how much it is."

That was true enough, Smoke supposed. But something still didn't feel right to him about this. His gut told him there was more to it than a simple attempted robbery, and he had long since learned to trust those hunches.

But the man was dead and nobody else was around, so it was unlikely there would be any explanation tonight. Maybe not ever.

"Roland's in no shape to stay out here by himself, ma'am," he told Bertha. "You need to take him inside, clean him up, and calm him down. I'll stay here in the barn to keep an eye on the coach and the horses, just in case anybody else comes around looking for trouble."

She nodded. Her face was flushed and tear-streaked as she said, "Thank you, Mr. Jensen. And thank you for savin' my boy's life. He . . . he's all I got left."

Smoke smiled and said, "I'm glad I came in when I did. If you'd tell Mrs. Jensen where I am and what I'm doing . . . ?"

"I sure will. You folks can have anything I got. You just ask for it, and it's yours."

"A good night's sleep for my wife and a good breakfast in the morning will do just fine."

"Don't you worry. I'll see to it."

Still fussing over Roland, whose sobs had subsided to whimpers, she led him out of the barn.

Burke canted the coach gun over his shoulder and said, "I'll stay out here and help you stand guard, Mr. Jensen."

"So will I," Horton said. "That way we can have two men watchin' and one gettin' a little shut-eye. What about this dead varmint?"

"We'll drag him into an empty stall for the night, I guess," Smoke said.

"The nearest law is in Stephenville," Burke said. "That'll be our first stop in the morning anyway. We can send the sheriff and the undertaker back up here to deal with the carcass. The weather's cool enough he ought to keep for that long without spoilin' too bad."

Smoke nodded. It was the best plan they could come up with. He still wished he knew exactly what was behind the attempt on Roland's life, though.

Unfortunately, the man on the ground wasn't going to be volunteering any answers.

Harlan Gunderson wanted to take a gun butt to his brother's head and bash it in, but he had promised their ma on her death-bed that he would take care of his little brother, so he couldn't do that. He settled for backhanding Karl instead, a hard enough blow to knock the smaller man off his feet.

"You were supposed to be standin' guard!" Harlan roared at Karl. "What'n blazes did you do, sleep all night?"

"I . . . I might'a dozed off a mite," Karl said as he cringed backward on the ground as if afraid that Harlan might kick him. That seemed to be a distinct possibility.

"You must've been sound asleep, Karl," Grady said. "Otherwise you would've heard Tioga when he saddled his horse and lit a shuck."

Harlan cast an angry glare at Grady that made the other outlaw look down at the ground. Harlan was not only the boss of this outfit, he was Karl's brother and would deal with what had happened.

"Go see if you can pick up the kid's trail," he ordered coldly. "Find out which way he went."

"What does it matter?" Jed Lavery asked. "He's gone, and it's not likely he's coming back. I'd say we're lucky he didn't steal all our horses."

Harlan Gunderson let out a disgusted snort.

"He knew better than that. He knew I'd

track him down and make sure he died slow and painful-like if he double-crossed us like that."

"Maybe he decided he just didn't want any part of that robbery," the middle-aged, normally quiet Simon Dawson suggested.

"Not want a share of ten grand?" Grady said. "That don't seem likely."

"Jed's right, it doesn't matter why he ran out on us or where he went," Gunderson said. "What's important is that there's still five of us, and that's plenty to hold up that stagecoach."

"So you don't want us to look for Tioga's trail after all?" Grady asked.

The anger inside Harlan Gunderson had blazed so fiercely for a few minutes that it had burned itself out. He shook his head and said, "No, to perdition with it. And to perdition with the kid, too. It's his loss."

Karl picked himself up and used his hat to slap dirt and dead leaves off his trousers. He said, "So we're still stoppin' the coach and takin' that money?"

"You bet we are. Get a fire going, Karl. We'll have some coffee, and then we'll find a good spot for the ambush."

"Might not be easy to find enough dry wood for a fire," Karl began. The drizzle that had fallen most of the night had stopped, but things were still wet. When his brother frowned at him, though, he went on hurriedly, "But I'll manage, Harlan, you can sure count on that."

They all put Tioga and his disappearance out of their minds. Whatever the young outlaw's fate might be, it was no longer any of their business.

The rest of the night passed quietly at the stagecoach station. Smoke got enough sleep in the hayloft during his turn to nap that he wasn't too tired the next morning. He was glad to see that the rain had stopped and that not enough had fallen during the night to make the roads much muddier than they had been to start with.

Bertha refused to take any payment for Smoke and Sally's breakfast. She gave them a sackful of biscuits to take with them as well.

"That ain't hardly enough to even start repaying the debt I owe you, Mr. Jensen," she told Smoke as the passengers began loading onto the coach in front of the station. "C'mere."

He grinned as she pulled his head down and bussed a rough kiss on his cheek. She hugged Sally, too, while Smoke shook hands with a cleaned-up and much more composed Roland.

"Thank you for savin' my life, Mr. Jensen," the young man said politely.

"I'm glad I was able to help, Roland," Smoke assured him. "You take care of your ma now."

"Yes, sir, I sure will."

A few minutes later, Floyd Horton cracked his whip and yelled to his team, and the stagecoach rolled out of Morgan Mill, following the road into the hills that rose south of the settlement.

CHAPTER EIGHTEEN

As the coach rocked along, Arley Hicks was still excited about what had happened the night before and kept talking about the killing. Finally, Donald Purcell glared at the young cowboy and snapped, "Can't you just shut up about that dreadful business? You're upsetting my wife."

Mildred Purcell's face was pale and drawn, and her lips were pursed in disapproval, Smoke noted, but she didn't seem that much more upset than usual. From what he had seen, that was pretty much her normal expression and attitude.

"Beggin' your pardon, ma'am," Arley said to Mildred as he took his hat off.

"That's quite all right, Mr. Hicks," she told him without looking at him.

"It's just that Mr. Jensen here's famous, and now I get to tell folks I was there — or at least close by — when Smoke Jensen killed a no-good owlhoot. You can't blame a gent for bein' a mite excited about some-thin' like that. I'll have me a good story to tell in the bunkhouse —"

"You're still going on about it," Purcell gritted.

"Oh. Yeah, reckon I am. Beg pardon again." Arley swung around so he was fac-ing Smoke and Sally. "Just how fast was your draw when you shot that fella, Mr. Jensen?"

"Fast enough to save Roland's life," Smoke said. "That was all I was worried about."

"Yeah, from what Floyd and Tom said, that varmint was about to slice the poor feller open from gizzard to gullet!"

Purcell reached out, grabbed Arley's shoulder, and jerked him around.

"That's enough!" he exclaimed. "I've asked you politely —"

"You best take your hand off me, mister," Arley said quietly. Smoke heard the menace in the young cowboy's deceptively mild tone. He saw Arley's hand move toward the opening of his coat and figured there was a knife or a pistol in his waistband. The wor-ried frowns on the faces of Langston and Mrs. Carter told him they had the same hunch.

"That's enough, both of you," Smoke said,

his voice firm with command. "Arley, we've hashed it all out enough. And Mr. Purcell, you need to understand that we're not back East now. Folks have different attitudes about most things out here."

"Including life and death?" Purcell asked in a challenging tone.

"Yes, sir. Maybe that more than anything else. Westerners know how many things there are in the world that can kill you, and we're used to running into them from time to time."

"I prefer civilization, where life is safe," Purcell said stiffly.

"Oh, it's not safe there, either," Smoke said with a smile. "Folks just do a better job of pretending it is."

A strained silence descended on the coach. Herman Langston broke it a few minutes later by asking Arley to name all the spreads where he had worked. The young cowboy seemed glad to do so, and he had a colorful story about every ranch.

With that tension eased, the journey went more pleasantly again. The coach's motion even began to lull Smoke into a half-sleep.

That drowsy state was shattered by the sudden blast of gunfire.

The terrain was so hilly through here that

when the road had been built, the men who'd put it in had used dynamite to blast openings through some of the ridges that left steep banks on both sides, mostly fifteen to twenty feet tall. The different layers of earth could be seen in those ridges, which were topped by juniper, mesquite, scrub brush, rocks, and cactus.

On top of the west bank of one of those cuts, Karl Gunderson swallowed and asked nervously, "You sure about this, Harlan?"

"What? Yeah, of course I'm sure. I ever steer you wrong, Karl?"

As a matter of fact, Harlan had made a number of questionable decisions over the years, but there was no way Karl was going to bring those up to his brother. Harlan was still a mite touchy about Tioga deserting them. Karl didn't want to give him an excuse to really get mad.

"No, no," Karl said quickly. "Your plans always work."

Harlan nodded, completely confident that this robbery would go off just fine.

He and Karl were on this side, hunkered far enough back from the cut's edge so they couldn't be seen. Jed Lavery and Simon Dawson were on the east bank. Grady Kirk was up ahead, waiting in some trees just past the cut.

The plan called for the men on the banks to open fire on the stage as it rumbled through, killing the driver and guard, then Grady would spur his horse out into the road and catch the team's harness before the horses could bolt. Once the coach was stopped, Harlan would call on the passengers to throw out their guns and get out, and if they refused, the men on the banks would just pour lead through the vehicle's flimsy walls until everyone inside it was dead.

What could possibly go wrong with that?

Harlan cocked his head to the side and said, "Listen. Hear that?"

Karl licked his lips and asked, "Hear what?"

"The stagecoach," Gunderson replied impatiently.

Karl frowned for a couple of seconds, concentrating so hard he looked like something was paining him. Then he nodded and said, "Yeah. Horses. And wheels. Got to be the stagecoach."

Harlan looked away so his brother wouldn't see him roll his eyes. He checked his Winchester. Fully loaded, with a round in the chamber.

They had to time this properly. The cut was at the top of a slope, so the stagecoach wouldn't be traveling very fast when it got here. The outlaws hidden on top of the banks had to stay out of sight until they were ready to open fire, so the driver wouldn't spot them and whip up the team to a faster pace as he went through the cut. But they couldn't wait until the coach had gone past them. Harlan listened intently, knowing that he had judged the right moment to strike by the sounds.

"Harlan, I —" Karl began.

"Shut up," Harlan snapped. "Not now, Karl."

"Sorry," Karl muttered.

Harlan heard the thud of hoofbeats getting louder, the creak of the wheels, the rattle of harness. . . .

"Now!" he called. He leaped to his feet, rushed forward to the bank's edge, brought the rifle to his shoulder, and started shooting.

Mildred Purcell screamed as the gunshots boomed. So did her husband. Smoke was sitting on the left-hand side of the coach, on the forward-facing seat, and his Colt was already in his hand as he leaned toward the window.

"Arley, if you've got a gun, cover the other side!" he barked.

The young cowboy reached inside his coat and pulled out an old Colt Navy. He lunged across the middle seat to the window on the right-hand door.

Smoke looked up, spotted two men on the cutbank on his side blazing away at the stagecoach with rifles. He leaned out far enough to draw a good bead and fired three swift shots that were deafening inside the coach.

One of the men on the bank dropped his rifle, doubled over as he clutched his belly where a slug had ripped into him, and plunged over the edge. He turned a somersault in midair and crashed onto the road on his back about ten feet behind the coach.

The other man on that side spun halfway around from the impact of a slug and stumbled back out of sight.

On the right side of the coach, Arley had just opened fire when he suddenly grunted and fell back from the window. He dropped the Navy, which clattered onto the floorboard.

Without hesitation, Sally bent down and scooped up the gun. Arley lay on his side on the bench, right hand pressed to his left shoulder where blood welled between his fingers. Sally leaned forward and to the side, in front of Mrs. Carter, and thrust the revolver's barrel out the window. She fired off the remaining rounds as fast as she could cock the gun and squeeze the trigger.

Smoke heard Floyd Horton yelling at the team, urging them on to more speed. He knew what was going on as well as he would have if he could see the whole thing. Outlaws had laid an ambush on both banks, intending to murder Horton and Burke and stop the stage. Possibly because of the rapid way Smoke had cut down their numbers, the desperados had failed so far. Horton was still alive.

And now it was a race.

Harlan Gunderson cursed sulphurously as the stagecoach swept past the spot where he and Karl were standing and blasting away at it. The coach hadn't stopped, hadn't even slowed down. In fact, it was going faster now as the jehu shouted at his team and slashed at them with his whip.

Harlan hadn't counted on somebody inside the coach being such a gun wizard. Lavery was lying dead in the road, and Dawson was down on the far bank, badly wounded from the looks of him. And somehow the driver on the coach seemed to be untouched by all the lead that had flown around him.

The guard couldn't say the same thing. He was slumped on the seat, the side of his head covered with blood where he'd been hit.

"Come on!" Harlan shouted to Karl. "We gotta catch up!"

He turned and started running along the top of the bank with the rifle held at a slant across his chest. His long legs carried him swiftly and kept him not far behind the coach. The problem was that he couldn't shoot at the driver while he was running like this.

Then Grady Kirk spurred out into the road at the end of the cut and opened fire on the stagecoach with his pistol. The driver's instincts made him haul back on the reins in the face of this unexpected attack. The coach slowed, allowing Harlan and Karl to catch up with it. Karl had lagged several yards behind his brother, and he was puffing and panting like a steam engine as they slowed.

Harlan brought the Winchester to his shoulder again and was about to drill the driver, who seemed unsure what to do as Grady charged the coach. Before Harlan could pull the trigger, though, the guard suddenly reared up on the seat. That took Harlan by surprise, because he'd thought the man was dead.

Before the outlaws could react, the guard thrust his weapon toward them one-handed and fired both barrels of the coach gun. Beside Harlan, Karl said, "Uh!" and took a quick step back.

Harlan looked over at his brother, saw the bloody ruin where the buckshot had caught Karl in the belly and chest, and roared, "No!"

"H-Harlan . . ." Karl managed to say before he sat down hard and then died, rolling onto his side.

Down in the cut, the guard had dropped the shotgun and collapsed again. A man stood in the open doorway on the coach's far side, leaned out, and blew Grady Kirk out of the saddle with a well-placed shot.

"Go!" he shouted to the driver, who whipped the team again and made the coach surge forward as Kirk's horse danced out of the way.

"No!" Harlan yelled again. They weren't going to get away with this, not with killing Karl. He dropped the rifle and sprinted along the bank after the coach. The fury he felt gave him incredible speed. He was about to run out of bank, so he did the only thing he could.

He left his feet and sailed out over the cut

in a desperate leap, his long duster catching the air and billowing out behind him like the wings of a giant bird.

CHAPTER NINETEEN

Smoke had holstered his gun and was about to climb out of the coach and up to the driver's box to check on Tom Burke and give Floyd Horton a hand when he saw the huge shape plummeting down from the sky. The man's boots struck the coach roof and jolted it so hard because of his weight that Smoke's grip on the side of the door was knocked loose. Off balance the way he was, he toppled out of the coach.

The only thing that saved him from falling in the road was a desperate grab with his other hand that caught the handle of the door as it flapped back and forth in the wind. Smoke twisted and hung there with just the toes of his boots still inside the coach. That and the perilous one-handed grip was all that held him up.

The outlaw who had jumped from the cut bank to the stagecoach had fallen to his knees when he landed on the roof. He lunged forward, wrapped his arms around Horton's neck from behind, and started choking the driver. Horton dropped the reins and pawed at the arms clamping down on his throat like iron bands, but he couldn't budge them.

The team had never come to a complete stop. Now, spooked and wild-eyed from all the gunfire, they started running hard again. As the road came out of the cut, it sloped downhill, so the coach began to pick up speed.

"Smoke!" Sally cried. He looked up and saw her leaning toward him as she held out a hand. Herman Langston was behind her with his arms wrapped around her waist. That familiarity with a married woman, normally unforgivable, was understandable under these circumstances. They were trying to get Smoke back into the coach.

Smoke flung his other hand up and clasped wrists with Sally. She was a strong woman, and with the drummer bracing her she was able to haul Smoke up from his precarious position. He got his feet inside the coach and wrapped his arm around the window frame as he let go of Sally's wrist.

They weren't out of danger, though. The way the stagecoach was careening down the hill with no hand on the reins to slow the horses, the vehicle might veer off the road and crash at any time. That outlaw was doing his best to choke the life out of Floyd Horton, too.

Smoke pointed up to let Sally know what he was doing, then reached for the brass rail that ran around the edge of the coach roof. He couldn't try a shot because there was too great a risk of hitting Horton. Instead he got a foot in the window, held on to the rail, and heaved himself on top of the coach.

A few pieces of baggage were lashed in place up here. Smoke clambered over them, drew his gun, and struck at the man who was attacking Horton. The coach lurched just as the Colt fell, and instead of hitting the man in the head and knocking him out, as Smoke intended, the blow slammed into his shoulder instead. The man bellowed in pain and anger, let go of Horton, and twisted around to swing a powerful arm at Smoke in a swift backhand.

Smoke pulled back to avoid the hit, but the outlaw's arm struck his forearm and knocked the gun out of his hand. The man threw himself at Smoke, crashed into him, and drove him backward.

Smoke landed with his shoulders at the back edge of the roof with his head hanging over the canvas-covered boot. The outlaw tried to knee him in the groin, but Smoke writhed aside at the last second and took the vicious strike on his thigh. Roaring curses, the outlaw knelt astride Smoke and began raining punches down on him.

Smoke jerked his head from side to side to avoid most of the blows, and as soon as he got a chance he shot up a short punch of his own that caught the man on the chin and rocked his head back. That gave Smoke an opening to grab the outlaw by the throat and heave him to the side.

The man fell against the railing and toppled over it, but he snagged it with a hand and a foot and clung there. Smoke rolled over, came up on his knees, and glanced back and forth between the outlaw who was struggling to pull himself back up onto the coach and the road ahead of them, which took a fairly sharp turn at the bottom of the hill.

If the coach hit that bend in the trail at the speed it was going now, there was a good chance it would turn over. Smoke had no choice except to try to slow it down.

He scrambled up to the driver's box. Tom Burke had slipped down into the floorboard and lay there either unconscious or dead. Floyd Horton had passed out from being choked and lay slumped across the seat. Smoke shoved the senseless driver aside and slid down onto the seat.

The loose reins coiled and writhed on the floorboard next to Burke like a nest of snakes. Smoke reached down and grabbed them, then straightened and hauled back on the leathers. The horses were still spooked, but they responded immediately to a human touch on the reins. They started to slow down.

Something hit Smoke from behind with such force he would have pitched forward off the seat if an arm hadn't looped around his neck and held him up. As that arm closed on his throat and cut off his air, he knew the outlaw had managed to climb back onto the coach and was trying to choke him to death, just as he had done with Horton.

As Smoke's head began to spin from lack of breath, he reached back and caught hold of the man's duster. Smoke was immensely strong, as his unusually wide shoulders indicated, and his position gave him a little leverage. He bent forward and pulled with all the strength he could muster. The outlaw let out a startled shout as Smoke heaved him up and over. The man came down on the singletree attached to the front of the coach, tried to get hold of it, but slipped off and fell under the hooves of the still galloping team. Smoke felt the jolt as two of the wheels rolled over him.

Smoke had been forced to drop the reins to deal with the outlaw. He lunged for them again and caught them just as they were about to slither out of his reach. Straightening, he planted his boot soles against the floorboard and pulled back on the reins with his left hand while he used his right to lean on the brake lever. The team slowed again and the coach shuddered to a stop about ten feet short of the turn that likely would have wrecked it.

Smoke looped the reins around the brake lever and dropped quickly off the box. He jerked the door on that side open and said, "Sally, are you all right?"

"I'm fine," she told him as she leaned out to give him a reassuring smile. "Bounced around quite a bit, but that's all. Arley's the only one who's wounded."

"How's he doing?"

"I think he'll be all right. It looks like the bullet went through cleanly. Mrs. Carter and I are trying to stop the bleeding."

"You get back to that, then. When you get a chance, check on the driver and the guard. I need to make sure none of those outlaws are still alive."

Smoke had lost his Colt in the struggle with the man who had jumped on top of the stage, so he went to the boot at the back, untied the canvas cover and pulled it aside, and reached in to get his Winchester that was stored there along with quite a bit of baggage. He knew the chamber was empty but the rifle was fully loaded otherwise. He worked the lever up and down so it was ready to fire, then walked grimly back up the hill toward the first body lying in the road.

He could tell before he got there that the man was no longer a threat. Several hooves had struck him in the head, battering it into a shape that was barely human. That would have been enough to kill him even if the stagecoach's iron-rimmed wheels hadn't crushed his midsection. Smoke's lips tightened as he looked at the grisly remains.

He went on up the hill, retrieving his Colt when he spotted it lying on the road on the way. The man who had ridden out and tried to stop the stage was dead, too, with a single gunshot wound to the chest, as was the first man who had toppled off the bank when two of Smoke's slugs punched through his belly.

That left two more men, one on each

bank. Smoke found places where the banks had collapsed a little and climbed up to check on them. Both were dead, the man on the east bank from one of Smoke's bullets, the other on the west bank shredded by the buckshot from Tom Burke's shotgun.

Smoke wondered briefly if they had any connection to the man he had killed at the stagecoach station in Morgan Mill. Chances were he would never know, since none of them were left alive to tell the tale.

When he got back to the coach, he found that Floyd Horton was sitting up, shaking his head, and rubbing his throat.

"Are you all right, Floyd?" Smoke asked.

"Yeah," the jehu rasped. "Be a mite hoarse for a while, but I'm fine. Can't say the same for Tom."

Burke was stretched out on the ground with a folded blanket under his head. Sally knelt beside him as she tried to wipe some of the blood away from the wound on his head.

"He's alive," she told Smoke. "It looks like the bullet just left a deep graze on his head, but I can't tell if it cracked his skull. He needs real medical attention."

"It's only about ten more miles to Stephenville," Horton said. "We'll put him in the coach and make him as comfortable as we can, then get him there right away."

The other passengers had gotten out of the coach, too. Arley Hicks had a crude bandage tied around his left shoulder and that arm was in a makeshift sling, but he didn't seem to be in too bad of a shape. Herman Langston was fine, and the Purcells were badly shaken up but otherwise unhurt.

"Wait a minute," Donald Purcell said. "Will there be room in there for the guard and the rest of us?"

Horton's eyes narrowed as he said, "I'm gonna forget you said that, mister. The ladies can ride inside. There's room for the rest of you on top of the coach."

"On top?" Purcell repeated. "Oh, no, I paid for my passage —"

"Tom Burke took a bullet trying to keep you safe," Smoke snapped. "You'll help us get him in the coach and then climb up there and keep your complaints to yourself."

Purcell opened and closed his mouth a couple of times, but he didn't say anything else. His wife just gave him a contemptuous look and said, "Give them a hand, Donald, like Mr. Jensen told you."

Langston said, "I suppose we'll leave the bodies for the sheriff?"

"Or the coyotes and the buzzards," Smoke

said. "Doesn't much matter to me who gets to them first."

The stagecoach station in Stephenville was a block away from the courthouse square. A man in a suit and top hat was pacing back and forth in front of the building when Horton brought the coach to a halt.

"There you are!" the man exclaimed. "I expected you earlier."

Smoke was riding on the seat next to Horton. He said, "Who are you, mister?"

The man ignored the question and rushed to the back of the coach. He fumbled with the ties on the canvas cover and then threw it aside. His hands shot into the boot and brought out a small valise that he clutched to him like it was something precious.

By this time Smoke had climbed down from the box. The station manager and a couple of hostlers came out to greet the stage, too.

"Tom Burke's inside the coach, got a bullet wound on his head," Horton said. "Somebody best fetch the doc right away."

One of the hostlers rushed off to do that while the manager said, "Good Lord, Floyd, did you get held up?"

"Yeah, they jumped us in one of those cuts a few miles this side of Morgan Mill."

"They didn't steal anything?"

"No. In fact, the varmints all wound up dead." Horton nodded toward Smoke. "Thanks to Mr. Jensen there."

The man holding the valise tried to step around Smoke, who blocked his path and said, "Wait a minute, mister. I asked who you are, and now I want to know what's so important about that bag."

"That's none of your business," the man snapped. "Now, get out of my way —"

Horton moved up beside Smoke and said, "I'd listen to this hombre if I was you, mister. You're actin' like what's in that bag is important enough to make a gang of owl-hoots come after this stage."

The man glared at them and said, "Well, if you must know, I'm the president of the bank here in Stephenville, and I arranged for a shipment of cash to be brought in —"

Smoke didn't let him finish. He pulled the bag out of the protesting man's hands, undid the catches, and opened it. Inside were bundles of greenbacks.

"Who knew about this?" he asked disgustedly as he shoved the valise back into the man's arms.

"Why . . . why, just Mr. Ferguson and myself —"

"You didn't tell the law, or the folks who

would be responsible for getting that cash here safely?"

"I thought it best to tell as few people as possible."

"Blast it," Horton said. "If I'd known we was carryin' all that loot, I would've brought the stage on into town yesterday evening. Didn't seem like there was any rush, though."

"And your secrecy almost got some innocent people killed," Smoke added.

The banker drew himself up and said stiffly, "I was just conducting my business as I saw fit, and you've no right to chastise me for it."

Sally had climbed down from the coach by now. She put a hand on her husband's arm and said, "Let's go, Smoke. I want to make sure Mr. Burke gets the attention he needs, and Arley could use having that shoulder wound looked at, too."

Smoke nodded slowly and turned away. Sally was right. There were more important things to take care of than punching that stuffed-shirt banker in the mouth.

But it sure was tempting.

CHAPTER TWENTY

Seth Barrett put the pen down next to the sheets of paper in front of him and leaned back to rub his eyes with both hands. He had been sitting here at his desk all evening, working on his sermon for the Sunday morning service. He looked at the words he had written in the light from the lamp at the corner of the desk, but the letters seemed to blur before his eyes until they no longer made sense.

He was worrying about it too much, he thought, putting too much pressure on himself. But this would be the first Christmas sermon he had ever preached, and he wanted it to be a good one.

That was one thing about hearing the Lord's call and coming to the ministry late, he mused. There were a lot of first times for everything.

He got a clean sheet of paper, picked up the pen, and dipped it in the inkwell. As he leaned forward again, he muttered, "Bethlehem . . . manger . . . wise men . . ."

Too bad that last didn't apply to him, he thought wryly. He was trying, but he didn't figure anybody would ever call him wise.

A gust of wind struck outside, causing the window in Seth's study to rattle in its casement. Bare branches tapped against the glass, and fingers of cold rain clawed down the smooth surface.

Seth was glad he was inside tonight. Even though the little whitewashed parsonage behind the Enchanted Rock Baptist Church had its share of drafts, the weather outside was a lot more miserable.

Seth scrawled a few lines on the clean piece of paper, then paused to read them over. Unsatisfied, he gave in to a sudden urge and crumpled the paper.

Then he chided himself for being wasteful, smoothed out the paper, and turned it over to make a fresh start again on the other side.

After a while he at least had an opening that he was satisfied with. Thinking that was enough for tonight, as well as something he could build on, he put the pen back in its holder and stood up to stretch after being hunched over the desk for what seemed like a long time. He winced as stiff muscles caught and twinged. He had some bruises and scrapes from the fracas with Felix Dugan the day before.

He wondered what the members of the congregation would think when they heard that their pastor had been brawling with the rancher. That wasn't a good thing for him to be doing, and he had known it at the time. He just hadn't been able to control that wild, reckless streak in him, especially knowing that Delta Kennedy was there watching. . . .

The thought of Delta made him frown. He didn't have any business being interested in the pretty widow. It would be a mistake for him to get involved with any woman, especially one as nice as her. What he needed to do was concentrate on the work that had called him here, ministering to the spiritual needs of the people in this area instead of worrying about himself and the loneliness that sometimes gripped him.

"You think too much," he told himself out loud this time. Picking up the Bible sitting on the corner of the desk, he leaned over and blew out the lamp. It was time for him to retire for the evening. Before he went to sleep, he would read for a while from the Good Book. The beautiful power of the language always soothed him. He would forget about the storm outside, forget about Felix Dugan, even forget about Delta . . . although the image of her beauty that was burned into his brain would make that more difficult.

Most of all he would forget about the things that had brought him here, the past that lurked behind him like a lobo skulking along after its prey.

Two men sat on horseback under the dripping trees about thirty yards from the parsonage. The bare branches didn't offer them much protection from the cold rain. In slickers and wide-brimmed hats, they hunched miserably in their saddles as they watched the window's glowing yellow rectangle and then saw the light go out.

"Looks like he's turnin' in for the night," one of the men said. "We could go in there and get him, Deke."

The man called Deke shook his head, causing more water to run off his hat brim.

"You know that's not what the boss told us to do, Packy," he said. "We're not supposed to do anything except keep an eye on him."

"Shoot, we ain't even sure he's the right fella, are we?" Packy asked.

"It's him," Deke said heavily. "It's got to

be. Nothin' else makes sen— Hold on." He stiffened and leaned forward. "Somebody's comin'."

It was true. Several riders were approaching the church and the parsonage. The two men under the trees drew their mounts back deeper into the shadows.

The newcomers rode around the church and into the small yard between the bigger building and the parsonage. They drew rein there. One man swung down from his saddle and went up the three steps to the porch. He pounded a fist on the door and yelled, "Preacher! You in there, preacher man?" His voice was loud enough that the watchers heard him clearly over the drip of the rain.

Packy edged his horse forward a step and said quietly, "Deke, we better do somethin' about this. That hombre sounds mad, and the boss won't like it if anything happens to that so-called preacher."

Deke lifted a hand to hold back his companion. He sounded amused as he said, "No, for now we're gonna just wait and see how this plays out. I don't think we have to worry. If we're right about that fella, those men have bit off more than they can chew."

Seth had lit a candle in his bedroom and

was about to get undressed and put on his nightshirt when the pounding came on the front door. He frowned as he swung around in that direction, wondering why anybody would be visiting at this time of night. Maybe someone was sick or hurt. . . .

Then he heard the raucous shout and recognized the voice. For a second, Seth closed his eyes and sighed.

He knew that hoping the caller would go away was asking for too much. He picked up the candleholder and started toward the front of the house.

The man was still beating on the door and yelling when Seth twisted the latch and pulled the panel open. The slicker-clad figure swayed forward a little when the door wasn't there for him to hit anymore. He caught himself and blinked at Seth, owl-eyed in the candlelight.

"What do you want, Andrews?" Seth asked the puncher who rode for Felix Dugan.

Whiskey-laden breath gusted in Seth's face as Andrews leaned toward him again.

"Come to settle up with you, preacher man," the cowboy said.

"You don't owe me anything."

That brought a harsh bark of laughter from Andrews. He said, "It's you that does the owin', Barrett! You laughed at the boss, and then you whipped him. You got to pay for that."

"I'm sorry I laughed at Mr. Dugan," Seth said. "I shouldn't have done that. It was un-Christian of me. And you can tell him I said so. Or I'll apologize to him myself the next time I see him." Seth paused. "As for the fight . . . he attacked me. I had a right to defend myself."

Andrews shook his head stubbornly and said, "You think a bunch o' words are gonna make it go away? It's gonna take more'n that, preacher man."

"You're drunk," Seth said, not bothering to keep the disgust out of his voice.

"Not too drunk to teach you a lesson."

Seth had the candleholder in his left hand. His right clenched into a fist. It was pure instinct, as was the urge to knock the drunken, loud-mouthed cowboy off his front porch.

Forcing himself to relax, Seth said, "I'm not going to fight you, Andrews. You might as well go home." He couldn't stop himself from adding, "Besides, in your condition, it wouldn't be a fair fight."

"Think I'm too drunk to whip you, huh? Well, maybe I am." Andrews moved back a couple of steps, to the edge of the porch, and pulled his slicker open, sweeping it back to reveal the butt of the revolver holstered on his right hip. "But I ain't too drunk to make you dance a hot lead jig!"

The cowboy's hand streaked toward the gun. Seth knew Andrews intended to blast some shots at his feet and make him jump to avoid the bullets. The thing of it was, Andrews probably wasn't good enough with the gun to do that even when he wasn't stinking drunk. The condition he was in now, his shots were more likely to smash Seth's legs and cripple him.

That thought flashed through Seth's mind in the time it took Andrews to grab his gun. As the weapon cleared leather, Seth flung the candle and its holder into Andrews's face. The cowboy shrieked and jumped back as the flame burned his face. A fraction of a second later, Seth's left hand closed around the gun's cylinder. His right fist crashed into Andrews's jaw and knocked the man backward off the porch. Andrews lost his grip on the revolver, which remained in Seth's left hand.

One of the two punchers who had ridden up with Andrews yelled, "Look out! The preacher's got a gun!"

They clawed out their own Colts. Seth could have jumped back into the house and slammed the door, but the thought never occurred to him. Instead, he flipped the revolver in the air with his left hand, and his right deftly plucked it from its flight. Colt flame spurted redly in the gloom as the cowboys opened fire on him. Seth crouched as a slug thudded into the wall near him and another sizzled through the air beside his head.

The gun in his hand roared as he triggered four swift shots. Even though he had never held this revolver until now, its grips felt natural and comfortable against his palm. The gouts of flame from its barrel lanced out, lighting up the yard between the church and the parsonage. He saw one of the cowboys topple out of the saddle, and the other man slumped forward as he tried to control his skittish mount.

Suddenly it felt as if the world had fallen away underneath Seth, even though his boots were still planted firmly on the porch planks. Dizzy horror engulfed him. What had he done?

Andrews scooted backward in the mud, crying, "Don't shoot me! Please don't shoot me!"

The man who had fallen off his horse reached up, got hold of the trailing reins, and climbed unsteadily to his feet. At least he wasn't dead, Seth realized as relief went through him. But there was still the other man to worry about.

He stepped back in the house and set the gun on a table just inside the door. The candle had gone out when it fell on the wet porch, of course, but a lamp sat on the table with a little box of matches beside it. Seth had it lit in a matter of seconds. He started to step out onto the porch with it, then paused and picked up the gun again as well.

The light from the lamp washed over the yard. Andrews, seemingly shocked sober now, was helping the unhorsed man to climb back into the saddle.

"How bad are they hurt?" Seth asked.

"Cole's got a hole in his arm where you drilled him," Andrews replied. "Your bullet knocked Jimmy's saddle horn off and it hit him in the belly, knocked the wind out of him. Reckon they'll both be all right." Andrews swallowed. "You've still got my gun."

"That's right, I do," Seth said, his voice hard and flat. It hid the vast relief he felt at knowing he hadn't killed anyone tonight, even though that was blind luck — or someone watching over him. "I'll leave it here on the porch. You can come back and get it tomorrow. Tonight I'm going to hang on to it while the three of you get out of here."

"We're goin', we're goin'," Andrews muttered as he reached for his own horse's reins. "Don't think this is over, though, preacher."

"You keep saying that," Seth responded coldly.

"Yeah, but now I know how good you can shoot."

They wheeled their horses and rode out, vanishing around the church.

Seth sighed and blew the lamp out, not wanting to stand there and make a target of himself. As the darkness closed in around him again, he thought that Andrews was right.

It wasn't over . . . and Seth had to wonder if it ever would be.

In the trees off to the side, Packy laughed softly and said in a half-whisper, "You were right, Deke. That's our man. Ain't no doubt about it now."

CHAPTER TWENTY-ONE

It was a cold, wet, miserable night on the trail for Porter and the Jensen boys, one of too many spent that way lately for Ace and Chance. Porter wasn't used to such hardships, and he looked forlorn the next morning as he sat on a stump while Ace tried to find enough dry wood for a fire.

"My health has never been all that good, you know," Porter said. "That's one reason I came to Texas. I thought the climate might be better here." He let out a laugh tinged with bitterness. "Little did I know!"

"I figure it's not always like this," Ace said. "We've never been down in this part of the country in December before, so we weren't sure what to expect."

"As close as Texas is to Mexico, though, I figured it'd be warmer," Chance added as he checked on the horses. "We just didn't realize how blasted *big* the place is."

"The state does stretch for a considerable

distance in all directions," Porter agreed.

After a while, Ace gave up on getting a fire started.

"It's just too wet," he said disgustedly. "We might as well ride on to Fredericksburg, if you're still bound and determined to go there, Will."

"I haven't given up on my dream," Porter said. "I can't."

"Well, then, let's saddle up and get started," Chance said.

Ace had some jerky in his saddlebags. As they rode, he passed around the dried, leathery strips of meat. They were better than nothing, but they would have gone down a lot easier with some biscuits and hot coffee.

The rain fell off and on all morning, sometimes just a drizzle and other times a downpour. However, as the middle of the day approached, the rain stopped falling, and a few patches of blue sky appeared.

"Don't believe it," Chance said scornfully. "The weather's just teasing us. Before you know it, the sky will turn black, and the bottom will fall out again."

"I'm afraid you're right," Ace agreed. "It's rained so much I'll believe it's going to dry out when I see it."

At least the better weather held until they

reached Fredericksburg, which was nestled in a valley surrounded by wooded hills. As they rode into town, Ace studied the houses they passed, most of which were built of stone with a coating of whitewash. Many of the doors had wreaths hung on them, reminders that Christmas was only a few days away.

They came to a large wooden building in a distinctive circular shape. A sign identified it as the *Vereins Kirche*. Ace couldn't read German, but the place looked like a church to him, so he figured that was what *Kirche* meant.

Everyone they passed, whether on foot, horseback, or in a buggy or wagon, smiled at them. Chance returned the smiles and commented, "Friendly folks around here, from the looks of it."

As they approached the town square, wreaths and garlands decorated with bright red berries and colorful cloth ribbons became more prominent. In the square itself, a large evergreen had been set up and decorated.

"That's one of those Christmas trees I've heard about," Ace said as he nodded toward the evergreen. "Folks all over are starting to put them up as part of celebrating Christmas."

On another corner of the square stood an elaborate, three-tiered carousel with Nativity scenes and other holiday decorations on it. None of the three newcomers had ever seen anything like it. They reined in and tried not to gape at the thing.

One of the townsmen paused and said, "You like our Christmas pyramid, *ja*?"

"Is that what you call it?" Chance asked.

"Yes. The *Social Turn Verein* builds one every year."

"Turn Verein?" Ace repeated with a frown.

"The local social and athletic club." The citizen hooked his thumbs in his vest and added proudly, "I am a member myself, you know."

"Well, you fellas do good work," Chance told him. "Looks like you've got the whole town decorated for Christmas."

"*Ja,* it is the biggest holiday of the year." The man frowned. "But this rain threatens to wash out all our plans."

"Maybe it'll dry up," Ace said, even though he wasn't convinced of that.

Porter asked the local man, "Could you tell us where the stagecoach station is?"

"You missed it. Go back a block and half a block to the left."

Ace touched a finger to the brim of his hat and said, "We're obliged to you, friend."

"How about a good place to eat?" Chance asked.

That put a grin on the man's face. He pointed and said, "A block that way. Opa's Haus. That's H-A-U-S. Try the schnitzel."

"We will," Chance said with a laugh.

Porter turned his horse back the way they had come. Ace and Chance followed suit. Porter said, "I think we should try the stage station first and find out what time the coach from Johnson City is expected."

"No matter what the schedule says, the coach isn't here yet," Ace pointed out. "It would have had to pass us on the road, and it didn't."

"But I want to be on hand when it arrives. You fellows go on and eat, if you'd like. I'll understand, since I know we all missed breakfast this morning."

"No, we'll stay with you for now," Ace said. He glanced at Chance, who shrugged and nodded. They both knew that Porter probably planned to confront Evelyn Channing and Oliver Hudson again, and if he did, no doubt it would provoke more unpleasantness. Neither of the brothers wanted Porter to have to face that by himself.

As they headed back to the stagecoach station, they passed the Nimitz Hotel, which looked like the biggest and best hotel in town. With their funds starting to run low, they wouldn't be able to stay there, Ace thought. But he was sure they could find some other inexpensive place to put up while they were here.

He wondered how long that would be . . . and if he and Chance would wind up having to hog-tie Porter, throw him on his horse, and take him back to Austin by force to keep him from getting shot.

Because from what he had seen so far, Ace didn't think there was a chance Evelyn would ever change her mind about marrying Oliver Hudson.

The rain and the bad roads had the stagecoach more than an hour behind schedule. Evelyn was willing to put up with the delay, though, in order to reach her destination and get started on the rest of her life — the life she intended to spend with Oliver Hudson.

She thought fleetingly about William Porter as she looked out the coach window at the wet landscape. William was a nice enough young man, and when he had first expressed a romantic interest in her, she had considered — briefly — seeing where that might lead.

But he was also a dreamer. Oh, he worked

at one job or another, she had to give him credit for that, but he was also content to spend most of his time singing or playing the guitar or envisioning a future where he was a rich, successful author. That was a ridiculous way to live, and Evelyn wanted no part of it. She was a practical young woman and had been for a long time, ever since she'd been on her own.

Now, Oliver was different. When Oliver promised that they would be rich and that she would never want for anything, she believed him . . . even though as far as she could recall, he had never mentioned *how* that was going to come about.

But all she had to do was look at him and see how handsome and strong and capable he was, and she believed every word he said.

"You look like you're lost in thought, Evelyn," he said, breaking into her reverie as they swayed a little on the coach seat. "What's going on in that mind of yours?"

"Oh, nothing," she said, not wanting him to know that she'd been daydreaming about him. Her future husband didn't need a swelled head even before they got married.

A snore came from the old, white-bearded man on the other seat, who was the only other passenger. He was going to visit his granddaughter and her family in Fredericksburg, he had explained to them, and then he had promptly dozed off. Evelyn didn't see how anyone could sleep in a bouncing, jolting stagecoach, but she wasn't as ancient as their traveling companion, either.

The rain had stopped, the coach was moving a little faster, and she hoped it wouldn't be long now until they were in Fredericksburg. She asked Oliver, "How much farther do you think it is?"

"Oh, I'd say about five miles," he replied as he looked out the window and studied the passing countryside. After a moment he added, "Almost exactly five miles."

Evelyn frowned, wondering how he knew that, but before she could ask him, the coach lurched and began to slow down. They shouldn't be stopping now, she thought, not if they were still that far out of town. She hoped there was nothing wrong with the stagecoach or the team that would delay their journey even more.

As the vehicle slowed and then came to a halt, the old man sputtered and roused from his sleep. He blinked rheumy eyes, looked around, and asked in a quavery voice, "Are we there yet?"

"Not yet, old-timer," Oliver told him.

From the box on the front of the stagecoach, the driver called, "You folks stay inside." Evelyn thought he sounded nervous. No, more than that.

He sounded scared.

A moment after that, a gun went off somewhere nearby. The unexpected boom made Evelyn cry out. Instinctively, she clutched at Oliver and exclaimed, "What —"

"Don't be frightened," he told her. "I won't let anyone harm you."

On the opposite seat, the old-timer just looked confused.

Hoofbeats thudded on the wet ground. A man on horseback loomed up at the window on the coach's left side, reached over from the saddle to grab the door latch, and jerked it open. He held a huge revolver with a barrel that looked as big around as a cannon to Evelyn. Pointing the gun at them, he growled, "Get outta there."

The driver had told them to stay in the coach, but Evelyn was afraid the shot she'd heard had been directed at the poor man. She shrank back against Oliver, but he said, "We'd better do what he tells us, darling."

He moved past her and stepped down from the coach to the muddy road, then turned to assist her. Evelyn's muscles didn't want to work, but when he held his hands out toward her, she drew strength from his calm demeanor. She swallowed hard, then took his hands and let him help her climb down from the coach. Once her feet were on the ground, he put his arm around her shoulders again.

"You, too, you old pelican," the man with the gun ordered. He wore a long, mud-splattered duster, and a bandanna was tied across the lower half of his face under a pulled-down hat.

While the old man was climbing awkwardly out of the coach, Evelyn risked a look around. She saw half a dozen more men, all wearing dusters and masks like the first one, sitting on their horses as they formed a line blocking the road. Some held rifles while others had pistols in their hands, but they all looked ready to kill at the slightest excuse.

Evelyn glanced at the box and saw the driver slumped on the seat, clutching a bloody left arm where he'd been wounded. She had been right about the target of the shot she'd heard.

"They're here," said the outlaw next to the coach. "Bring up the horses."

One of the other masked men rode toward them leading two saddled, riderless horses. Evelyn's eyes grew huge as she realized what was happening.

She and Oliver were about to be kidnapped!

William Porter, she thought wildly. As insane as it sounded to her, he must have put these terrible men up to this. He had hired desperadoes to kidnap her and Oliver. They probably had orders to kill Oliver!

"All right, you two," the man who seemed to be the leader said. "Get on these horses. You're comin' with us."

"We're not going anywhere with you," Oliver said bravely.

"You better think twice about that, mister." The outlaw's tone was hard and menacing.

At that moment, the old man, who had still been looking around as if he didn't comprehend what was going on, suddenly yelped, "Road agents!" Moving with surprising speed for someone so decrepit, he reached under his coat and hauled out a long-barreled pistol that looked almost as ancient as he was.

The man on horseback turned his gun and fired. Flame spurted from the barrel, close enough to the old man that the sparks started his coat smoldering as the bullet slammed into the frail body. The old-timer was blown off his feet and landed like a bundle of sticks at the edge of the road.

"Blast it!" the outlaw shouted. "Why'd the crazy old coot do that?" Without waiting for an answer, he pointed the gun at Evelyn and Oliver again and snapped, "Get mounted!"

Evelyn could barely control the shuddering that went through her. She couldn't have climbed on the horse if Oliver hadn't been there to help her. Quietly, he said, "Don't be frightened, dear. You won't be hurt, I swear."

She didn't see how he could prevent these men from doing whatever they wanted to, though. Obviously, they were all brutal killers.

A couple of the masked men dismounted, picked up the old man's body, and put it back in the coach. The boss outlaw told the driver, "You can still handle the reins. Get this coach outta here now, unless you want another bullet!"

The driver was pale from pain, but he was able to slap the reins against the horses' rumps and get them moving again. Jerkily, the coach rolled away with its grim burden as the outlaws galloped toward the hills. Surrounded as they were, the prisoners had no choice but to go with them.

One of the men was leading Evelyn's horse. All she could do was hold on to the saddle horn with both hands for dear life and moan as she tried not to fall off.

They rode hard for half a mile before slowing to a walk. Evelyn's hat had come off, and some of her hair had fallen loose around her face. Breathing hard, she looked over at Oliver and was shocked to realize that he was grinning.

That was when the man who had seemed to be in charge pulled down his bandanna, returned Oliver's grin, and asked, "How was that, boss? You reckon we fooled that jehu just like you wanted."

CHAPTER TWENTY-TWO

The manager at the stagecoach station in Fredericksburg assured Ace, Chance, and Porter that there was nothing to worry about, even though the coach should have been there already.

"With the weather and the roads like they are, you expect it to be runnin' late," the man said. "Gil Burnley's a good driver. He'll bring the coach on through just fine, and it'll be here in a little while. You just wait and see."

But another half-hour passed, and there was still no sign of the stagecoach.

Porter was getting frantic by now, and Ace could tell by the look on the station manager's face that he was worried, too. Ace asked the man, "There's only one main road between here and Johnson City, isn't there?"

"Yeah, that's right. The coach wouldn't have had any reason to go any other way."

"Well, then, why don't we ride back and

see if we can find out why it hasn't shown up yet?" Ace suggested.

"Maybe it broke an axle or a wheel or something," Chance added.

Porter nodded eagerly and said, "Yes, I think we should go and look for it."

"You fellas do what you want," the station manager said. "Actually, I'd be obliged to you. I hate to say it, but ol' Gil's late enough now that there really could be something wrong."

Ace, Chance, and Porter headed for their horses. Porter was more agitated, but the Jensen brothers had grim looks on their faces to show that they were worried, too.

Before they could mount up and ride out, however, the station manager exclaimed, "Wait a minute! I think I hear the coach comin'."

The four men walked a short distance out into the street to look to the east where the street turned into the stage road. They spotted the vehicle coming toward them about a quarter of a mile away, moving fast.

"Gil's in a hurry for some reason," the station manager commented. "And something about him doesn't look right . . . Good Lord! I think he's been hurt. Look at the way he's driving with just one hand."

It was true. The driver was slumped to the

side, too, as if he weren't able to sit up straight.

"Something's happened, all right," Ace said. "Maybe we'd better ride out and meet the coach."

"Time we get mounted up, it'll almost be here," Chance pointed out.

"I don't care!" Porter cried in a ragged voice. "I've got to see if Evelyn is all right!"

He practically flung himself into the saddle and galloped toward the oncoming stagecoach. Ace and Chance exchanged a glance and then went after him. It wasn't likely that Porter would need help, but the hombre did seem to have a knack for getting into trouble.

They caught up with him by the time he reached the stagecoach. Ace and Chance saw that the driver was hurt, just as the station manager thought. The left sleeve of the jehu's coat was red with blood.

Porter reined his horse next to the coach's windows and bent down to peer inside. He popped back up and said to the driver, "Your passengers! Where are your passengers?"

"One's in there dead," the man replied. His strained voice showed the pain he was in from the wounded arm.

"Dead!" Porter yelled. "Stop! Stop right here!"

The driver kept the team moving. He said, "Mister, I'm gettin' this coach to the station 'fore I pass out."

Ace moved his horse alongside the box, pulled his left foot out of the stirrup, and rested it on the floorboards. He grabbed hold of the railing at the edge of the box and pulled himself from the saddle onto the seat.

"Take my horse, Chance," he told his brother, then went on to the driver, "I've handled a stagecoach team before. Let me take them on into town."

"Normally, I wouldn't do it, youngster," the jehu said. "But this ain't normal circumstances. I've lost more blood than I like to think about, and this arm hurts like blazes." He passed over the reins. "I'm obliged to you."

"The passenger who's dead," Porter said. "Is . . . is it a woman?"

The driver shook his head and said, "Nope, some old-timer who got on in Johnson City."

Porter closed his eyes, evidently almost overcome by the relief flooding through him.

"What about the other passengers?" Ace asked as he kept the stagecoach rolling into the outskirts of Fredericksburg.

"There were only two of 'em, a man and a woman. Married couple, I reckon."

"No, they're not," Porter snapped. "What happened to them?"

"The same bunch of no-good owlhoots who killed the old-timer carried 'em off."

"They were kidnapped?" Porter looked stricken again now.

"Yeah, I reckon that's what you'd call it. They made 'em get off the stage and had a pair of horses waitin' for them. Looked to me like the whole thing was planned out ahead of time."

"They say anything to give you any idea why?" Chance asked as he rode alongside the coach.

The driver shook his head.

"Nary a word. They shot that old man when he pulled a gun on 'em, threw his carcass back in the coach, then rode off into the hills after tellin' me to get out of there."

"Which direction did they go?" Ace asked.

"They headed north. Whether they kept goin' that way, I don't have no idea. I was too busy keepin' the coach movin' to pay any attention to the varmints after they rode off."

"Where did this happen?"

"About five miles back."

"Come on," Porter said to Ace and Chance. "We have to trail them. Maybe we can rescue Evelyn!"

"I sort of had the same thing in mind," Ace said. "But we need to get this coach to the station first and see that Mr. Burnley here gets some medical attention."

Nodding, the driver said, "I'm obliged to you for that, son."

Porter didn't like it, but he said, "All right, we can do that. But then we go after those outlaws!"

"Then we go after those outlaws," Ace agreed solemnly.

Evelyn could only stare in shock and horror at the man she had thought she knew.

"You did a fine job, Tate," Oliver Hudson told the now unmasked outlaw who had murdered the old man. "When the driver gets to Fredericksburg, he'll tell everyone how you took us off the stage against our will. It might have been a little better if the old man was still alive to say the same thing, but I can't blame you for what you did. He pulled iron on you, after all."

"Yeah, when I saw that gun o' his come out, my gut told me to shoot him," the man called Tate agreed. "I didn't have time to think about anything else."

230

"Well, no matter," Hudson said, his voice breezy and casual as if the old-timer's death meant less than nothing to him.

And that was the truth, Evelyn realized as sick astonishment hollowed out her insides even more. Oliver *didn't* care that the old man had been gunned down. He didn't care one little bit.

That meant he was just as bad as these other men. No, worse, because he had pretended to be a good man. He had fooled her into believing that he was honest and upright and . . . and really wanted to marry her . . . and. . . .

He turned toward her, smiled, and said, "See, I told you everything would be fine, my dear. You *are* all right, aren't you?"

Evelyn gave him the only answer she could.

Her hand flashed up and cracked across his face in as hard a slap as she could muster.

Hudson's head jerked back and anger flared in his eyes for a second before he controlled it with visible effort. He lifted his reins and brought his horse closer to hers.

"I understand why you're upset, Evelyn, but I can't have you doing things like that in front of my men. They'll lose respect for me if I let my woman get away with such an insult."

His hand shot out and closed around her left wrist. A cruel twist sent pain shooting up her arm and brought a cry to her lips.

"So let's not have any hysterics, all right," Hudson went on in a low, dangerous tone. "The last thing in the world I want is for you to be hurt. I don't want to see you upset or unhappy, either. I promised you a comfortable life, and that's what I intend to give you. But I can't have you interfering in my efforts to do that, either."

She tried to pull away from him, but she couldn't escape his grip. She said, "I . . . I'm not going to have any kind of a life with you, Oliver Hudson. Not after what I've seen today."

He let go of her wrist and smiled, but there was no warmth in the expression.

"You're wrong about that, darlin'," he drawled. "We're still going to be married, just as we planned. Soon now, you'll be my faithful wife, and we'll be happy together."

She started to spit out a furious reply, but she thought twice about it and managed to stop before any of the angry words came out of her mouth. Her wrist already hurt, and there was no telling what else he might do to her if she continued to defy him in front of his men.

And these outlaws *were* his men. There was no escaping from that conclusion. She had thought she was marrying an honest man, but in reality he was the leader of a bandit gang. Just the thought of that made her head spin. With no warning, her whole world had been upended in a matter of moments.

She looked down at her horse without saying anything. After a few more seconds went by, Hudson said, "Well? Are you all right now?"

"I'm fine," Evelyn forced herself to say. "I . . . I was just confused, Oliver, that's all."

Hudson sat back in his saddle and looked satisfied with himself. He said, "I knew you'd listen to reason. You're a smart girl, Evelyn. You'll see that I know what I'm doing. And when we're rich, you'll be glad that I took the necessary steps to accomplish that goal."

"Of course," she murmured, still not looking at him. "I'm sure I will."

Hudson nodded as if the discussion was over, but it wasn't, thought Evelyn. Not really.

She didn't intend to cooperate. As soon as she had a chance to get away from him and his murderous companions, she was going to seize it.

She should have listened to Will Porter, she thought gloomily.

Hudson turned to Tate and asked, "What about that other matter you were tending to?"

"It took a while, but we found him," Tate reported. "At least, we were pretty sure we had. Deke and Packy have been keepin' an eye on him." Tate turned in the saddle and waved over two of the other men. "Tell the boss what happened last night."

"We were watchin' the fella's place," one of the men said. "Some cowboys came ridin' up late and called him out. From what we could hear, there was some sort of bad blood between 'em. One of the punchers was up on the porch, and when he slapped leather, the hombre we've been keepin' an eye on knocked him down and took his gun away. Snatched that Colt right outta the air, clean as a whistle. The other two opened up on him, but they didn't come close. He drilled one and knocked the saddle horn into the other one's belly."

"You ask me, that was a lucky shot," the second outlaw said. "He was trying to feed that fella a slug in the guts."

Hudson nodded and said, "Of course he

was. Once it came down to gunplay, every-thing was automatic for him. Did he kill all of them?"

"Didn't kill any of them," the first man said. "He just sent 'em on their way."

"That's odd," Hudson said with a frown. "Not like him, either."

"I reckon he didn't want to kill 'em, what with him bein' a preacher and all."

Hudson's eyebrows rose in surprise.

"A preacher?" He sounded like he couldn't believe it.

"That's right. We've done plenty of askin' around. Calls himself Seth Barrett now. He's the pastor of the Enchanted Rock Baptist Church."

Hudson sat there for a long moment, evidently digesting what he had just been told, before he finally threw back his head and let out a loud, raucous laugh.

"A preacher!" he said. "That's actually pretty smart. A church is just about the last place anybody would think to look for the likes of Sam Brant."

That drew chuckles from the rest of the men. Evelyn, still sitting there on her horse, didn't see what was so funny about it, but the outlaws were certainly amused.

Hudson turned his head and eyed her speculatively. He said, "You know, that gives me an idea. We're going to need someone to perform our wedding ceremony and join us together forever as husband and wife. What better person to do that than my old friend and partner, since he's gotten religion and become a sky pilot?"

Evelyn didn't say anything, didn't tell him that she would die before she ever became his wife.

It was easy to say things like that in the heat of anger, but she worried that when the time came, she would be too terrified to follow through on that resolve.

"You really think he'll do that, boss?" Tate asked.

"Of course he will, if he wants to live a little longer," Hudson replied. "But once the ceremony is over — and once he's told us what we want to know — he's going to die anyway, and I'll take great pleasure in killing him."

CHAPTER TWENTY-THREE

Holding his black bag, the doctor was already waiting at the stagecoach station when Ace brought the vehicle to a stop in front of the building. The station manager had sent someone running to fetch the physician.

Ace and Chance helped Burnley down from the box. He grumbled, "I don't know why ever'body's makin' such a fuss over me. I just got a bullet hole in my arm, that's all."

"Take him inside and put him on the sofa in the office," the manager said. "You'll be all right, Gil."

"I know that, dadblast it. But the fella who shot me won't be, happen I should ever catch him in my sights."

Porter didn't dismount while Ace and Chance half-carried the wounded jehu into the station. He was walking his horse back and forth impatiently when they emerged

237

from the building a couple of minutes later.

"Now can we go?" he asked.

The Jensen boys swung up into their saddles. Ace said, "Yeah, let's go see what we can find out."

The fact that the outlaws had kidnapped Evelyn Channing and Oliver Hudson was pretty troubling, Ace thought as he, Chance, and Porter rode out of Fredericksburg. Road agents hardly ever did that. They just robbed their victims of any valuables and left them with the stagecoach.

The only reason Ace could think of why outlaws would carry off a couple of passengers would be to hold them for ransom. That seemed unlikely in Evelyn's case. If she or her family had enough money to make that feasible, she wouldn't have been working as a waitress at that café in Austin.

That left Hudson. He'd been well-dressed, but he hadn't struck Ace as a rich man.

There was really only one way to find the answers, he told himself, and that was to track down the outlaws and their prisoners.

It wasn't difficult to locate the spot where the gang had stopped the stagecoach. No other traffic had come along the road since then, and the welter of hoofprints in the mud told the story well enough to the Jensen brothers' eyes.

"Is this where it happened?" Porter asked as he reined in, following the lead of Ace and Chance.

"Yeah," Chance said, pointing to the tracks. "You can see where they rode out and blocked the stagecoach."

"We've come about five miles from town, too, and that matches what Mr. Burnley told us," Ace added.

"What else can you tell?" Porter asked.

Chance pointed at the road and said, "Bootprints there, and some smaller prints, too. Looks like a lady's shoes."

"Those have to be Evelyn's prints," Porter said grimly.

"Yeah, but there's not very many of them," Ace said. "Of course, we already knew from what Mr. Burnley told us that they put her on a horse and rode off with her, but this confirms it."

Chance had reined his horse to the side of the road. He said, "Looks like here's the trail where they headed north."

"Can we follow it?" Porter wanted to know.

"I don't see why not," Chance told him. "The ground's soft enough from the rain that the horses left a lot of prints."

The three young men started north. As they rode, Chance commented, "You know, with everything that's going on, we forgot about getting something to eat."

"Yeah, and we didn't have much of a breakfast, either," Ace added.

Porter glared at them and said, "How can you be worried about your bellies when the woman I love has been kidnapped?"

"Just because we're hungry doesn't mean we don't care about Miss Channing," Chance said. "We'll do everything we can to rescue her from those owlhoots. But you've got to remember, Will . . . she's a grown woman. It was the decisions she made that got her into this mess."

"So you're saying it's all her fault!" Porter responded indignantly.

"Nope, not at all. I'm just saying I wish we'd had a chance to try that schnitzel the fella was talking about before we rode out on this rescue mission."

"I suppose I can't be too upset about that," Porter said with a shrug. "Evelyn's not the future wife of either one of you, after all."

Ace and Chance exchanged a glance without Porter seeing. They weren't convinced that Evelyn was Porter's future wife, either, but no purpose would be served by pointing that out. Anyway, the young lady's matrimonial plans were irrelevant right now, while she was in the hands of bandits. Saving her life was a lot higher priority.

But if Porter was part of that effort, it might make her think more kindly toward him, Ace mused. Maybe she wouldn't be so set on marrying Oliver Hudson, who had allowed them to be captured. From the sound of what the driver had said, there really hadn't been anything Hudson could have done to prevent it, but a woman might not take that into account.

Ace broke out the last of his jerky and shared it with his two companions as they followed the trail deeper into the rolling, heavily wooded Hill Country.

There were still patches of blue sky overhead, but clouds were gathering, too, as they seemed to almost every afternoon recently, and promised more rain later on.

Evelyn Channing had to bite her lip to keep from whimpering. She was a mass of pain from the waist down, but of course it wasn't proper for a lady to acknowledge that or even think too much about that region of her body.

Every step the horse took made her discomfort worse, though. She had ridden before, but never for so long and never astride like a man. That humiliation was bad enough, but the way it made her hurt was worse.

Weren't they ever going to reach their destination, whatever it might be?

Hudson looked over at her and asked, "Are you all right, my dear? You look a little pale."

Why wouldn't she look pale, she thought, snatched off a stagecoach the way she had been and forced to endure hours of torment?

She wasn't going to give him the satisfaction of admitting just how miserable she really was, though, so she gritted her teeth instead and said, "I'm fine. I'm just ready to get wherever it is we're going."

"It shouldn't be much longer," Hudson told her. "Tate, how much farther?"

"Another mile or so, I'd say, boss," the outlaw responded.

It still boggled Evelyn's mind when she heard one of the hard-bitten criminals address Hudson as "boss." Yet she accepted that he really was the leader of this gang. There was no possible mistake about that.

"The hideout's a good one?"

"You bet," Tate said. "We got all the comforts of home in that cave."

Cave? Evelyn thought. They were taking her to a *cave?*

A short time later, she found that was true. They rode across a creek and then up a slope toward a rocky bluff that bulged out like a grotesquely deformed skull. As they came closer, Evelyn saw a dark opening at its base. The sight caused a shiver to run through her. The skull-like formation made the opening resemble a mouth. A mouth waiting for an unwary victim to come close enough before snapping shut. . . .

She tried to put that thought out of her mind. It was just a cave, she told herself. Just a feature of the landscape that had nothing sinister about it.

She didn't quite succeed in making herself believe that.

Besides, from what Hudson and Tate had said, this was where the outlaws had their headquarters and that was sinister enough in itself.

A man appeared on top of the bluff, holding a rifle in one hand. He used the other hand to take off his hat and wave it back and forth over his head.

Tate said, "That's the all clear. We've got guards up there around the clock."

"Excellent," Hudson said. "Have any lawmen come poking around up here?"

Tate shook his head as they continued walking the horses toward the bluff.

"Not so far. Of course, stoppin' that stagecoach today is really the first job we've pulled in these parts. We've spent our time findin' a good place to hole up and lookin' for Brant."

"And now you've found both."

"Yeah. The church is a few miles from here. You want us to go ahead and grab him?"

Hudson appeared to think about it for a moment and then shook his head.

"Not yet," he said. "I know how stubborn Sam can be. If we try to force him to tell us what we want to know, he's liable to get all stiff-necked and refuse."

"Give me a sharp knife and an hour, and I'll bet I can make him talk," Tate said with an evil grin.

"Maybe, maybe not. I can see him being so stubborn that he'd die before telling us. I'd like to have something better to use against him than just torture."

"What've you got in mind, boss?"

"I'll have to think on that," Hudson said. He tipped his head back and looked up at the thickening clouds as thunder rumbled in the west. "It's going to start raining again soon. Let's get inside out of the weather."

Now that they had almost reached the cave, Evelyn could see that the opening was about twenty feet tall and maybe twice that wide. The bluff loomed over it for sixty or seventy feet. It was impressive, no doubt about that. The light was fading, but she could see far enough into the opening to know that there was an actual cave beyond it, not just an overhang. She couldn't tell how far the chamber went into the earth.

"You're keeping the horses in there, too?" Hudson asked.

"Yeah," said Tate. "It's plenty big enough. There are some natural chimneys farther back, so the air moves through all the time and keeps it from smellin' too bad. That takes care of the smoke from the fire, too."

"You'll need to put up some blankets and make a separate area for Miss Channing. She'll need some privacy."

Tate grinned and said, "Already ahead of you, boss. We've got that done. Fixed up a nice bunk for the lady and everything."

Hudson looked over at Evelyn and smiled.

"You see?" he said. "It's not going to be so bad. In fact, I'm sure you'll be quite comfortable here."

"I'm sure I will be, too," she said. She hoped her words didn't sound as hollow and despairing as she felt.

She saw a red glow up ahead as they rode into the cave. That made her think it was like riding into the mouth of hell.

The glow turned out to be a campfire that cast its light over a large chamber. The outlaws had used poles made from saplings to build a fence on one side of the cave. That formed the corral for the horses. Crates and kegs were scattered around to use as seats, and the men had rolled barrels into the cave to serve as tables. Blankets were spread over branches brought in from outside, then bedrolls were arranged on top of them to form bunks. Bags and boxes of supplies were stacked against a wall.

Ropes were stretched and more blankets flung over them to make the private room Hudson had talked about, on the opposite side of the cave from the horse corral. The blankets were pushed back at the moment to reveal several crates arranged to form a rectangle, with blankets and padding on top of them. That was the bunk they had made for her, thought Evelyn.

As crude as it was, she was so tired and sore right now it looked as inviting as a feather bed to her. She would have loved to throw herself on it, groan, and not move for a while.

Instead she dismounted awkwardly, allowing Hudson to help her even though her skin crawled at the touch of his hand, and then stood there stiffly as she waited to see what was going to happen. Her leg muscles screamed in pain from the ride, but she ignored them.

Thunder boomed again outside, so loud that Evelyn felt the stone floor vibrate a little under her feet. Rain began to fall so hard that it was a continuous roar.

"Aren't you glad you're snug and warm in here instead of out in that downpour?" Hudson asked her.

"Yes, I am," Evelyn said, and that was true, anyway. Getting soaked would have just made her more miserable, if that was possible.

"We'll have supper in a bit," Hudson went on, "and then I'm afraid I'll have to leave you for a while."

"Leave me?" Evelyn couldn't hold in her surprise or her fear. As much as she had come to despise Oliver Hudson in the past few hours, at least she knew him. These other men were strangers and ruthless outlaws as well.

"Don't worry," he told her as he smiled. "You can go behind those blankets, and no one will bother you."

"How can you be sure of that?"

"Because every man here knows that I'll kill anyone who lays a finger on you," he said. "You'll be safer here than you would be in the best hotel in Fredericksburg."

"But . . . but where are you going?"

Hudson still smiled, but an icy glitter appeared in his eyes as he said, "To see an old friend who thinks he's left us all behind."

CHAPTER TWENTY-FOUR

"And there were shepherds abiding in the fields by night," Seth Barrett said as he stood in the little study in the parsonage, "keeping watch over their flocks. And lo, an angel of the Lord came unto them —"

He stopped and looked down at the paper in his hand, annoyed with himself for not being able to remember exactly what came next in the Scripture. Of course, he was at a disadvantage compared to most preachers, he reminded himself. He had come to this rather late in life. He hadn't grown up going to church and studying the Bible.

He had been too busy trying to stay alive and not starve to death.

A frown creased his forehead. He didn't like to think about those days when he had been a boy alone in the world, no family, nobody to care for him. He had done things to get by that he was ashamed of now. Stealing from stores had been the start, and it had just gotten worse from there.

He gave a little shake of his head. Tomorrow morning he would be preaching his first Christmas sermon. He thought what he had written was pretty good, but he had to commit it to memory, or at least enough so that he wouldn't get lost and have to stand up there in the pulpit with a blank look on his face like an idiot. The members of the congregation had accepted him as their pastor, and he didn't want to disappoint them.

"Glad tidings," Seth muttered to himself. "Unto you this day —"

Pounding on the front door interrupted him.

Seth stiffened. He thought about the confrontation with Andrews and the other two cowboys from Felix Dugan's ranch. Maybe Andrews had come back to take up the fight again.

Then he heard a familiar voice calling through the door, "Seth! Seth, you in there?"

That was Hoyt Larrabee, one of the church's deacons. Hoyt wouldn't be here to cause trouble. Seth dropped the pages of his sermon on the desk and hurried through the house to the front door.

Hoyt stood there on the porch in slicker

and dripping hat with the downpour behind him. He said, "Sorry to bother you, Brother Seth, but the creek's startin' to rise. Some fellas are headin' down here with sandbags to make sure it don't get into the church buildin'."

Seth reached for his own slicker and hat and said, "How close is the creek to getting out of its banks?"

"Pretty close, I think. We'd best hurry."

Seth felt some guilt as he put on his slicker and hat and followed Hoyt into the rain. He was right here, less than a hundred yards from the creek, and he hadn't realized that it posed a danger to the church. He had been concentrating on his sermon and the possibility of flooding hadn't even occurred to him.

His eyes adjusted somewhat to the darkness as he and Hoyt hurried around the church. The creek ran between tree-lined banks on the other side of the road, about fifty yards away. Seth heard something that sounded a little like a train in the distance and asked Hoyt, "Is that the creek I hear?"

"Yeah, it's runnin' good," the deacon answered.

A wagon with a pile of sandbags in its bed pulled up at the side of the road nearest the creek just as Seth and Hoyt got there. The man at the reins called, "Howdy, Preacher!"

"Hello, Dave," Seth responded, raising his voice a little to be heard over the rain and the swift-flowing creek. "Thank you for coming out on such a terrible night!"

Dave Buckland was another of the deacons. He swung down from the wagon seat and said, "Keepin' the flood waters out of the Lord's house is doin' the Lord's work, I reckon."

"It certainly is!" Seth agreed. He reached into the wagon and took hold of one of the heavy sandbags. Grunting with the effort, he lifted it out and started toward the creek.

Hoyt and Dave joined him, each with a sandbag as well. Hoyt said, "We'll start stackin' 'em up about five yards back from the edge. Don't want to get any closer than that 'cause the bank might wash out in places. I reckon this little low spot here by the church is all we really got to worry about. Ground's high enough east and west of here to hold back the water."

The three men worked steadily, forming a line of sandbags about fifty yards long. Then they began adding to it on top, building it up into a rampart.

More men arrived, some on horseback, some driving wagons loaded with more sandbags. The work quickly turned into a team effort, with men lining up to pass the sandbags from the wagons to the makeshift barrier.

All the while, rain sluiced down and the rumble and roar from the rising creek grew louder.

Women had come with their husbands to help out, and while the men were dealing with the heavy sandbags, the ladies went into the church and lit the lamps. Seth wasn't sure what they were doing in there until some of the women came out later to bring cups of coffee to the men.

One of the ladies, shrouded in a hooded slicker and carrying a cup with a piece of oilcloth over it to protect it, came up to Seth and said, "Drink this, Mr. Barrett. It'll help warm you up a little, I hope."

Seth recognized Delta Kennedy's voice. He leaned closer and saw her lovely face peering out from under the hood. That made warmth go through him that had nothing to do with the coffee she was offering him.

He caught a whiff of the coffee, though, and instantly craved it. He took the cup from her, and the heat that seeped through it to his half-numb fingers felt wonderful. He moved the oilcloth back enough to take a sip of the potent brew and savored the taste and warmth of it.

"Did you make this?" he asked her.

"I did."

"It's the best cup of coffee I've ever had."

She laughed and said, "You're just saying that because of the circumstances."

"Doesn't make it any less true," Seth told her.

"Do you think the church is going to flood?"

Seth glanced at the wall of sandbags, which was now about three feet tall in places.

"I doubt it. If we can make that barrier a little higher, it would take a flood of, well, biblical proportions to get over it."

"You mean like Noah."

"Exactly."

"I'll bet no one around here has thought to build an ark."

That brought a laugh from Seth. He said, "If it looks like it's going to keep raining, maybe I should suggest that in my sermon in the morning."

"Maybe you should," Delta agreed with a laugh of her own.

Seth drank the rest of the coffee, handed the cup back to her, and said, "Thank you. You've restored my strength. I can get back to work now."

"Can I help?"

"I think these sandbags might be too heavy for you," he said.

"You'd be surprised." She set the cup on the lowered tailgate of a wagon, reached into the bed, and took hold of a bag. She pulled it closer, got her arms around it, and lifted it, swinging around to plop the heavy bag into Seth's waiting arms. "See?"

He passed it on to the next man in line and told her, "I see that it wouldn't be wise to underestimate you."

"That's right." Delta reached for another bag.

Seth put a hand on her shoulder to stop her. He knew he was being forward but hoped she would forgive him.

"There's really no need for you to do this, though. We have plenty of men out here working on the wall."

"Well . . . all right. I suppose I should go check on Charlie, anyway. I left him in the church."

"That's a good idea. I'll see you later." Seth's hand still rested lightly on her shoulder. Since he had already been daring enough to touch her, he went one step further and squeezed, just for a second.

That made Delta look down, but Seth caught a glimpse of her face in the light

255

coming from the church and thought she looked pleased. She picked up the cup and headed toward the building but not without glancing back at him.

Seth was still cold, wet, and miserable on the outside, but what he was feeling inside made the sandbags seem a little lighter as he resumed his efforts to block the rising waters.

The creek overflowed its banks, but the higher ground to the south, plus the wall of sandbags, forced it to spread mostly over the fields to the north. When the rain tapered off to a drizzle and then finally stopped, Seth knew the water wouldn't get much higher before it began to go down. The threat was over . . . for now.

The members of the congregation who had come to fight the flood now gathered inside the church to dry off and warm up. There were four stoves, one in each corner of the sanctuary, and the ladies had fires going in all of them. Water dripped from the men's soaked clothing and formed puddles on the floor that the women began mopping up.

"That can wait," Seth told them. "I'd like for us all to sing a hymn. I think 'Amazing Grace' would be appropriate, since it was the Lord's grace that saved our church to-night."

"And some mighty hard work from all of us, Brother Seth," one of the men said.

Seth smiled as he asked, "And who was it that gave us the strength to do that work, Brother Fred?"

The man just shrugged, grinned sheepishly, and said, "I reckon you're right, Pastor."

One of the ladies sat down at the piano and began to play, and a moment later the beautiful strains of "Amazing Grace" filled the church.

Since the rain had finally stopped, the man sitting on horseback under the trees about a hundred yards from the sanctuary could hear the music. It was faint, but he recognized the tune. It put a grin on his face.

"You once were lost, Sam," Oliver Hudson said, paraphrasing the lyrics of the hymn, "but now you're found. And you're going to wish you had kept running instead of stopping here where I could find you."

CHAPTER TWENTY-FIVE

The stagecoach carrying Smoke and Sally on their journey rolled on steadily from Stephenville to Brownwood to Brady, through a couple of days of off-and-on rain. Some of the storms were torrential and forced the new driver, Jonas McClaren, to pull to the side and wait because water was running across the road too swift and deep for the stagecoach to risk it.

Smoke had been watching the streams they crossed. Luckily they were all spanned by bridges, because the creeks and rivers were swollen. The ground was saturated from the weeks of intermittent rain, and any downpour lasting more than a few minutes was enough to make the streams rise.

Sally saw her husband frowning out the window and asked quietly, "Do you think we're going to get there all right, Smoke?"

"I'm sure we will," he said. "McClaren seems like a careful man. He won't take the stage into anything that seems too risky."

Herman Langston had left the coach in Brownwood to make sales calls on the accounts he had there, but the Purcells, Mrs. Carter, and Arley Hicks were still aboard. Arley's wounded shoulder was bandaged properly now, and a black silk sling supported his arm. He hadn't lost any of his youthful enthusiasm.

"I hope this whole part of the country ain't been washed away by the time I get to Bandera," he said. "Won't be any use havin' a ridin' job if there ain't nowhere to ride."

Donald Purcell said, "I could teach you how to speak properly, you know, young man."

"You sayin' there's somethin' wrong with the way I talk?" Arley asked with a frown.

"I mean no offense, but . . ."

"You understand what I'm sayin', don't you?"

"Of course I do," Purcell said.

"Then I don't see what could be wrong with it. That's the whole point of talkin', ain't it? To make folks understand what you're sayin'?"

Sally said, "I think Mr. Purcell means that there are rules to language that people are supposed to follow."

"Well, there you go. I ain't never been

much o' one for followin' the rules."

"Believe me, I understand about that," Sally said, her eyes twinkling with amusement as she looked over at Smoke. "I married a man who's never minded breaking a rule if he needed to."

"Just doing what needs to be done," Smoke said with a chuckle.

"But I was a teacher, too, like Mr. Purcell," Sally went on, "so I understand why he said he could help you to speak in a more proper manner."

"You taught school, Mrs. Jensen?" Purcell said. "You never mentioned that before."

"Yes, I was working at a school in Idaho when Smoke and I met," Sally said.

The settlement of Bury, Idaho, held a lot of memories for both of them, mostly bad. That town had been under the thumb of the three men responsible for the death of Smoke's father Emmett. A lot of blood had been spilled when Smoke caught up to them and settled that score.

But there were good memories, too, because that was where the two of them had met and fallen in love. Neither of them would ever forget *that,* either.

Arley said, "Well, I reckon if you was to think I oughta learn how to talk gooder, Mrs. Jensen, I might give it a shot. I ain't promisin' nothin', though."

Purcell said, "You could start by not using the word *ain't* anymore. That sentence you just spoke should be phrased like this: I am not promising anything, however."

"Dadgum! If I was to talk like that, I'd sound just like I had a stick up my — Beg your pardon, ladies. Almost said too much there."

"Yeah, you did," Smoke said.

Arley took his hat off, scratched his head, and said, "I ain't — I mean, I'm not sure a feller like me could ever be edjimicated, but I'll give 'er a try."

"See?" Sally said with a smile. "That's the first step."

A short time later, the stagecoach crossed another bridge. It was raining hard by now, and the shutters over the windows were closed to keep out as much of the dampness as possible. Smoke opened one slightly to look out as the coach rattled across the bridge. The creek was high, with muddy brown water roiling along less than a foot below the planks.

Half a mile later, McClaren slowed his team and brought the stagecoach to a stop. He dropped down on one side of the vehicle while the guard, Ike Plumlee, got off on the other side. McClaren opened the door on his side and said, "Cougar Creek Station, folks. Usually we just change teams here, but I reckon we'd best spend the night and give the rain a chance to stop so maybe the streams'll go down. Bridge back yonder was almost flooded, and the south fork of this creek crosses the road another mile farther on. That bridge is lower than the one we just went over, so there's a chance it's washed out already. Even if it ain't, I wouldn't dare take the coach over it with the creek up like it is. Too big a chance we'd get swept off."

Mildred Purcell sighed and said, "I'm beginning to despair of ever reaching our destination."

"Oh, we'll get there, ma'am," McClaren told her. "May take us longer'n what we figured, that's all. Better to get there safe than on time, though."

Mildred sniffed and looked like she wasn't sure if she agreed with that idea or not.

McClaren went on, "Ladies, let me go in the station and get some canvas you can hold over your heads to keep from gettin' too wet whilst you run in. It's a real toad-strangler out here."

Smoke could tell that was true without even seeing the rain, just from its constant drumming on the coach roof.

A few minutes later, the passengers made the dash to the station, which was a sprawling structure with walls made from large chunks of red sandstone and a slate roof. A barn and a corral sat to one side.

Sally held a square of canvas over her head while Smoke grasped her arm and helped her along so she wouldn't slip and fall in the mud. Donald Purcell did the same with his wife. Smoke had told Mrs. Carter to stay in the coach and he would come back for her, but Arley gave the woman a hand.

"My right arm's still all right, so I don't mind pitchin' in," the young cowboy declared.

Once all the passengers had disembarked, Jonas McClaren pulled the coach over to the barn and drove inside.

The station was run by a spade-bearded man named Olmsted and his wife. Their three sons worked as hostlers, and their daughter helped her mother with the cooking. The station's large main room was a little drafty, but the air was much warmer inside than out, and the roof was nice and tight, allowing no leaks.

"You folks gather around the fire and dry out," Mrs. Olmsted said, pointing to a huge stone fireplace on one side of the room. "I've got coffee brewing and a pot of stew simmering, along with fresh bread in the oven. You'll be warm inside and out in no time."

"That sounds wonderful to me," Sally said. "It seems like we've been damp and chilled forever."

The heat from the fireplace made the passengers' clothes steam as they stood around it, basking in the warmth. McClaren and Plumlee came in from the barn, shed their slickers on the enclosed porch, and joined the group.

By the time everyone was relatively dry, Mrs. Olmsted had supper on the long table in the center of the room.

As they began to eat, Olmsted pulled on his beard and said, "It's a good thing you decided to stop for the night, Jonas. I sent one of the boys down to the south fork bridge a while ago, and he came back and said the water was already washin' over it a little. Probably a foot deep on the bridge by now."

"Think it's likely to wash out?" McClaren asked.

"Don't know about that. Bridge is pretty sturdy. It's been through some floods before without washin' out. But it sure wouldn't be safe to drive over it right now. I wouldn't risk either of those bridges, to tell you the truth."

"But if there are bridges on both sides of the station," Mildred Purcell said, "doesn't that mean we're stuck here?"

"Only until Cougar Creek goes down," McClaren said. "Maybe tomorrow, if the rain will stop."

"And if it doesn't," Mrs. Olmsted said, "we have plenty of supplies here, and we'll be glad for the company so you can stay as long as you need to, ma'am."

Neither of the Purcells looked happy about that prospect, but there was no use arguing with the weather. There was nothing they could do to change it.

The Olmsted boys came in a few minutes later, having finished unhitching and caring for the team. They were big, strapping, blond-headed youngsters who appeared to take after their mother instead of their sparsely, dark-haired father.

The food was good, and as Smoke washed down the meal with a cup of excellent coffee, he started to grow a little drowsy. Despite the relatively early hour, it was already dark outside. Folks would be turning in early tonight, he thought. This was good sleeping weather.

Christmas was only a few days away now.

Smoke and Sally had intended to spend the holiday at Chester Fielding's ranch, but the delays had them running a couple of days behind schedule. They would reach Mason tomorrow, Smoke reminded himself, and it was only a day's ride from there to Fielding's spread on the Llano River, so they ought to be at their destination by Christmas Day.

Assuming nothing else happened. . . .

After supper, Olmsted packed his pipe and lit it, then said, "If you gentlemen want to gather around the fire again, I've got a bottle of good brandy, and it seems like a fine night to open it up."

"Good brandy?" Purcell repeated. "Out here in the middle of nowhere?"

Olmsted's teeth clamped down a little harder on his pipe stem, Smoke noted. The stationman said, "Why don't we just try it, mister?"

"That's fine with me. I'd like to be persuaded."

Smoke wasn't much of a drinker, but a small glass of brandy might not be bad on a night like this, as Olmsted had said.

"I'll join you fellas in a few minutes," McClaren said as he stood up. "I want to check on the horses."

"My boys do a good job," Olmsted said.

"I'm sure they do. It's just a habit of mine to look in on my animals before I settle down for the evenin'."

"Well, in that case, go right ahead."

McClaren put his hat on and went onto the porch to shrug back into his slicker. He closed the door and went out into the night.

A dark figure stood in the rain, apparently not even feeling it as the big drops pounded at him. He was practically invisible in the darkness. In fact, the man who came out of the station and trudged toward the barn passed within ten feet of him and never saw him.

The young men who had come out of the barn earlier had left a lantern burning inside. The watcher saw light spill out as the man from the station pulled one side of the door open. The glow silhouetted his burly frame. He went inside, leaving the door ajar.

The watcher glided toward the light, and as he did, he reached down to the bone handle of the knife stuck behind the sash around his waist.

Death smiled in the darkness.

CHAPTER TWENTY-SIX

Smoke was no expert on such things, but he thought the brandy was pretty good, just as Olmsted claimed. Even Donald Purcell admitted that, although grudgingly. The men didn't talk much, but an air of camaraderie began to steal over the group gathered by the fireplace. Ike Plumlee got a pipe going, too, and Purcell took a cigar out of his vest pocket and lit it with a burning twig he retrieved from the fire. He didn't offer a cigar to anyone else, though, Smoke noted.

After a few minutes, a frown creased Plumlee's forehead. The shotgun guard said, "Jonas should've been back by now. That barn's close by. It wouldn't take him long to walk over there, check on the horses, and get back here."

"Maybe there was a problem with the animals," Purcell suggested.

"Shouldn't be," Olmsted said. "Like I told you, my boys do a good job takin' care of the teams. They been doin' it since they was just little sprouts." The station manager's three sons were sitting at the table, enjoying second helpings of their mother's stew. "Boys, did all those horses look all right when you left 'em out there?"

"They were all fine, Pa," one of the young men answered. "Shouldn't be no problems with 'em."

"Maybe Mr. McClaren slipped in the mud, fell down, and hurt hisself," Arley said.

Plumlee set his pipe aside, stood up from the chair where he'd been sitting, and said, "I'm gonna go make sure he's all right."

"He's bound to be back in a minute —" Olmsted began.

"I don't care. Jonas and me been partnered up on the stagecoaches for a while now. He's a good friend."

Smoke got to his feet as well and said, "I'll come with you." Some instinct had begun stirring at the back of his mind. He couldn't have said why, exactly, but he felt like something might be wrong.

As he headed for the door, Sally called from the other end of the room where she'd been talking to the other women, "Smoke, where are you going?"

"Just out to the barn for a few minutes," he told her.

"Is something wrong?"

He smiled and shook his head.

"Hope not."

"You're finally dried off. Try not to get too wet again," she said.

On the porch, Smoke put on his slicker and hat. Most of the water had dripped off both of them by now. Plumlee followed suit. He picked up his double-barreled coach gun, too, and put it under the slicker to keep it dry.

"Don't like to go too many places without it," he explained to Smoke. "Reckon I'm in the habit of packing it."

"I feel the same way about my Colt," Smoke told him.

The rain wasn't falling as hard now, they discovered as they stepped out into it, but there was still a steady drizzle. Even if it kept that up all night, the creeks might go down a little. Maybe not enough to make it safe to cross the bridge over the south fork of Cougar Creek, though. It might take a day without any rain at all for that to happen.

One of the barn doors was standing open a couple of feet. Lantern light came from inside the big building and washed across the open space between the barn and the station. There was no sign of Jonas Mc-Claren.

"He must be inside," Smoke said.

Plumlee grunted and said, "Yeah, I reckon."

As they neared the barn, Smoke heard the horses inside whinnying, as if something had spooked them. He slowed and said, "Wait a minute, Ike."

"Yeah, I hear 'em, too," Plumlee said worriedly. "Somethin's sure got 'em bothered. There are wolves in this part of the country. I wonder if one of 'em's prowlin' around." He paused, then went on, "But even if that was true, Jonas'd be in there tryin' to calm the horses down again."

Unmindful of the rain, Smoke unbuttoned his slicker and moved it back enough that he could get to his gun. He said, "Let me have a look first. Probably be a good idea to have that scattergun of yours ready, too."

"I was just thinkin' the same thing, Mr. Jensen," Plumlee said, his voice grim now.

Smoke drew the revolver as he stepped up to the open door. He stopped for a moment just outside and listened intently, but he didn't hear anything except the restless horses. Something definitely had disturbed them. They were bumping against the walls of their stalls as they moved around.

Smoke went into the barn in a low, fast crouch. Once he was inside he twisted away from the door and swung the Colt from side to side as he searched for any intruders who might be lurking in the barn. The lantern hung from a nail driven into one of the posts that supported the hayloft and lit up the aisle in the center of the barn.

He didn't see anyone, but he smelled something besides the usual barn odors of straw, manure, and horseflesh. This was a strong coppery scent that made the skin on the back of Smoke's neck prickle.

What he smelled was freshly spilled blood and a lot of it.

As Smoke stood there, he heard a steady *drip-drip-drip.* His gut told him the sound didn't have anything to do with the rain. Warily, he followed it until he reached an empty stall where the light from the lantern didn't reach. A shape loomed in the darkness, but Smoke couldn't tell what it was until he fished a lucifer out of his shirt pocket with his left hand and snapped it to life with a flick of his thumbnail.

The harsh light from the match's glare revealed a hideous sight. Jonas McClaren hung from one of the ceiling joists, a rope around his neck supporting his limp body. Smoke could tell that the jehu had already been dead when he was strung up there, however, because of the amount of blood that had pooled underneath his dangling feet. A corpse wouldn't lose that much blood; it required a still-beating heart.

So Smoke knew that McClaren had suffered the torments of the damned as someone worked him over with a knife, inflicting several wounds that would have been fatal even if nothing else had been done to him. Then the killer had put the rope around his neck and hauled him up there to finish draining. That was the dripping Smoke had heard, as blood ebbed from the wounds and trickled down McClaren's legs to finally plop into the gory pool on the ground.

Some men would have been sickened by this gruesome sight and lost the supper they had eaten a short time earlier. Smoke had witnessed too much death in his relatively young life, so he didn't react that way.

Instead, his discovery of the murdered stagecoach driver angered him. His first thought was to avenge McClaren's death.

And the killer might still be here in the barn.

Smoke dropped the match into the pool of blood, which snuffed out the flame. He turned quickly and lined the Colt in front of him. His eyes swept the barn, searching every corner he could see. He didn't spot anything out of place. The horses were upset, but the smell of blood would have done that.

"Mr. Jensen?" Ike Plumlee called from the entrance.

"Come on in, Ike, but be careful," Smoke told him.

Plumlee stepped into the barn, holding the shotgun ready for instant use. He saw Smoke standing in front of the stall toward the back of the barn and asked, "What's wrong?"

"Jonas is in here. He's dead."

Plumlee's eyes widened and he started to take a step forward as he exclaimed, "Dead!"

Smoke stopped him with an upraised left hand. He didn't want Plumlee rushing into an ambush if the killer was still in here.

"We need to search the barn to make sure nobody else is here," he said.

"You mean somebody murdered Jonas," Plumlee said. "It wasn't an accident."

"No," Smoke said. "It was no accident. You take that side of the barn and I'll take this side. If you see anything suspicious, blast it."

Plumlee nodded. Like Smoke, he knew that all the other travelers were inside the station, as were the members of the Olmsted family. That meant the killer had come from somewhere outside.

The search took only a few minutes. Satisfied that he and Plumlee were the only human beings alive in the barn, Smoke holstered his gun and said, "He's back here, but I don't know if you want to see him, Ike."

"I gotta know what happened," Plumlee said. A bleak expression settled over his rugged face as he joined Smoke in front of the stall and looked up at McClaren's hanging body as Smoke lit another lucifer.

Plumlee started breathing hard. In the light from the match, his face turned dark with rage. A little shudder went through him as his hands tightened on the shotgun he held.

"Whoever did this," he said, "I'm gonna kill 'em. I'm gonna make 'em die hard and painful."

"Let's cut him down," Smoke said. "We'll cover him up and then get back to the station."

"You mean to just leave him out here by himself all night?" Plumlee snapped.

"Nothing can hurt him anymore, Ike," Smoke said gently. "And since whoever did this isn't in here anymore, that means they're out there somewhere."

He inclined his head toward the doors as he spoke. For a couple of seconds, Plumlee still looked stubborn and angry, but then he sighed and nodded.

"You're right. The rest of those folks may be in danger. We need to warn 'em." He hesitated. "Unless the varmint who killed Jonas was a robber and is long gone."

"That doesn't seem likely to me," Smoke said. "A thief might have killed him . . . but he wouldn't have taken the time and trouble to do . . . what he did."

"You're right. Whoever did this was like a hydrophobia skunk, killin' for the pure savagery of it."

That was the way it looked to Smoke, too.

And he had a strong hunch that Jonas Mc-Claren's death wouldn't be enough to satisfy the killer's blood lust.

CHAPTER TWENTY-SEVEN

They cut the rope and lowered McClaren's body to the ground as carefully as possible. Smoke knew they wouldn't be able to keep from getting the dead man's blood all over them, but that couldn't be helped. They placed him on a blanket they found in the tack room and wrapped it around him, tucking the blanket in securely to protect the corpse from rats.

That wasn't much, but it was all they could do for Jonas McClaren right now.

"Lord, I hate to leave him like this," Ike Plumlee muttered as they left the barn.

"I know, but it'll be better for him to stay out here where it's cool," Smoke said. "If we took him inside, it might not be pleasant by morning."

"I know that," Plumlee said with a sigh.

Both men were alert as they walked quickly toward the station building. Smoke had his Colt in his hand underneath the half-open slicker.

No one bothered them. The night seemed dark and empty except for the continuing drizzle.

Smoke knew that wasn't the case, though. His instincts told him the killer wasn't far away.

While Plumlee had been getting the blanket to wrap McClaren's body, Smoke had taken a look around the barn. The hard-packed dirt floor didn't take prints well, and besides, a lot of people had been in and out of there today. It was impossible to make any sense out of the few tracks he found.

Something struck him as odd about a few smudges he noted as he hunkered on his heels next to them, however. They might be footprints, he thought, but they hadn't been left by someone wearing boots.

The only explanation that suggested itself to him was that if the marks really were the killer's tracks, then the man must have been wearing moccasins.

Most of the time that meant an Indian.

When Smoke had first come west, in the days immediately following the Civil War, battles between the whites and the Indians had been breaking out all across the frontier. He had traded shots with painted and buckskinned warriors on many occasions. In fact, it had been after a battle with a Pawnee war party that the old mountain man called Preacher had dubbed young Kirby Jensen "Smoke," because of the deadly speed with a gun he had demonstrated during that clash.

But in recent years, conflicts with the Indians had tapered off. The massacre of Custer and the Seventh Cavalry at Little Big Horn had seemed like a huge victory for the Plains Indians, but in reality it had been the high-water mark of their resistance to what they considered an invasion. Ever since, they had suffered defeat after defeat, and many of them had fled north into Canada or surrendered and gone to the reservations.

Likewise here in Texas, the fierce Comanche had been bested by the cavalry under Colonel Ranald Mackenzie at the Battle of Palo Duro Canyon. The Comanche hadn't lost that many warriors, but their horse herds had been destroyed. Without their mounts, their fighting ability was diminished to the point that they couldn't continue their war against the whites. Like their cousins to the north, most of them had either retreated or accepted life on the reservations.

Smoke had heard all about that, but he

knew not all the warriors were ready to give up. Some of them, now regarded as renegades, were still out there, clinging to their hatred of the white-eyes and determined to fight to their last breath.

Smoke had to wonder if one of those renegades had visited the barn at Cougar Creek Station tonight.

Most of the blood was on the slickers the two men wore, but they had gotten quite a bit of it on their hands, too, and as they came into the station, Sally spotted the crimson stains, stood up sharply, and said, "Smoke, what's wrong? What happened out there?"

"Is that blood?" one of the Olmsted boys asked in a shocked tone.

"It's not ours," Smoke said.

Quickly, everyone in the room gathered around Smoke and Plumlee. Smoke looked at them and said solemnly, "We found Jonas McClaren's body in the barn. Someone killed him."

Mrs. Olmsted gasped and put her hand to her mouth. As employees of the stagecoach line, all the Olmsteds knew the drivers on this route well, including McClaren.

Mildred Purcell turned pale. Her husband said, "You mean the man was murdered?"

"That's right," Smoke said.

Olmsted said, "But . . . but who could've done something like that? Jonas McClaren didn't have an enemy in the world, not that I know of, anyway. And everybody in these parts tonight was inside the station!"

"Not everybody," Smoke said. "Somebody had to be out there in the barn with him."

Out of respect for the ladies' sensibilities, he wasn't going to go into the grisly details of McClaren's death. It was enough for them to know that someone had killed the driver.

He pondered whether he should say anything about the tracks he had found. Some folks would panic at the mere mention of the word "Indian." Decades of raiding and killing by the Comanches had left people on the Texas frontier with an instinctive fear of their war parties.

"We need to see if we can find whoever done this," Olmsted blustered.

"We can't track anyone with it raining like this," Smoke pointed out. "Not to mention the fact that with a killer on the loose, if we start blundering around out there in the dark, we're practically inviting him to strike again."

"Are you sayin' we should just do nothin'?"

"I'm saying we need to have some common sense," Smoke said as he reined in the annoyance he felt at the station manager's attitude. Olmsted probably knew better than to act rashly; he was just too upset about McClaren's murder to be thinking straight right now.

Smoke went on, "Come morning, we'll take a look around and see if we can find anything. In the meantime, we'll stay in here where folks will be safe. We can bar the door and take turns standing guard. I don't think the killer will try to get in here, but if he does, we'll be ready."

"I reckon what you say makes sense, Mr. Jensen," Olmsted admitted grudgingly.

The preparations went quickly. The door was barred, and shutters were fastened over all the windows. Olmsted broke out several rifles and ammunition for them and made sure he and his sons were armed.

Sally came over to Smoke, laid a hand on his arm, and smiled as she said, "You hate being the voice of reason, don't you? You'd rather be out there tracking down that killer and avenging poor Mr. McClaren's death."

Smoke shrugged. His wife knew him better than anyone else on this earth.

"Figured it was more important to make sure you and all the rest of these folks are safe," he said quietly. "Besides, I meant what

I said about nobody being able to track in this weather. I don't reckon even Preacher could manage it."

"So we wait for morning."

"Don't see what else we can do," Smoke said.

Sally nodded and said, "I have a feeling it's going to be a long night, and nobody's going to get much sleep."

Sally's prediction proved to be true. The air of tension that gripped nearly everyone in the station prevented most of its occupants from doing more than dozing fitfully. Smoke, who probably had faced more dangerous situations in his life than all the rest of them put together, was cool-nerved, but he took a shift on guard duty and the rest of the time slept only lightly, in case of trouble.

Morning couldn't have come too soon to suit any of the people in the stagecoach station.

Unfortunately, it didn't bring much relief. The rain was falling hard again. When Smoke opened one of the shutters and looked out, he saw that there was so much standing water around, it looked like a lake between the station and the barn. Any tracks McClaren's killer had left behind were long since washed away.

Ike Plumlee would probably insist on searching anyway, Smoke thought. He couldn't blame the man for wanting to settle the score for his friend and partner.

The mood at breakfast was subdued, but even under the circumstances, the meal Mrs. Olmsted and her daughter Betty prepared was very good. The hot food and coffee seemed to raise people's spirits a bit.

After everyone had eaten, Olmsted said, "Somebody's gonna have to go out there to the barn and take care of the animals."

"No one goes anywhere alone," Smoke said. His experience and personality made it logical that he would take charge as long as the station was under siege — if indeed it was. They had no way of knowing if the killer was still within miles of there.

Olmsted nodded and said, "That's what I was thinkin'. The boys and I will go tend to the chores. We'll all be armed, and two of us will stand guard while the other two take care of what needs to be done."

Smoke said, "All right. While you're doing that, Ike and I will take a look around."

Everyone put on slickers and picked up rifles. Smoke's Winchester was in the boot on the stagecoach, but Olmsted had one to spare. Plumlee carried his shotgun and was armed with a revolver, too.

They went out into the rain, everyone staying together at first as they headed toward the barn. Smoke and Plumlee veered off from the Olmsteds to circle around the big building and the corral. Their boots splashed in the puddles, which were a couple of inches deep most places. The sky overhead was a leaden gray without a trace of the sun. Gloom was thick in the air.

Plumlee said, "How in the world are we gonna bury poor Jonas in this muck? Even if it stops rainin', we go to dig a hole in the ground and it'll just fill up with water. Probably be that way for weeks. But he's got to be laid to rest. Anything else just ain't fittin'!"

"I know," Smoke said. "Olmsted's got some boards in the barn. We'll hammer together a coffin, put McClaren in it, and take him on to Mason as soon as the creek goes down enough to get across. The undertaker there will be able to deal with the problem."

"That could take days!"

Smoke grimaced at the unpleasant thought, but he didn't see any other solution.

He and Plumlee walked completely around the barn and then behind the station without seeing anything out of the ordinary. They paused and stood there looking out over the gray, misty, rain-shrouded hills, and Plumlee let out a frustrated curse.

"Whoever butchered Jonas like that is gonna get away with it," he said. "There ain't no way we can find —"

That was when a woman screamed, followed by the boom of a gunshot in the stone building behind them.

CHAPTER TWENTY-EIGHT

Instantly, Smoke whirled and sprinted toward the front of the building. He knew the back door had been barred earlier, and he didn't want to waste time trying to open it when he probably couldn't get in that way.

Water flew up around his boots. He heard the splashes as Ike Plumlee lumbered along behind him. As Smoke rounded the corner of the station, he saw that the men in the barn must have heard the shot, too. Olmsted and his sons were running toward the station, but Smoke leaped onto the porch and reached the front door well ahead of them.

He grabbed the latch with his left hand and threw the door open. Instead of charging into the station, he twisted aside and pressed his back against the wall next to the door, with the Colt held up ready for use.

No bullets came through the opening. In fact, it was quiet inside the building now . . . quiet enough, at least, that Smoke couldn't hear anything over the steady sound of the rain.

Then a guttural voice called, "Come in, white man."

The mocking invitation was followed by what sounded like a gasp of pain from a woman. Knowing that Sally was in there and might be suffering at the hands of the man who had butchered Jonas McClaren made anger blaze up inside Smoke.

He fought down the urge to charge into the station. He might run right into a bullet if he did that, and his death would endanger Sally even more because there wouldn't be anything else he could do to help her.

Instead he said, "Send the women out, and I'll come in and talk to you, whoever you are."

At the same time, he motioned for Plumlee and the Olmsteds to stay back out of the line of fire from the doorway.

The mocking voice came again, saying, "The women stay where they are, white man. Do as I say, or they will never leave."

The fact that the intruder kept calling Smoke "white man" confirmed his earlier hunch that an Indian might have murdered Jonas McClaren. The man spoke English well, but that didn't mean anything. All the reservations had schools, and these days plenty of Indians spoke "the white man's tongue," especially the younger ones.

Fear for Sally's safety was strong inside Smoke. He wanted to call out to her, but he didn't want to risk what the intruder might do if she replied.

He wondered as well how the man had gotten into the station, but there was no point in pondering that now. They could figure it out later, after the threat was dealt with.

"All right," he said. "I'm coming in." He had to see what the situation was like in there in order to know what his next move needed to be.

"Leave your gun outside," the man ordered.

"So you can shoot me as soon as I step in the door?"

"I will not shoot you." The man paused. "I like to kill white-eyes with a blade."

Having seen what was done to McClaren, Smoke could believe that.

He didn't have any choice in the matter. He turned and extended his right arm into the doorway so that whoever was inside could see the gun in his hand. He bent down and placed the Colt on the porch, still in plain view. He set the borrowed Winchester beside it.

"Those are all the guns I have," he said.

"How do I know you speak the truth?"

"The same way I know you won't shoot me as soon as you lay eyes on me."

That brought an actual grim chuckle from the intruder.

"Very well. Come in. But if you try any tricks, the woman I hold will die a very painful death."

Smoke drew a deep breath and then stepped into the doorway, unsure what he was going to see. Relief flooded through him as he spotted Sally standing near the fireplace, unharmed. Mrs. Olmsted and her daughter were on the other side of the room.

A buckskin-clad Indian stood beside the table in the center of the room with his left arm around Mildred Purcell's neck as his right hand pressed the keen edge of a Bowie knife to her throat. Her husband was off to the side, white as a ghost and obviously too terrified to move.

Arley Hicks lay on the puncheon floor, blood staining his midsection. He was either unconscious or dead; Smoke couldn't tell which. Arley's revolver lay near his outstretched hand. Smoke figured Arley had taken a shot at the Indian when the man burst in, but it appeared that he'd missed. The intruder didn't seem to be wounded.

Smoke had never seen the man before. He was pretty sure he would have remembered if he had. The intruder had an odd mark on his cheek, a dark, half-moon-shaped disfiguration of some sort.

Mildred Purcell looked like she might faint at any moment. Smoke didn't want that to happen. If she started to collapse, the Indian might go ahead and cut her throat. Smoke put a reassuring smile on his face and said, "It's going to be all right, Mrs. Purcell."

"Do not lie to the white woman," the Indian said. "She will die. All of you will die. The only question is how slowly and painfully."

"Mister, you've got a mighty high opinion of yourself. There are five more armed men outside. You're not going anywhere. The only chance *you* have of getting out of here alive is if you let the woman go, put that knife down, and surrender."

A smile appeared on the man's face as he said, "Your weapons cannot harm me. All those who rode with me from the reservation are dead, but Black Moon still lives because the spirits watch over him."

"That's your name? Black Moon?"

"That is what the white-eyes call me," the man said with a sneer. "I bear the brand of their hatred."

Smoke guessed he was talking about the half-moon-shaped mark on his face. It was a scar of some sort, maybe embedded powder grains from a close range gunshot. It seemed to him that Black Moon might have adopted the name because he regarded the mark as a badge of pride, or a reminder of the hatred he bore for the whites.

"Well, listen, Black Moon, you may think you have some sort of medicine magic that protects you, but it won't stand up to a .44-40 round or a load of buckshot. That's what you'll be facing if you walk out of here without surrendering. And there's no other way for you to get out."

"I come and I go like the wind and the rain," Black Moon countered. "Your bullets and your buckshot cannot hurt me if they cannot find me."

"How'd you get in here, anyway?" Smoke asked. As long as he could keep Black Moon talking, the man wasn't hurting anybody.

Black Moon didn't answer. Sally did. She said, "He was hiding on the roof, I think. He waited until all of you left, then dropped down and came in."

Black Moon scowled and snapped, "Stop talking, woman."

Smoke thought he understood why Black

Moon was annoyed. Sally's hardheaded, practical answer didn't go along with the Indian's mystical ranting. It reduced Black Moon's "medicine" to what it really was, a figment of his fevered imagination.

Arley groaned. The young cowboy was still alive, thought Smoke. But he definitely needed medical attention if he was going to stay that way.

"What is it you want?" Smoke asked.

"To kill as many whites as I can," Black Moon answered without hesitation. "To make them feel the same pain I feel."

"Nobody tortured you, like you did with Jonas McClaren."

"The man in the barn?" Black Moon smiled again, but it was more of a wolfish sneer. "His death was sweet to me, like food and drink. Spilling his blood was like cold water on a hot day."

"The man never did anything to you."

"He was white. Your kind drove my people from our home, put us on reservations, gave us food that sickened us. Many of my people died —" For the first time, Black Moon's voice caught a little. "Like my woman. She sickened from the spoiled beef and died."

"Listen," Smoke said. "A lot of the mistreatment of your people can be laid at the feet of certain men in Washington and elsewhere. They did it for profit, pure and simple. Some of us have tried to stop them."

That was true, not a ruse. Several times in the past, Smoke, his brother Matt, and the old mountain man known as Preacher had battled the so-called Indian Ring, a group of politicians and financiers who would stop at nothing to enrich themselves. Those schemers were stubborn, though, and not easily defeated. Every time it looked like their plans had been put down, they popped up again somewhere else.

"Your words are empty and mean nothing to me," Black Moon said. "Tell all the other men to leave their guns outside and come in."

"Why? So you can butcher us one by one? You really think we're going to stand still for that?"

"Do as I say and the women will die quickly, with as little pain as possible."

Slowly, Smoke shook his head. Black Moon was loco, no doubt about that. No matter what the reasons behind it, he had sunk so far into his madness that he just couldn't think straight anymore. All he could do was hate and lash out, like a rabid dog.

"Let Mrs. Purcell go," Smoke said quietly.

"Then you and I, we can settle this, man to man."

"Smoke . . ." Sally said.

"It's the only way," Smoke went on. "Think about it, Black Moon. You're smart enough to know the rest of the men aren't going to cooperate with you. They'll just gun you down. But you fight me . . . you kill me . . . I give you my word you can ride away from here."

Black Moon sneered again.

"Why would I believe you?"

"Because it's the only chance you have to live through this." Smoke looked at his wife. "Sally, you heard what I said. You tell the others. You make them stick to it."

He could tell she wanted to argue with him, but she knew it wouldn't do any good. Once Smoke Jensen made up his mind, nothing could sway him.

"You have no weapon," Black Moon said.

"Don't need one," Smoke said.

The warrior couldn't resist that challenge. His face twisted with rage as he suddenly shoved Mildred toward her husband. With a hoarse cry, Black Moon leaped toward Smoke with the knife upraised, ready to deliver a killing stroke.

CHAPTER TWENTY-NINE

As the blade flashed down at Smoke, his left hand shot up and caught Black Moon's wrist, halting the thrust in midair. The Indian had already built up too much momentum for Smoke to stop him completely, though. Black Moon barreled into him. Smoke went over backward, still holding off the knife.

They hit the floor and rolled toward the doorway. Smoke's right hand shot up and closed around Black Moon's throat. An instant later, Black Moon got hold of Smoke's throat with his left hand in a similar grip. Both men surged to their feet and swayed back and forth as they struggled.

Mildred Purcell screamed hysterically as she was finally able to give in to her terror. She clutched and clawed at her husband, who still stood as if frozen by shock and fear. Mrs. Olmsted and Betty rushed toward

them, while Sally moved with swift ef-
ficiency to scoop up Arley's gun from the
floor. She turned toward Smoke and Black
Moon with the weapon.

Sally hesitated with her finger on the trigger. The two men were so close together she
couldn't risk a shot. There was too great a
chance she might hit Smoke.

But if she had an opening, she would be
ready to take it.

Smoke was vaguely aware of what else was
going on in the room because his peripheral
vision was so good he saw it happening. He
didn't pay much attention to it, though,
because he was too busy fighting for his life.
Black Moon was lean but possessed a wiry
strength, and the madness that gripped him
gave him even more. Smoke had to struggle
to keep the renegade from plunging the
knife into his body, and red spots were starting to dance in front of his eyes from lack
of air. His blood roared in his veins like a
raging river.

Black Moon had to be going through the
same thing. Smoke had immense power in
his grip, and as he closed it tighter and
tighter around Black Moon's throat, he
wondered how much more the man's windpipe could stand without collapsing.

Of course, the same thing could be said

about *his* windpipe. . . .

Suddenly, Black Moon took him by surprise by letting off on the arm holding the knife and lunging against him. The impact drove Smoke backward again. This time they staggered across the porch and off the steps, toppling into the muddy yard in front of the station.

Puddled water flew up around them, drenching Smoke's face and momentarily blinding him. With slick mud now coating them, it was impossible for either man to maintain his grip. They writhed and twisted apart. Smoke came up and threw himself backward as the Bowie knife streaked past his face, missing him by no more than an inch.

He kicked Black Moon in the belly. The blow made the Indian double over. Smoke clubbed his hands together and swung them in a powerful punch that caught Black Moon on the jaw and straightened him up. In that instant, Smoke saw that Plumlee and the Olmsteds had formed a circle around them. The men leveled rifles and shotguns at the fighters.

"Hold your fire!" Sally shouted from the porch. "Smoke promised him a fair fight!"

After what had been done to Jonas Mc-Claren, the men probably didn't care about fairness. Smoke couldn't blame them if they riddled Black Moon with lead. But he would have to get out of the way for them to do that, and that would mean retreating.

When the Good Lord made Smoke Jensen, he didn't put in any back-up.

One way or another, this would be a fight to the finish.

As Black Moon staggered back from the powerful two-handed punch, Smoke bored in after him and kept him off-balance by peppering him with short, sharp blows to the face and body. Unable to get himself set, all Black Moon could do was flail desperately back and forth in front of him with the knife. That forced Smoke to break off his attack.

Even though the respite lasted only a second, that was enough for Black Moon to get his feet under him and go on the offensive again. Smoke darted out of the way as the blade came at him. He raised his left arm, and the knife passed under it. Smoke clamped his arm down on the Indian's forearm, pinning it. He pivoted and at the same time used his right hand to catch hold of Black Moon's right arm, just below the shoulder. Black Moon had no choice but to go with him as Smoke continued turning. Smoke threw his hip into it. Black Moon left his feet and sailed through the air, then smashed down in the mud on his back.

The throw, taught to Smoke by Preacher — who had, ironically enough, learned it from Indians in his youth — had wrenched Black Moon's arm so violently that he had lost his grip on the knife. It lay in the mud near Smoke's left foot. He kicked the Bowie to the side, well out of reach of either of them.

Now the fight really was man to man, hand to hand — *mano a mano,* as they said south of the border.

Black Moon rolled and came up on his hands and knees, then without climbing the rest of the way to his feet launched himself in a diving tackle at Smoke's knees. Smoke couldn't get out of the way in time. He went down as Black Moon wrenched his legs out from under him.

The renegade hammered a punch into Smoke's face, stunning him for a second. Black Moon grabbed his shoulders, rolled him over, and planted a hand on the back of Smoke's head, forcing his face down into the mud where there was no air to breathe.

A man could drown in this soupy mud, just the same as he could in water.

Smoke wasn't going to let that happen. He got his hands and knees underneath him and tried to buck upward, but he slipped in the slick mud and went down again. The next time he dug deeper with his hands, ignored the mud that tried to clog his mouth and nose, and heaved himself up and back. Black Moon lost his hold and toppled off.

Still on his knees, Smoke twisted around and dived after the Indian. He rammed his left elbow into Black Moon's belly, got his right hand under the man's chin and thrust up as hard as he could. Black Moon's head went back so far it seemed impossible that his neck didn't snap. He writhed away, though, before Smoke could finish him off.

Slowly, both men climbed to their feet and faced each other with six feet separating them. Their chests heaved from the exertion and strain of this epic combat. Then with an inarticulate cry of hatred, Black Moon leaped at Smoke again.

Black Moon went high so Smoke went low, ducking under the attack and catching hold of the renegade around his knees. Smoke straightened and dumped Black Moon over his head. He whirled around, summoning his last reserves of strength and speed to do so and dropped to his knees to catch hold of Black Moon from behind. His right arm went around Black Moon's neck.

His left hand caught the right wrist, clamped the arm in place. Black Moon squirmed and flailed but couldn't get free.

The muscles under Smoke's coat bunched like giant cables as he heaved upward. Over the pounding of the rain sounded a sharp crack, like a branch breaking. A final shudder went through Black Moon, then he hung there limply in Smoke's grip as the rain washed down over both of them.

Smoke let go. Black Moon toppled forward to land facedown in the mud. He didn't move again.

Smoke looked up and was surprised to see that a horseman now sat in the yard in front of the stagecoach station. In the heat of battle, Smoke hadn't noticed the man's arrival.

He was even more surprised to realize that he knew the man.

His brother Matt leaned forward in the saddle. Water dripped from the brim of his black Stetson as he said, "Never expected to run into you down here, Smoke. It looks like you've done my job for me."

Smoke sat close to the fireplace, wrapped in a blanket as he warmed up. He had scrubbed off as much of the mud as he could from his hands, face, and head. Mrs.

Olmsted had his clothes soaking in a pot of hot water in the kitchen.

One of the Olmsted boys helped Arley Hicks over to another rocking chair near the fire. Arley was wearing a borrowed shirt over some bandages wrapped around his midsection, since his shirt had been soaked with blood from the wound in his side. Sally had cleaned and dressed the injury, which she had said looked worse than it really was.

"I'm startin' to wonder if there's gonna be anything left of me by the time I get to Bandera," Arley said with a rueful grin. "Done been shot and stabbed already. I'm afraid to ask what's gonna happen next."

"You probably don't want to know," Smoke said.

That brought a laugh from Arley, whose spirits seemed undaunted by the bad luck dogging his trail. Or maybe it was good luck, Smoke reflected, because as the young cowboy had pointed out, somebody had tried twice now to kill him, and he was still breathing.

Sally and Mrs. Carter sat at the table, drinking coffee. The Purcells were on the other side of the room, not saying anything to each other or anyone else. Donald Purcell wouldn't meet his wife's eyes, but she seemed to have no trouble glaring at him.

Smoke guessed Mildred wasn't too happy about the way her husband had frozen in fear.

Of course, if Mr. Purcell had tried to put up a fight against Black Moon, the renegade probably would have killed him in less time than it took to talk about it.

Smoke heard boots stomping on the porch. A minute later, the door opened and Matt and Ike Plumlee came inside after hanging up their slickers and hats. Matt said, "Good news. It's stopped raining, and I think the creek has gone down a little already. If it keeps dropping, the stage might be able to make it on into Mason by late this afternoon."

"Yeah, if it don't start rainin' again," Plumlee added.

The two of them had ridden down to the south fork bridge to check on the level of the creek. Smoke was glad to hear what they had to report. The sooner they got Jonas McClaren's body to the undertaker, the better.

"You boys need some coffee," Mrs. Olmsted said. She picked up the pot from the stove and began filling cups.

Matt carried his coffee over to stand between the rocking chairs occupied by Smoke and Arley. He said, "Now that I think about it, Smoke, I recall you saying in one of your letters that you planned to come down here to Texas to see about buying a bull. I didn't expect you to do it at Christmastime, though."

"Chester Fielding wrote me that he had other folks interested in that bull," Smoke explained, "so I'd better come on down if I wanted first crack at it. We've agreed on a price, and if I like the looks of the animal, we have a deal. If he's as fine as Fielding claims, he'll improve my herd."

Matt had already told Smoke about how he had been on Black Moon's trail for several days, having followed the renegade south from the Palo Pinto Mountains.

"I guess he saw the stagecoach and figured it was stuck here by the high water," Matt had said. "He just couldn't pass up the chance to kill that many white folks."

He had also told Smoke about tracking down the war party of Comanche renegades with Major Macmillan and the cavalry patrol. Matt hadn't gone into detail about the atrocities Black Moon and his companions had carried out.

He didn't need to. Smoke had seen the renegade's work for himself, and it was going to be a while before those grisly images faded from his mind.

Sally walked over to join them and asked, "What are you going to do now, Matt?"

"Well, I figured I'd ride shotgun on the stagecoach the rest of the way into Mason," Matt said. "I've done that job before." He shrugged. "After that, I don't have any plans. You know how fiddle-footed I've always been."

"I have an idea," Smoke said. "Come with us to Chester Fielding's ranch. We'll all spend Christmas there."

Matt grinned and said, "Christmas and trouble seem to go together for us, don't they, Smoke? This won't be the first one we've spent with varmints trying to kill us."

"Bite your tongue," Sally scolded him. "All the trouble's over now. And I agree with Smoke's suggestion. You should come with us, and we'll all enjoy the holiday together."

Matt nodded and sipped his coffee. He said, "I reckon that's a good idea. And I'm sure that's the way things will turn out."

The adventuresome twinkle in his eyes as he looked at Smoke, though, made it clear he wasn't convinced that what he said was true.

CHAPTER THIRTY

After overflowing its banks, the creek next to Enchanted Rock Baptist Church went down quite a bit overnight. As the water receded, it left large puddles in the fields that had been flooded the night before.

The members of the congregation left the wall of sandbags in place, blocking the low spot that would threaten the church if the creek rose again. That possibility seemed all too real. Dark gray clouds still hung over the Hill Country landscape. Old-timers afflicted with the rheumatism said their bones told them there was more rain in those clouds, and no one disputed that prediction.

As people began to gather at the church for the Sunday morning service, though, no rain was falling. Everyone seemed happy and relieved to see each other, Seth Barrett thought as he stood just inside the door and greeted them as they filed in. They all drew comfort from their shared faith.

Besides, it was only two days until Christmas, one of the most joyous days of the year, a day to celebrate the birth of the Lord.

Seth shook hands, smiled, and nodded to everyone, old and young alike. The lady who played the piano sat down on her bench and began quietly playing "Shall We Gather at the River."

"Good morning, Mr. Barrett," Delta Kennedy said as she appeared in the doorway, herding Charlie along in front of her. The little boy looked uncomfortable in his Sunday clothes, and although his mother had tried to slick down his hair, a cowlick stood up stubbornly at the back of his head.

Delta looked fresh and beautiful, thought Seth. She showed no signs that she had been here at the church until late the night before, not leaving until everyone was satisfied there was no more danger of flooding. She took Seth's hand when he extended it, and even though she wore gloves, he felt the warmth of her grip through them. He smiled and closed his left hand around hers as well.

"Good morning, Mrs. Kennedy," he said. "I hope you and Charlie are well this morning."

"We're fine, thank you."

Seth looked down at the boy and asked, "Are you about ready for Christmas to get here, Charlie?"

That made the boy perk up. He smiled, nodded, and said, "I sure am." Then he grew serious and added, "Except for one thing."

"What's that?" Seth asked.

"We don't have a Christmas tree."

Cutting down a tree, bringing it into the house, and decorating it was a fairly new custom in these parts, Seth knew, brought over from Germany by the many settlers from there.

Delta frowned and said, "I've tried to explain to Charlie that I can't really do that. Besides, we have more important things to worry about."

Charlie looked crestfallen as he muttered, "Yeah, I guess so."

Delta mouthed *Sorry* to Seth as she steered Charlie on up the aisle to their usual pew. He smiled to let her know it was all right.

When everyone was seated, Seth walked up the aisle to the pulpit, carrying his Bible in his left hand. He set it on the pulpit and opened it to the passage he had marked in the Gospel of Luke covering the Nativity. He motioned for everyone to stand for the opening prayer. Once every head was bowed, he led the prayer in a powerful voice that filled the sanctuary. Then, while everyone was still standing, they sang a hymn.

After Seth welcomed the congregation, he went on, "I want to say a special thank you to everyone who came here last night to help tame the raging floodwaters and turn them back from entering our church. It was a valiant effort, and we might not be in here this morning enjoying this service if not for all the hard work of so many people. And the Lord was truly with us last night, struggling right alongside us."

A chorus of "Amen" came from several places in the sanctuary.

Seth led them in another couple of hymns, including "Hark, the Herald Angels Sing" because of the season, then launched into his sermon. As usual, all the fretting he had done about it proved to be for nothing. He began by reading from the Scripture, and the power of the beautiful words filled him and transported him out of himself. At moments like this, he knew the Lord truly was speaking through him.

No one came forward during the altar call, but Seth didn't allow himself to be disappointed about that. Winning people over to the Lord was an effort that had no real end.

He would go on doing that good work as long as he drew breath. That was why he had been led to this place and inspired to put his old life behind him.

He called on one of the deacons to lead the benediction, and while that prayer was going on, Seth walked to the rear of the church and took up his place by the door again. The service's conclusion was the same process in reverse, as Seth shook hands, smiled, and talked with the members of the congregation as they departed. He was glad to see that no rain was falling. Maybe folks would be able to get home on their horses and in their wagons and buggies without getting soaked.

As Delta and Charlie came to the door, Seth smiled down at the boy and said, "I've been thinking about that Christmas tree you were talking about, Charlie. Maybe if your mother doesn't object, you and I could go up in the hills this afternoon and get one."

Charlie's eyes widened as he exclaimed, "You mean it, Preacher?"

"I do," Seth said solemnly, then glanced at Delta. "But only if it's all right with your mother."

She was frowning a little, and he suddenly worried that he had put her in a bad position by giving in to the impulse he'd felt.

311

Maybe she had some good reason she didn't want to have a Christmas tree.

But then she smiled and said, "That's very kind of you, Mr. Barrett. But wouldn't chopping down a tree mean that you'd be doing work on the Sabbath?"

Before Seth could answer, Charlie said, "Shoot, no, Ma, choppin' down a tree is fun, not work."

"Well, I guess that would depend on how big the tree is," Seth said with a grin. "But I don't reckon a nice-sized sapling would be too much of an effort."

"Are you sure?" Delta asked. "I wouldn't want to put you to any trouble."

"No trouble at all," Seth assured her. "I wouldn't have said anything about it if it was something I didn't want to do."

"Well, then . . . I suppose it would be all right. But only if you'll come and have Sunday dinner with us first."

"I could do that," Seth said, nodding.

"And then you can use our wagon to bring in the tree," Delta went on.

"Good idea, since all I have is a saddle horse."

"All right. Give me an hour?"

"I'll be there," Seth promised. He couldn't seem to wipe the grin off his face. The idea of having dinner with Delta and Charlie and then spending the afternoon with them had put it there, and he didn't figure it was going away anytime soon.

Seth felt a little bad about praying for the rain to stay away Sunday afternoon, but he did it anyway. He didn't want anything to interfere with the outing he had planned.

So far, so good, he thought as he hitched up the team of mules to the Kennedy wagon after a fine dinner of fried chicken, potatoes, greens, and berry cobbler. The food was good.

The company was better.

A feeling of warmth filled Seth as he sat at the table with Delta and Charlie. A cloth of fine Irish linen covered the table, and Seth could tell that Delta had brought out the best china and silver she had for the meal, too. This was the sort of normal family experience Seth had never had in his hardscrabble life before coming to the Hill Country.

Charlie talked most of the time he wasn't eating, mostly about trees he had seen that he thought would be good for the Christmas celebration. Delta didn't say much, but she smiled a lot at Seth, and that was more than enough for him.

Now as Seth finished hitching up the

mules, Charlie hurried out of the house wearing his hat and coat. Delta followed him and stood in the doorway with a shawl around her shoulders.

Seth smiled at her and said, "Why don't you put a coat on and come with us?"

"I don't know. It still looks like it might rain again."

"It'll be less likely to if you come with us."

Delta laughed and asked, "How do you figure that?"

"Rain wouldn't dare fall on someone as pretty as you."

"Aw, Preacher!" Charlie exclaimed. "Don't go talkin' like that to my ma."

"Hush, Charlie," Delta said. "Let Mr. Barrett say whatever he wants. He's our guest, after all."

"Yeah, yeah," Charlie muttered.

"I suppose I could get my slicker," Delta said. "Charlie should take his, too, just in case."

"Sounds good," Seth said with a nod. "You don't mind your ma coming along, do you, Charlie?"

"No, I reckon not," the boy said, but he didn't sound all that sincere about it.

A short time later, Seth helped Delta climb onto the wagon seat and take her place beside Charlie. Again, the feel of her gloved hand in his sent a definite tingle through Seth.

He went around the wagon and swung up onto the seat from the other side, so that Charlie was sitting between him and Delta. No one could accuse them of behaving improperly. He picked up the reins, slapped them against the mules, and got the team moving.

He had a pretty good idea where to look for a Christmas tree. A hill not far away was covered with junipers that weren't too big yet. One of them ought to do just fine, Seth thought. There was an ax in the back of the wagon he could use to cut down the tree they chose. He would let Charlie have a few swings, so the boy would feel like he'd contributed, but Seth intended to do most of the work himself.

"This looks like it may be a good Christmas, despite the weather," Delta commented as the wagon rolled along.

"Maybe the best ever," Seth said. That grin was back on his face.

A few hundred yards away, a man on horseback lowered the field glasses through which he had been watching the three people on the wagon.

This Christmas looked like it might be a

lucrative one indeed, Oliver Hudson thought with a satisfied smirk.

CHAPTER THIRTY-ONE

Evelyn Channing had been afraid that Hudson would try to come into her blanket-partitioned area of the cave the night before, but neither he nor any of the other men had intruded upon her privacy. She couldn't have stopped him, no matter what he tried to do, but maybe there was still a spark of something decent buried deep inside him. There must have been, she tried to tell herself, or else she never would have fallen in love with him to start with.

Of course, all that was finished now. No matter how much he talked about how he was going to marry her and how she would come to accept that, she knew she never would.

After the things she had seen, there would never be anything in her heart for Oliver Hudson except hate and fear.

Once she had realized that no one was going to bother her, she had fallen into a deep, exhausted sleep that left her feeling drugged this morning. When she dared to venture out, she found herself alone in the cave except for two men whose names, she recalled, were Deke and Packy.

They were sitting on crates beside the fire, drinking coffee, Evelyn saw as she tentatively pushed aside one of the blankets and looked out. Deke noticed her and immediately came to his feet, motioning for Packy to do likewise.

"Mornin', ma'am," Deke said.

"Yeah, mornin'," Packy rumbled. He was shorter and more ruggedly built than Deke, who had a certain rough-hewn handsomeness to him. Both men were outlaws, though, cold-blooded killers, and Evelyn couldn't ever allow herself to forget that.

"How about a cup of coffee?" Deke went on.

Evelyn didn't want to act the least bit pleasant or friendly to them. They had helped kidnap her, after all. But the coffee smelled so good she couldn't stop herself from saying, "Yes, please. That sounds wonderful."

It was a little chilly in the cave, even with the fire burning. Evelyn was glad for the jacket she wore. She must look terrible, she thought, after sleeping in her clothes the way she had. Even though she didn't have a mirror, she knew her hair had to be a tangled mess.

Using a thick piece of leather to hold it, Deke took the coffee pot from the edge of the fire and filled a tin cup for her. He turned toward her and held it out. Evelyn swallowed her fear and walked out of the partitioned-off area. They were only blankets, she thought; they didn't offer her any real protection.

Her hands shook a little as she took the cup from Deke and lifted it to her mouth. She sipped the coffee, found it to be hot and bitter but very bracing.

"Sorry it's nothin' fancy," Deke told her.

"That's all right. It's very good."

"We saved you some bacon and a couple of biscuits from breakfast, too."

"Thank you. That was very nice of you." She looked at the gray daylight outside. "What time is it?"

"When it's this cloudy, it's hard to tell, ain't it? Got to be close to the middle of the mornin', though."

"That late? I . . . . I must have been really tired."

"I expect so, if you're not used to riding a lot," Deke said.

Packy sat back down on his crate. Evidently he wasn't interested in making small talk.

"Where are all the others?" Evelyn asked. She noticed that most of the horses were gone.

"Oh, they're around," Deke said with a casual wave of his hand. "Some are standin' guard, others are scoutin'. The boss said he had to run an errand and rode off a while ago. He left Packy and me to look out for you."

To keep her from escaping, that was what he meant, Evelyn thought.

It was still a little disconcerting, too, to hear Oliver Hudson being referred to by one of these hard-bitten outlaws as "the boss." How could she have been so foolish, so blind?

Deke told her to sit down on the crate where he'd been sitting. Evelyn hesitated, but then she realized there was no reason not to. She couldn't get away, but for the moment these two men were treating her decently. They were probably too afraid of Hudson to do otherwise.

She sat down while Deke took some bacon from a skillet and put it on a tin plate along with the two biscuits he had mentioned. He gave the plate to Evelyn. Just as the smell of the coffee had made her realize how thirsty she was, the aroma and the sight of the food made her ravenously hungry. She dug in.

After several minutes she asked, "Is it still raining?" She had heard the roar of the storm for much of the night.

"No, it's stopped," Deke told her.

"But not for good, I'll bet," Packy put in.

"It's got to stop and dry out one of these days," Deke said. "Otherwise this whole part of the country is gonna be underwater pretty soon."

"Like the great flood in the Bible," Evelyn said.

Deke frowned and said, "Uh, yeah, I reckon. To be honest, I don't remember much about that. Been a long time since I set foot in a church and heard the Scriptures read. Goin' on twenty years, I'd say."

"That's a shame. I haven't been as diligent a church-goer myself as I should have been."

Packy said, "No time for it when you're always on the dodge."

"Come to think of it, though," Deke mused, "I believe the boss mentioned somethin' about goin' to church when he left."

That wasn't possible, Evelyn thought. If a man as evil as Oliver Hudson ever set foot in a church, hell would surely freeze over.

But it *was* Sunday, she reminded herself.

321

Somewhere, services were going on right now. Maybe Hudson had meant what he said.

If he had gone to church, though, it wasn't because he cared about his immortal soul. That was already doomed.

No, he had to have more wickedness in mind . . . although what could that have to do with church services? Evelyn had no idea.

Just as Seth had thought, there were plenty of trees the right size growing on the hill he had in mind. He brought the wagon to a halt at the edge of the road, waved a hand at the juniper saplings, and said, "There you go, Charlie. You go pick out a good one."

"All right!" Charlie said as he stood up, moved past his mother, and jumped to the ground.

As he ran up the hill, Delta called after him, "Try not to get too muddy!"

Charlie didn't seem to hear her. He was too excited.

With the boy running around in the trees on the hillside, that left Seth and Delta sitting together on the wagon. Seth smiled and said, "Maybe I shouldn't have sent him to do that. He was our chaperone."

"I'm a grown woman who was married

322

for a good number of years, Mr. Barrett," Delta said with a smile of her own. "I don't exactly require a chaperone. And you're a minister, so it goes without saying that your morals are above reproach."

Seth couldn't help it. He threw his head back and laughed.

Delta cocked her head a little to the side and asked, "Did I say something amusing?"

"No . . . No, not really. It's just that you don't know me as well as you think you do, Mrs. Kennedy."

"I doubt that," she said. "I regard myself as an excellent judge of character, and you strike me as a fine man, Mr. Barrett."

"Seth," he said. "Why don't you call me Seth?"

"Because if I did that," she answered, "I'd have to ask you to . . . to call me by my given name, and I'm not sure . . . I'm not sure that would be a good idea."

Seth's expression was serious now as he looked at her and said, "I don't see why not. I don't see how it would hurt a thing in the world if you and I became better friends."

"Mr. Barrett . . ."

"Seth," he reminded her gently.

"All right . . . Seth." She drew in a breath. "As I just mentioned, I was married for quite a few years —"

"And it's been three years since your husband passed away," Seth broke in. "I mean no disrespect to the late Mr. Kennedy. From everything I've heard about him, he was a very fine man, and I know that must be the case or else you never would have married him. I can see that in Charlie as well. His father raised him right."

"He would have," Delta said softly, "if he hadn't been taken from us so soon. Too soon."

"I agree. But you're still a young woman, Delta." Seth knew he was being too forward, but he charged straight ahead. That was the way he had been in the life he'd led before coming here, straight ahead no matter what the odds, and it wasn't something he could change the way he had changed his name. "You shouldn't have to spend the rest of your life alone."

"I'm not alone. I have Charlie."

"You know what I mean. And someday Charlie will grow up and leave to live his own life."

"Of course he will."

"I'm not asking you to make up your mind about anything. I'm just asking you to think about the things the future could hold . . . for both of us —"

"Hey!" Charlie's eager shout floated down

the hill. "How about this one?"

Seth and Delta both looked up the slope and saw Charlie standing next to a well-formed juniper about five feet tall. Seth said, "Do you think we can get that in your house?"

"I don't see why not," Delta said.

"All right, I'll get the ax —"

She stopped him by reaching over and resting her hand on his arm. She said, "Seth . . . I'll think about it. I promise."

The grin came back to him as he said, "That's all I ask." He swung down from the seat, reached into the back of the wagon, and picked up the ax. "You'd better stay here. It's too muddy for you to go clambering up that hill."

"Can the two of you manage the tree by yourselves?"

"I reckon we can," Seth said.

Soon the countryside rang with the sound of the ax blade biting into the juniper's trunk. Seth and Charlie traded off on the chopping, although Seth made sure he did most of the actual work. It took about half an hour to fell the tree. Once it was down, Seth handed the ax to Charlie and got hold of the trunk where they had cut it. He dragged the tree to the wagon, trying to avoid the worst of the mud as he did so.

Charlie climbed up into the back of the wagon to help as Seth lifted the tree into the bed. He arranged it so that the end of the trunk was braced against the back of the seat. The tree's conical shape angled back and rested on the tailgate. Seth didn't think it was going anywhere, but he tied it down anyway, just in case.

"You can sit on the outside this time," Delta told the boy as she slid over to the middle of the seat. "I don't want you stomping on my feet with those muddy boots."

"All right," Charlie said, "as long as you don't think the preacher'll mind sittin' next to you."

Delta glanced over at Seth as he settled himself on the seat beside her and smiled.

"I don't think he'll mind."

No, he sure didn't, Seth thought as he picked up the reins and got the mules moving. He didn't mind one bit.

In fact, as he swung the team around and got the wagon started back toward Delta's house, he thought there was a good chance this right now, being with Delta and Charlie, smelling the scent of that fresh-cut juniper, feeling the warm pressure of her hip against his, was the happiest moment in his life so far.

He didn't see how anything could ruin it.

CHAPTER THIRTY-TWO

The stagecoach rolled into Mason on Sunday, two days before Christmas. Once the south fork of Cougar Creek had gone down enough for the bridge to be passable, nothing else happened to slow down the coach's journey.

Smoke, Sally, and Matt said farewell to the other travelers while the teams were being switched at the stagecoach station. Smoke shook hands with Arley Hicks and told the young cowboy, "If you ever drift up Colorado way, Arley, stop in at the Sugarloaf. There'll be a riding job waiting for you."

"I appreciate that, Mr. Jensen, I truly do," Arley replied, "but I reckon I'm a Texan, born, bred, and forever. Don't really have much interest in leavin' the good ol' Lone Star State. But I'll sure remember your kind offer."

The Purcells weren't nearly as effusive in

their farewells. Smoke didn't expect that to be a very happy marriage from here on out, if it ever had been to start with. He didn't figure Mildred would ever get over the grudge she held against her husband for what had happened at the Cougar Creek Station.

Mrs. Carter gave Sally a hug and Smoke a peck on the cheek.

"It's been exciting traveling with you two young people," she said. "It'll be quite a memory to hang on to. But I think I've had just about enough excitement for my age!"

Once the stagecoach had rolled on south, Smoke checked into renting a buggy for the trip the rest of the way to Chester Fielding's ranch. He asked the liveryman about it.

"Don't have a buggy, but I got a buckboard you can use, Mr. Jensen," the man said after Smoke introduced himself. "It's in good shape, and it'll get you there if there ain't too much high water betwixt here and Chet's spread."

"You know Fielding?"

"Sure," the liveryman said. "He was one of the first ranchers in these parts, just like I was one of the first businessmen. Pioneers, I reckon you could call us."

"Then you can tell me how to find his place. I've got directions in the letter he sent me, but I've found it's always good to talk to somebody who knows the ground."

"Yes, sir, it is. Take the main road, the one that goes to Kerrville, and about ten miles south of here, after you cross the Llano River, you'll veer off to the left on another trail that'll take you to the CF Ranch. That's Chet's spread. Runs for miles along the river. Prettiest place you'll ever see."

"I'm obliged to you," Smoke said. "If we could get a team hitched up to that buck-board . . ."

"I'll take care of that," the liveryman promised. "You can fetch your wife and your bags over here from the stage station, and I'll have you all fixed up by the time you get back."

The man was true to his word. Less than half an hour later, the buckboard rolled out of Mason with Smoke at the reins and Sally beside him on the seat. Their bags were sitting on the back of the vehicle, covered with canvas in case it started to rain again . . . which, judging by the slate-gray sky overhead, seemed to be a distinct possibility.

Matt rode alongside the buckboard on his own horse. He said, "I hope that bull's as good as you think it is, Smoke, after you've gone to this much trouble to get him."

"Well, we didn't know the weather was

going to be this bad," Smoke said. "This is Texas. I thought they were supposed to have mild winters down here."

"I reckon it's mild compared to some places. We're not in the middle of a blizzard."

Smoke couldn't argue with that.

Since the stage road from Mason to Kerrville was well-traveled, it had the advantage of having a bridge spanning the Llano River. That was good, Smoke thought when they came to the stream, because otherwise they couldn't have crossed the rain-swollen river. The Llano ran between sheer sandstone bluffs, and after all the downpours of the past few weeks it was a swiftly flowing torrent of muddy brown water full of driftwood and debris. The crest was still below the top of the bluffs by several feet, but Smoke eyed the river warily as he drove the buckboard across the bridge.

Matt had ridden ahead. He reined in and waited for them on the south side of the bridge, and as the buckboard came up to him, he said, "If that river ever busts out, a lot of this country's gonna be under water."

"I'm afraid you're right," Smoke said. "But at least with all these hills, there's plenty of high ground."

Sally asked, "Didn't the liveryman back in

Mason say that Mr. Fielding's ranch is on the river?"

"He did," Smoke said. "But the ranch house is probably set back far enough that it wouldn't be in any danger. That's the way I'd do it, anyway."

"Not everybody is as well prepared for trouble as you are, Smoke."

Matt chuckled and said, "He's had to be, as much as he gets into it."

Smoke just smiled, flicked the reins, and kept the horses moving.

A short time later, they came to the road that branched off to the east, just like the liveryman had said. There was even a sign nailed to a tree with the legend CF RANCH written on it, along with an arrow pointing east.

As Smoke turned the buckboard onto the smaller road, thunder rumbled in the west.

"Tater wagon rolling over," Matt said. "Sounds like more rain coming."

"Maybe it'll hold off until we get where we're going," Smoke said.

That was what happened. They passed quite a few cattle standing forlornly in soggy fields, then half an hour later came in sight of a large, two-story house set in some trees atop a knoll to the right of the road. Surrounding the knoll were barns, corrals, and half a dozen outbuildings. The road curved and climbed the slope toward the ranch house.

Someone must have noticed their approach, because three men on horseback rode out to meet them when they were still a couple of hundred yards from the house. Several big, shaggy dogs trailed the riders, barking at the visitors.

Smoke pulled back on the reins and brought the team of horses to a halt. When you were a stranger riding up to somebody's place, the polite thing to do was to stop and introduce yourself.

The three horsebackers halted about twenty feet from the buckboard. They wore range clothes and looked like typical cowhands, but they also carried Winchesters across their saddles and eyed the visitors warily. Smoke saw them relax a little and attributed that to Sally's presence. She didn't look like the sort of lady who would be consorting with troublemakers.

"Good afternoon to you," Smoke called. "If you fellas ride for Chester Fielding, your boss is expecting us. My name's Smoke Jensen. This is my wife Sally and my brother Matt." He inclined his head toward each of them in turn.

That information made the attitude of the

three cowboys ease even more, but they still looked worried about something. One of them told the dogs to hush, then edged his horse a little in front of the others and thumbed his hat back.

"It's an honor to meet you, Mr. Jensen," the man said. "That's right, the boss told us you were comin' down here to see about buyin' that Diablo Rojo bull from him, but we didn't know for sure when you'd show up." More thunder boomed in the distance. "Seems like you beat the latest bout of rain. We'll take you up to the house so you can introduce yourselves to Miz Fielding."

Something about the man's voice made Smoke frown slightly. He asked, "What about Mr. Fielding?"

"The boss ain't here," the puncher replied, and the look on the man's face told Smoke that was what had them a little spooked.

"Where is he?"

"Best you talk to Miz Fielding about that, I reckon," the man said as he turned his horse. The others followed suit.

Quietly, Sally said, "Smoke, something odd is going on here."

"Yeah, I got the same feeling," Smoke agreed as he flicked the reins against the team and got the horses moving again.

"Trouble, more than likely," Matt put in.

Smoke had a hunch his brother was right.

As they pulled up in front of the house, the cowboy who had done the talking said, "We'll take care of your horses and the buckboard, Mr. Jensen."

"Much obliged to you," Smoke said.

He was helping Sally down from the buckboard when a woman came out of the house onto the verandah that ran along the front of the whitewashed dwelling. She was middle-aged but still attractive with only a touch of gray in her brown hair. The worried frown she wore matched those on the faces of the punchers.

"Hello," she said. "I'm Louise Fielding."

"Smoke Jensen, ma'am," Smoke said as he pinched the brim of his Stetson. "My wife Sally and my brother Matt."

The woman surprised him a little by exclaiming, "Oh, I'm so glad you're here, Mr. Jensen! I knew you were supposed to be on your way, but we weren't sure when you'd get here."

Smoke took Sally's arm and helped her up the steps to the verandah. Matt followed. Both men took off their hats as Smoke said, "I get the feeling that something's wrong here, Mrs. Fielding."

"That's right."

"Would it have to do with your husband?"

"Yes, it . . . Oh, forgive me. I'm so flustered I've forgotten my manners. Please come in out of this cold weather."

It was pretty raw outside, and Smoke didn't want Sally catching a chill, even though he was curious about Chester Fielding's whereabouts. He smiled and nodded, and the three of them followed Louise Fielding into the house.

A Mexican servant was waiting inside. Mrs. Fielding told her, "Bring coffee to the parlor, Mariquita." She looked at the visitors. "You haven't had dinner?"

"No, ma'am," Smoke said.

"Set three more places for dinner, too," Mrs. Fielding told the woman. "Our guests will be staying with us for a while."

The servant withdrew, and Mrs. Fielding ushered them into a comfortably furnished parlor. There was nothing fancy about the place, but it struck Smoke as a good place to live.

When they were all sitting down, Smoke and Sally on a sofa, Matt in an armchair, and Mrs. Fielding in a rocking chair near the stone fireplace, Sally said, "You have a lovely home here, Mrs. Fielding."

"Thank you. You should call me Louise."

"I don't want to rush you, Mrs. Fielding . . . Louise," Smoke said. "But some-

335

thing's wrong, and Matt and I would sure like to help you if we can."

"That's right," Matt said.

"Is this about your husband not being here?" Smoke asked.

Louise Fielding took a deep breath. Smoke could tell that she was struggling to keep her emotions in check, but suddenly that control slipped.

"I don't know where Chester is," she said in a ragged voice. "He's vanished."

Then she put her hands over her face and started to sob.

CHAPTER THIRTY-THREE

The servant came in just then, carrying a tray with four coffee cups on it. Quickly, she set the tray on a sideboard and hurried to Mrs. Fielding's side. Sally was already there, patting Louise on the shoulder and trying to comfort her.

"It is all right, señora," Mariquita said as she put her hand on Louise's other shoulder. "Nothing has happened to Señor Fielding. I am sure of it."

"I . . . I wish I could be sure," Louise said as she lowered her hands from her tear-streaked face.

"Maybe you'd better tell us what's happened," Smoke suggested. Sally frowned slightly at him, as if she thought he shouldn't be bothering the upset woman right now, but he and Matt couldn't do anything to help until they knew what the situation was. Smoke sympathized with Mrs. Fielding, but at the same time he was practical.

"Chet . . . Chet's been worried about the stock," Louise said. "With all this rain, he was afraid that some of them might have bogged down in the low places. He and the men have been going out every day to check on them. But then yesterday . . . he couldn't find Diablo Rojo."

Smoke exchanged another glance with Sally. That was the bull he had come to see about buying from Chet Fielding.

"He loves that bull," Louise went on with a weak smile. "I'm surprised he ever agreed to even think about selling him. But we've had a run of not so good luck and have been a little cash-poor . . . you know how it is to be a rancher, Mr. Jensen."

"I sure do," Smoke agreed. "And call me Smoke."

Louise looked up at him and went on, "He said he'd heard enough about you to know what a fine man you are and that he was sure you'd do right by Diablo Rojo. That was the only reason he'd consider selling. But then, like I said, Chet couldn't find the bull, and it really upset him. It wasn't just what Diablo Rojo's worth."

"I understand," Smoke assured her. "He was afraid something had happened to the bull. I reckon he went looking?"

Louise nodded and said, "That's right. He came back in, got a fresh horse and some supplies, and set off by himself. He said there was plenty of work around the place for the hands to do, so he didn't take anyone with him. He didn't figure he needed to, since he knows every foot of this range better than anybody else."

"I understand about that, too," Smoke said. "I feel the same way about my spread."

"I told him not to stay out overnight, and he promised he wouldn't unless he had to. He said he'd be back this morning, one way or another. But we haven't seen any sign of him."

Matt said, "No offense, ma'am, but it's only the middle of the day. Your husband might've gotten delayed by any number of things. Seems a mite early to be this worried."

"I know. I'm being silly."

"Now, that's not what I meant at all," Matt said quickly as Sally glared at him for a second.

"It's just that Chet and I have been together for a long time," Louise continued. "We've got a . . . connection, I guess you'd call it. I can tell when something's wrong, when he's in trouble. And I've been feeling it all day."

Smoke said, "It sounds to me like some-body needs to go and look for him."

"Chet left orders for all the hands to stay close to home . . . in case the river and the creeks start to rise and threaten to get out of their banks . . ."

"Matt and I can go."

Matt nodded to show that he agreed with Smoke's suggestion.

"We don't know the range, but we're pretty good at finding our way around," Smoke went on. "Which way was your husband headed when he left yesterday?"

"South," Louise said. "That was the last place anybody saw Diablo Rojo, down close to the southern edge of the ranch, not far from Enchanted Rock."

Matt frowned and said, "Seems I've heard of Enchanted Rock."

"You can see it for miles around. It's not actually on our land, but our southern border is close to it."

"Sounds like we'll be able to tell if we're headed in the right direction, then," Smoke told her with another reassuring smile.

"Yes, you can't miss it."

"I don't have a saddle horse with me, and Matt will need a fresh mount . . ."

"Take any of our horses you want. The men can tell you which ones are the best."

Smoke figured he and Matt would be able to tell that just by looking at the animals, but he didn't say that. Instead he said, "Maybe you could have Mariquita put together some supplies for us . . . ?"

"Of course."

Smoke looked at his wife and said, "You don't mind staying here and keeping Louise company, do you, Sally?"

"Certainly not," Sally replied, although Smoke saw a hint of worry in her eyes, too. She might not like the idea of him and Matt setting out into bad weather and what might be even more trouble, but she wasn't going to argue about it. For one thing, she knew how futile that would be.

"I really don't see how you're going to find him," Louise said as she took a linen handkerchief from her pocket and dabbed at her eyes. "It's such a big country out there."

"Maybe so," Matt said, "but Smoke and I have a knack for finding things."

He didn't mention that what they found was usually some sort of danger — and Smoke was grateful for his brother's discretion.

Smoke and Matt ate a quick lunch before they set out from the headquarters of the

341

CF Ranch. Smoke rode a sturdy dun, while Matt was mounted on a high-spirited roan. They trailed an extra saddle horse behind them. It was possible that Chet Fielding had lost his own mount somehow and would need a horse to ride when they found him.

Assuming they did find him, and Smoke wasn't going to allow himself to consider any other possibility. But at the same time, he knew how big this country was, and even though it was relatively settled these days, there were still plenty of things out there that could kill a man if he was careless or unlucky.

A steady drizzle began to fall not long after they rode out of sight of the ranch house. Both men were already wearing their slickers, because it had been obvious from the clouds that the weather wasn't going to stay dry for much longer.

While they were getting the horses ready to ride, they had talked to several of the CF hands and found out exactly where Diablo Rojo had been seen last. That was where Chet Fielding would have started his search.

"You won't be able to pick up his trail," one of the cowboys warned Smoke and Matt. "Not as much as it's been rainin'. There was a good downpour last night, like there's been 'most every night lately."

"We're not expecting to pick up his trail," Smoke had said. "We'll just range back and forth looking for him."

"We can fire a shot now and then, too," Matt had added. "If Mr. Fielding's in some sort of trouble and hears that, he'll know somebody's looking for him. Maybe he can fire some shots and lead us to him."

"It's worth a try," another of the ranch hands agreed. "But if you fellas don't find him by tomorrow, the whole crew's liable to head down there to look, orders or no orders."

"Tomorrow's Christmas Eve," Matt said.

"Yeah, well, findin' the boss all right would be a pretty good Christmas present, let me tell you," a grizzled old puncher said. "I've rode for a lot of spreads and a lot of bosses, but never any better than the CF and Chet Fielding."

Smoke remembered those words now as he sent the dun plodding along a trail that wound between wooded hills. Water stood in all the low places, so the horses kicked up little splashes with every step.

After an hour or so, Matt reined up and pointed.

"Look there," he said. "Is that Enchanted Rock?"

Smoke peered through the misty afternoon and saw a large, dark hump looming over the hills in the distance to the south. Judging by the size of it, even though it had to be several miles away, the rock formation was quite massive.

"Reckon that's got to be it," Smoke said. "Don't know if it's enchanted, but it's a mighty big rock, no doubt about that."

"Those punchers said we need to steer straight for it when we see it, and we'll come to the range where Diablo Rojo roamed most of the time."

Smoke nodded and nudged his horse into motion again.

More than anything else, Enchanted Rock looked like the humped back of some huge animal, one of those land leviathans from prehistoric times that he had heard Sally talk about. Or maybe the biggest buffalo that ever lived, Smoke mused with a faint smile. He knew more about things like that.

They came to a broad, shallow valley between two ridges. Matt said, "This looks like the place those cowboys told us about, the one where the bull was."

"We'll comb it good," Smoke said.

Every ten or fifteen minutes, they paused in their search. Smoke pointed his Winchester at the sky and fired a shot. The clouds and the drizzle seemed to muffle the sharp crack a little, but Smoke knew the sound would carry for a good distance anyway. If Chet Fielding was within earshot, the regular reports ought to alert him to the presence of a search party.

After every shot, Smoke and Matt listened intently for the sound of a reply. They didn't hear anything except the steady whisper of the rain.

Searching the valley took most of the afternoon. They didn't find any sign of Chet Fielding or the huge, reddish-colored bull Diablo Rojo.

"That dang bull wandered off somewhere, and Fielding went after him," Matt said as they paused to take stock of the situation.

Smoke glanced at the sky, where the grayish light was already fading, and said, "We don't have much time left. Looks like we're going to be out overnight after all."

"Reckon we can find a dry place to do it?"

"I wouldn't be too optimistic," Smoke said.

A creek cut through the far ridge and led on south toward Enchanted Rock. They followed it, and as they did Smoke kept an eye on the trunks of the trees they passed on the bank. After a while he stopped and pointed to a live oak.

"Something's been rubbing on that trunk in the past day or two," he said.

Matt studied the faint marks on the tree and nodded.

"Diablo Rojo, you think?" he said. "Bulls like to do things like that."

"Seems a good bet to me. It probably would seem like that to Fielding, too."

"So we're on the right track."

"Maybe," Smoke said. "That's what we've got to go on, anyway."

He cast a glance at the creek. It was flowing fast, and it was high in its banks.

Overhead, lightning crackled, thunder boomed, and the rain started to fall harder. That wasn't good, Smoke thought grimly.

Like Matt had said, it wasn't going to take much more to put a big chunk of the Hill Country under water.

CHAPTER THIRTY-FOUR

"We might as well admit it," William Sydney Porter said gloomily. "We're lost. We have no idea where we are or where we're going."

"That's not exactly true," Chance said as he stretched in the saddle to ease tired muscles. "We're somewhere north of Fredericksburg. As long as you know where you are, you can't say that you're lost."

"That's ridiculous," Porter snapped. "If you don't know where you're going, you're lost."

Chance shook his head and said, "That's not the way I see it. We know if we turned around and rode south, sooner or later we'd come to Fredericksburg, or at least we'd hit the road between there and Johnson City. And if we headed north, sooner or later we'd come to some other town. So you can't say that we're —"

"Oh, shut up, both of you," Ace said

disgustedly. "Arguing about whether or not we're lost doesn't accomplish a blasted thing."

"Maybe not," Chance admitted. "But still —"

"We've lost the trail," Ace said. "I know you don't want to admit that, Will, but we don't have any idea where Miss Channing is or where to find her. We're just riding around in circles. We might as well go back."

Porter got a stubborn look on his face as he said, "And abandon poor Evelyn to whatever fate awaits her at the hands of those desperadoes? I can't do that, Ace. I don't need to remind you of the danger she's in."

"No, but there's nothing I can do about it, either."

Chance sighed and thumbed his hat back as he said, "Besides, it's Christmas Eve. Leastways I think it is, if I've counted the days up right."

"I hope you don't think I feel like celebrating," Porter said as he scowled at the Jensen brothers.

"Nobody said anything about celebrating," Ace told him. "But we've been out here for several days on short rations, we've gotten soaked more than once by rainstorms, and we're no closer to finding Miss

Channing than we were when we started out. We need to head back to town and at least pick up some supplies before we start looking again." Ace paused, then added, "Anyway, it's possible the sheriff took out a posse and found Miss Channing. She could be sitting there in Fredericksburg right now, warm and safe, while we traipse around these hills and just get more miserable."

Porter frowned in thought for a long moment, then finally sighed and nodded.

"I suppose that's possible," he admitted. "Still, it feels like I'm giving up. I don't like that."

"Consider it a strategic retreat," Chance told him.

"Very well." Porter looked up at the overcast sky. "But how are you going to tell which way is south, so we can find our way back to Fredericksburg? I have no idea where the sun is."

Chance grinned and said, "Ace is pretty good at knowing which direction is which, even if he doesn't have much to go by. It's just a natural talent of his, sort of like the way I am with cards and women."

"I think I'm better at finding my way around than that," Ace said dryly as he started to turn his horse. He stopped short, though, and frowned. "Hold on a minute."

"You hear something?" Chance asked.

"No. I *smell* something. Wood smoke."

Chance lifted his head and sniffed the damp air. After a moment, he nodded.

"Yeah, me, too," he said.

"Well, I don't smell a thing," Porter said. "I don't doubt that you're right, though. Your senses are sharper than mine. One of the drawbacks of being a city boy at heart, I suppose. Do you think the smoke means anything?"

"Not necessarily," Ace said. "There are plenty of farms and ranches in this part of the country. It might be worth checking out, though. Most folks are pretty hospitable. Maybe we could buy some supplies from them."

Smiling, Chance said, "They might even ask us to stay over and have Christmas dinner with them."

"I suppose that would be better than going all the way back to Fredericksburg," Porter said. "I'm game, if you think you can follow the scent."

"Don't worry about that," Chance told him. "Old Ace is like a bloodhound. Once he's got the scent, he won't lose it."

" 'Old'?" Ace repeated. "We're the same age, remember?"

"You were born a few minutes earlier,"

Chance said smugly. "You reminded me of it often enough when we were kids, Grandpa."

Ace ignored the gibe. He lifted his reins and said, "Come on."

The three young men rode across the hills, under the leaden sky. The smell of burning wood got stronger, until even Porter could recognize it.

"That must be coming from somebody's chimney," Chance said.

"Or a good-sized campfire," Ace replied. "If that gang of owlhoots is still in this part of the country, they have to be holed up somewhere. And it wouldn't surprise me if they were, since the weather has been terrible for traveling."

That was certainly true. All three of them were starting to feel like they might never dry out completely again.

The smell led them up a long, fairly steep slope covered with thick stands of trees and rocky outcroppings. Ace held up a hand in a signal to stop as the slope came to an end about twenty yards ahead of them, falling away to become the face of a bluff that overlooked a valley with a creek running through it.

"There's nothing up here," Porter said. "The smoke must be coming from somewhere down in that valley."

Ace frowned and said, "Maybe. But the smell is pretty strong here."

Porter looked around, twisting a little in his saddle as he did so.

"I don't see a thing! There's no cabin or camp."

"No," Ace agreed, "there's not. But the smoke could be coming out of the ground."

Porter looked at Ace like he'd lost his mind. Chance nodded slowly, though, and said, "You're thinking there's some sort of natural chimney around here."

"That makes sense," Ace said. "That smoke has to come from somewhere. We could be right on top of a cave with its mouth in that bluff up ahead."

"A cave?" Porter repeated.

Ace nodded and said, "I've heard tell that there are caverns all over this part of the country."

"And a place like that would make a good hideout for, say, a gang of stagecoach robbers and kidnappers," Chance added.

A look of excitement appeared on Porter's face. He said, "You mean they could be holding Evelyn prisoner right here below our very feet?"

"It's a mite far-fetched," Ace said with a shrug, "but we can't rule it out. What we need to do —"

A voice from behind them suddenly said, "What you need to do is put your hands up!"

Ace and Chance started to twist around in their saddles. Instinct made their hands move toward their guns. But before they could touch iron, a shot blasted, echoing over the damp, hilly countryside. The brothers froze.

Not Porter, though. He panicked and started to yank his horse around. The man who had told them to lift their hands yelled, "You loco fool! I warned you!"

Ace knew Porter was about to be blasted out of the saddle. He kicked his feet free of the stirrups and hauled his horse around so that it rammed against Porter's mount. At the same time he dived from horseback and tackled Porter just as another shot slammed through the air. The slug hummed past Ace's head as he and Porter crashed to the muddy ground.

That was enough of a distraction for Chance to get turned around and draw his gun. He spotted the beard-stubbled, slicker-clad man who stood next to a bush holding a Winchester. Chance snapped a shot at him and came close enough to make the man jump for cover.

Another gun roared, off to Chance's left. The bullet whipped past his ear. He tried to turn in that direction, but with a sinking feeling he knew he was probably going to be too late.

Several yards away, Ace rolled over and came up on one knee in time to see the second man step out from some trees and fire a rifle at Chance. Ace's Colt was still in its holster, which was a stroke of luck because it could have fallen out when he and Porter toppled to the ground. The weapon seemed to spring into his hand. Flame licked from the muzzle as he triggered a round at the second rifleman.

The man's Winchester cracked, but the bullet screamed off into the overcast sky because he was already falling backward from the impact of Ace's slug drilling through his shoulder. He howled in pain as he flopped into the mud.

The first man was still a threat, though. He fired at Chance, who yelped as the bullet tore the sleeves of his slicker and coat and burned the flesh of his left forearm. The man leaped up and rushed at him, ramming the rifle's barrel into Chance's chest hard enough to knock him off the horse. The animal leaped out of the way. The man angled his Winchester down at the momentarily helpless Chance, who was gasping for breath after having the wind knocked out of him.

"Drop it, mister!" the man yelled at Ace, who still held his Colt as he knelt beside Porter.

Ace calculated his chances of dropping the hombre before the man could squeeze the trigger and kill his brother and decided they weren't good enough to risk it. He said, "Don't shoot."

"I told you to drop that gun!"

Ace leaned forward and placed the revolver on the ground.

"Get the other fella's gun, too," the rifleman ordered.

Ace slid Porter's gun from its holster and placed it next to his.

"Now both of you get up and back away from 'em."

The second man, who was now sitting up and clutching his wounded shoulder, said, "Blast it, Tully, go ahead and shoot 'em!"

"Not yet," the hardcase called Tully said. "I want to find out who they are and what they're doin' here. The boss might want to know."

Porter appeared to be pretty shaken up by the fall, but he was able to say, "This so-called boss of yours is no doubt Oliver

Hudson."

Both men gaped at him, and Tully said, "How in blazes did you know that? Who are you, mister?"

This unexpected revelation made Ace catch his breath. It also confirmed what had seemed like wild suspicions on the part of William Porter. Porter had insisted Hudson was really the leader of the gang that ostensibly had kidnapped him and Evelyn Channing from the stagecoach, but the idea seemed pretty far-fetched to Ace.

But evidently Porter had been right all along when he tried to convince Evelyn and anyone else who would listen that Hudson was no good.

Stubbornly, Porter remained silent, refusing to answer the outlaw's question. After a moment Tully jerked the rifle barrel at the prisoners and went on, "We need to get this all sorted out."

"And I need to get this blamed hole in my shoulder tended to," the other man said bitterly.

"Move, you three," Tully ordered Porter and the Jensen boys. "There's a trail down the bluff right over there."

"What about our horses?" Ace asked.

"Somebody'll take care of them. Now move, before I lose my patience! And keep those hands where I can see 'em!"

At gunpoint, the three young men trudged down the trail. As it curved around an outcropping of rock, Ace caught sight of a large cave mouth and knew his guess about where the smoke was coming from had been right.

Not that it did them a lot of good now.

The two gunmen followed them, and as they stepped into the cave, another pair of outlaws were waiting for them with guns drawn. One of them said sharply, "We heard the shootin'. Who are these varmints, Tully?"

"They came snoopin' around up on top of the bluff, Deke," Tully answered. "So far they ain't said who they are or what they were lookin' for —"

A cry of "William!" interrupted the man. Evelyn Channing, looking disheveled but otherwise unharmed, thrust aside some blankets that closed off a portion of the cave and rushed toward them.

"Evelyn!" Porter exclaimed.

Then they were in each other's arms, holding on tightly as they embraced.

"Yeah," Deke said as he watched them, "the boss is gonna be real interested in this when he gets back."

CHAPTER THIRTY-FIVE

Delta Kennedy never would have expected it, but she had to admit that the tree looked rather festive once it was set up in a washtub full of dirt in the front room of her house. Maybe the German settlers in the area had a good idea about this Christmas tradition after all.

The day before, after Seth Barrett and Charlie had set up the tree in the house, Delta had decorated it with as many bows as she could make from her supply of ribbons. That made the tree colorful, and its sharp but pleasant scent filled the house. Charlie had asked if they could do this every year. She had told him that they would have to wait and see, but it wasn't a bad idea, she mused now as she sat at the table, lingering over a second cup of coffee. Charlie had gone out to the henhouse to collect the morning's eggs. That was one of the chores he always handled.

Delta smiled to herself as she thought about how nice the previous afternoon had been. Charlie and Seth seemed to really like each other, and there was no denying the warm glow she felt inside when she was around the pastor.

As he was leaving, he'd clasped her hand for a second and smiled at her, and the tingle that went through her told her he was right. Maybe it really *was* time for her to get on with her life, and if that included a good man . . . well, she truly didn't believe her late husband would have objected even a little.

The sound of a horse splashing through the puddles outside made Delta lift her head. Maybe Seth had come for another visit, she thought as she stood up. She looked down at the thick robe she wore and wished she had already gotten dressed this morning. Usually she had by this time. She ran a hand over her dark brown hair, trying to smooth it.

Someone knocked on the door.

Delta had a smile on her face as she turned the latch and opened the door. That smile faltered as she realized her visitor wasn't Seth Barrett after all.

Felix Dugan stood there on her porch, water dripping off his slicker. He clutched his wet hat in both hands. His horse stood in front of the house with its head drooping.

"Good mornin', Miz Kennedy," the burly rancher said. He put a smile on his face, but it didn't look too comfortable on his bulldog features. "Merry Christmas to you, ma'am."

"Merry Christmas to you as well, Mr. Dugan," Delta said. She was sincere in the wish. Dugan's manner could be arrogant and overbearing at times, and she didn't return the romantic interest he obviously felt for her, but she didn't harbor any ill feelings toward the man. "What brings you here this morning?"

"I've come to extend an invitation to you, ma'am. I'd be mighty pleased and honored if you and your boy would come over to my ranch and have Christmas dinner with me tomorrow."

The invitation took Delta by surprise, but she didn't have to think about what her answer was going to be. She had already decided that she and Charlie would take the wagon to the church later today and ask Seth to share Christmas with them. What she had to do now was figure out a way to turn down Felix Dugan without insulting and angering him.

Her mind raced as she tried to do that, but before she could say anything her train of thought was interrupted by the sound of a sudden cry from the henhouse.

Her head jerked in that direction as her heart leaped in fear. Charlie sounded like he was hurt or scared or both. She saw him burst through the henhouse door and start toward her at a run.

"Charlie!" she exclaimed.

The boy had taken only a couple of steps when a figure appeared behind him, moving fast. Delta had never seen the man before. He wore a dark suit and hat and a holstered gun hung at his hip. He lunged after Charlie, reached out, and clamped his left hand on the youngster's shoulder. Roughly, he jerked Charlie to a stop and slung him on the ground at his feet.

"What in blazes!" Dugan roared. He dropped his hat on the porch and reached for his own gun. "Leave that boy alone, you no-good sidewinder!"

Dugan had reached the top step and his revolver had just started to clear leather when the stranger's gun appeared in his hand almost as if by magic. A shot crashed as flame spurted from the muzzle. Dugan grunted and rocked back against Delta, who was instinctively trying to get to her son as well.

The collision almost made her fall. She tried to grab Dugan and hold him up, but he weighed too much. He slipped out of her hands and slumped to the porch at her feet, rolling onto his back so she could see the spreading bloodstain on his shirt. Delta clapped her hands to her cheeks and screamed in shock and horror as she realized that Dugan was badly hurt.

But the rancher's gun had slid out of its holster as he collapsed, and when Delta's gaze fell on the weapon, she started to bend down and reach for it.

"Don't do it, lady!" the stranger warned. He grabbed Charlie by the collar and hauled the boy to his feet again. Charlie seemed dazed now, as if he barely understood what was going on.

Delta didn't understand, either. She had no idea who the man was or why he was here, why he wanted to threaten her son and shoot Felix Dugan.

Delta gasped as the man pressed the barrel of his revolver to Charlie's head.

"You step clear of that gun, ma'am, and don't even think about making a try for it," he ordered in a powerful voice. "I don't want to hurt you or your boy, but I will if I have to."

Despite the dampness that hung in the air, Delta's lips had gone dry as a bone from fear. She had to lick them a couple of times before she managed to say, "Please . . . please don't shoot. Whatever you want . . . just take it."

The man grinned, but it was more of a self-satisfied smirk. He said, "I've got what I want . . . for now. The boy's going with me."

"Ma!" Charlie wailed. "Ma, don't let him take me!"

Delta's heart hammered so hard it seemed like it would burst out of her chest. She wanted to scream and cry, but she forced herself to remain calm.

"You can't do that," she told the stranger. "He's just a little boy."

"I reckon I can do whatever I please," the man said. "I've got the gun."

At Delta's feet, Felix Dugan groaned in a vivid reminder of just how much damage that gun could do. Delta glanced down at the rancher. His face was pale and drawn in lines of pain. His eyes were open but unfocused. Delta could tell that he didn't know what was going on around him. He was probably dying.

She wanted to do what she could to help

him, but Charlie was more important to her. She turned her attention back to the stranger and said, "Take me instead. Let my son go."

The man clucked his tongue and shook his head.

"It's a tempting offer, Mrs. Kennedy. You're a very beautiful woman. But I'm engaged to be married."

Under the circumstances, that seemed like a ludicrous thing to say. Delta couldn't imagine any woman agreeing to marry this monster, no matter how smoothly handsome he might be on the surface.

"No, the boy will do just fine for my purposes," the man went on. "Besides, I have another job for you."

"I'll do anything you want. I give you my word. Just let Charlie go."

He went on as if he hadn't heard her, "What you need to do is go see Sam Brant and tell him what's happened here this morning. Tell him to ride toward Enchanted Rock and to bring what he took from me. He'll be met along the way. When I've got what's mine, you'll get what's yours . . . your boy, safe and sound."

Delta stared at him, still struggling to control the hysteria she felt edging into her brain. She said, "I . . . I don't know anyone named Sam Brant. This is all some sort of terrible mistake —"

"It's no mistake," the man cut in, and now his lips curled in a feral snarl. "You know Sam Brant, all right. He calls himself Seth Barrett now and tries to make everybody think he's some sort of sky pilot. But he's really just a no-good outlaw, and he always will be."

Delta had to put a hand down on the porch railing to steady herself as the stranger's words rocked her. Seth . . . an outlaw? That didn't seem possible. She had seen his goodness demonstrated time and again.

"You go tell him what I said," the gunman went on as he began moving toward the trees. "You tell him to come by nightfall, or else I won't be responsible for what happens."

"No!" Delta cried. She started down the porch steps, and as she did, she felt a hard drop of rain strike her cheek. "No, please —"

Big drops hit her, again and again, as more men appeared, coming out of the trees on horseback. Several of them pointed guns at her as she stumbled toward them.

Charlie began to struggle. His captor holstered the gun and used both hands to lift the boy and swing him up in front of one of the other men. That one clamped an arm around Charlie so tight that he cried out in pain.

Delta screamed and rushed toward the stranger while his back was turned. He swung around, caught her arms as she tried to claw at him, and threw her down in the mud. It was raining hard now.

"You know what you've got to do," the man told her as he looked down at her. He turned away and took the reins of a rider-less horse that one of the other men handed to him. Delta lay there whimpering as they mounted up and rode away, taking Charlie with them.

Slowly, she forced herself to her feet, then stumbled toward the porch where Felix Dugan still lay bleeding.

Seth was doing some preliminary work for the next Sunday's sermon — it was never too early to start thinking about such things — but he was having a hard time keeping his mind on the Scriptures he studied. He kept thinking about what a wonderful time he'd had with Delta and Charlie the day before. It would have been easy just to stay there, basking in the warmth of their companionship, instead of coming back here to this empty parsonage. . . .

"All right," he said out loud as he forced his attention back to the Bible open on his lap as he sat in the rocking chair near the fireplace. "Sunday will be two days before the new year starts, so there's got to be some verses somewhere about how we need to renew our faith. The first day of the year is a perfect time for that."

Rain hammered on the roof. It was so loud, in fact, that at first he didn't realize someone was pounding on the front door, too.

Who would come out in a deluge like the one moving over the Hill Country today? Seth asked himself. Then he sat up straighter as he thought that maybe someone had come to warn him the creek was rising again. It wasn't just possible, it was likely the way the rain was falling. He was confident that the wall of sandbags would hold, but it wouldn't hurt to check.

He closed the Bible, set it aside, and stood up. As he started toward the door, he called, "I'm coming."

The sight that greeted him as he swung the door open shocked him to his core. Delta Kennedy stood there, soaked to the skin, her head uncovered so that her hair was plastered to her head in limp strands. She glared at him with something very much like hatred in her eyes.

"Delta!" Seth exclaimed. "What . . . why. . . ."

A saddled horse stood in the yard between the church and the parsonage. The animal seemed familiar to him, and it was with another shock that Seth recognized it as the big, black horse Felix Dugan usually rode.

"He took him," Delta said in a hoarse voice.

"Took . . . who?"

"Charlie. The man took him. The man with the gun."

It was cold outside, as it ought to be in December, but the chill that suddenly filled Seth's body had nothing to do with the temperature.

"He told me to come here and talk to you," Delta went on. "He said he would kill Charlie unless you rode toward Enchanted Rock and brought what you stole from him with you."

Seth didn't have to ask her to describe the man who had kidnapped Charlie. There was only one man Seth knew who was evil enough to do a thing like that.

"What else did he say?" Seth asked in a flat, hard voice.

Delta glared wildly at him. She said, "He told me your name is really Sam Brant. He said you're nothing but a no-good outlaw!"

"He's right," Seth said.

CHAPTER THIRTY-SIX

Even as furious and terrified as Delta obviously was, Seth's words penetrated to her brain and made her stare at him in disbelief.

"You can't be an outlaw," she said. "You're a preacher."

"Only since I came here. Before that . . . I was everything that man said I was."

Cold wind whistled through the open doorway. Seth realized that Delta was standing there soaked to the skin. She ran the risk of catching a chill. She probably didn't care about that right now, but he did.

"Come inside," he told her. "You need to sit over by the fire and dry off some."

Without thinking, he reached out to put his hand on her upper arm and guide her into the house. She jerked away from him. Her lips twisted, and for a second she looked like she wanted to spit at him.

"Don't touch me," she said in a low voice. "Don't you dare touch me, you liar."

The harsh accusation made Seth want to bristle. Maybe he had never told her the truth, but he had never actually lied to her, either.

He controlled the reaction and kept his voice calm and soft as he said again, "Please, come over by the fire. Tell me everything that happened, and I'll do anything to help."

"He's dead, you know," Delta said.

"Charlie?" That was a shock like a physical blow. "No, that can't be. He's too valuable —"

"Felix Dugan," Delta interrupted. "He's dead. He's lying on the porch of my house with a bullet hole in his chest where that man shot him."

"Hudson," Seth breathed. "His name is Oliver Hudson. I don't have to see him to know that."

"I don't care what his name is. All I know is that he has Charlie."

Seth was sickened by the knowledge that his former partner had gunned down Felix Dugan. In a way it was his fault, he thought. Dugan would still be alive if Sam Brant hadn't stopped here in the Hill Country and dared to hope he could make a new life for himself here, with a new name.

Delta was shuddering from the cold as Seth said for the third time, "Please, come

371

over by the fire."

This time she did it. She sat down in the same rocking chair where Seth had been studying the Scriptures a few minutes earlier. Almost immediately, the heat from the fire made her wet clothes start to steam.

Seth knelt in front of her and said grimly, "Tell me what happened."

"We don't have time for that," she insisted. "You have to go after them. You have to help Charlie."

"I will, I swear. And I promise that Hudson won't hurt the boy. He's pure evil, but he's smart. He knows he has to keep Charlie alive in order to get me to do what he wants."

"What is it he wants? What is it you stole from him?"

Seth took a deep breath and said, "Money, of course. When I left the bunch that had been riding with me, I took all the loot we had cached from the jobs we'd pulled."

"You mean the robberies."

Seth shrugged.

"You're a vile, contemptible man."

"I won't argue with that, either," Seth said in a half-whisper.

Delta stared at him for a moment, breathing hard, then said, "He was waiting in the henhouse, I guess. He must have been spying on us. He knew that would be the easiest place to grab Charlie. He was out there when Mr. Dugan came to call on us. Then Charlie must have gotten away from him. . . . He came out and caught Charlie, and Mr. Dugan tried to draw his gun, and the man shot him. . . . There were other men with him, and he put Charlie up on a horse with one of them. He told me to tell you to ride toward Enchanted Rock and someone would meet you. He said you had to bring what you stole with you or he . . . he would kill Charlie."

"He's not going to kill Charlie," Seth said. He made his voice as firm and reassuring as he could. "He's a cold-blooded murderer, yes. That's one reason I knew we couldn't ride together anymore. But he only kills for a good reason. He won't hurt Charlie."

"How can you be sure of that?"

"Because Hudson wants the money. Nothing is more important to him than that."

"Then give it to him!" Delta cried.

Seth looked at her as a couple of long seconds went by, then he said, "I can't. I don't have it anymore."

"What?" Her eyes widened in disbelief. "What happened to it?"

"It's here," Seth said. He moved a hand to indicate their surroundings. "Well, only a little here in the parsonage. A lot more of it went to fix up the church. That's what paid for all the repairs I've done since I came here. And the rest of it went to folks in the congregation who needed it. There are a lot of families around here who need help in little ways. It all added up." He hesitated. "Like when your bill at the store was paid, and Mr. Truesdale wouldn't tell you who did it."

"You paid that bill?" Delta asked. Her tone hardened. "With stolen money?"

"Money that I was trying to make do some good."

"If you really wanted to do good, you'd have given it back to who it belonged to!"

"I thought about that," Seth said honestly. "But most of it came from the railroads and the banks, and I knew they'd already made good on most of the losses. I know it wasn't right . . . but it just seemed better this way."

"You didn't want to go to jail, that's all," Delta said.

"I never fancied spending years behind bars," Seth admitted.

"So you pretended to be a preacher —"

This time Seth couldn't stop himself. He broke in, "No. I haven't been pretending. I answered the Lord's call. I *am* a preacher."

"You expect me to believe that?"

"I don't expect anything, but it's the truth." Seth straightened up, reached over to take hold of a ladderback chair, and swung it around so he could sit close to Delta. He lowered himself onto the chair and clasped his hands together in front of him, between his knees. Peering earnestly at her, he went on, "I was on my own ever since I was a kid. I learned how to steal and do whatever I had to in order to get by. I'm not making any excuses, though. A lot of youngsters have hard lives and don't grow up to be outlaws."

"That's right, they don't," she said coldly.

"But that's what happened with me. I was good at it, too. Turns out I had a knack for figuring out the best way to pull a job. Other fellas threw in with me because of that."

"You mean you put together a gang."

"You could call it that," Seth said. "And one of them was Oliver Hudson. We got along well, worked together just fine. But he always had a mean streak in him, and that worried me."

"Because you were so innocent."

The words were scathing. Seth almost winced as they lashed at him. He said, "No, I wasn't innocent, but I never killed anybody, either. I stole plenty. I wounded some lawmen who were chasing us. I have blood

375

on my hands, no doubt about that. But Hudson shot to kill, and he didn't need much provocation to do it, either."

"And that's why you abandoned the gang?"

She didn't sound quite so skeptical now. Seth nodded and said, "I won't lie. When I left and took the money with me, I didn't have any intention of trying to do good with it. I just wanted to use it to start a new life somewhere. It wasn't until I came to Enchanted Rock that I changed my mind."

Delta frowned slightly, looking confused, as she said, "The church?"

"The rock," Seth replied with a faint smile. "The actual Enchanted Rock. When I first laid eyes on it, something about it seemed to call to me. I'd never seen anything so . . . so big and impressive. I left my horse there at the little creek that runs beside it and climbed to the top. I remember it was a beautiful day and I could see for miles and miles around." Seth took a deep breath. "And while I was standing there, just looking, it was like a voice spoke to me. I could hear it clear as a bell inside my head. It told me that the Lord made everything I was looking at, and if He could do something so magnificent, He could save a no-good outlaw like me." A shudder ran through him. "I dropped to my knees right there, Delta, on top of that big old rock, and I asked the Lord to forgive me and show me what I needed to do, and by the time I walked back down to my horse, I knew He'd take me in the right direction. I turned around and rode back this way, and a little while later I came to the church. . . ." He smiled and spread his hands. "You know the rest of the story."

She had listened intently to him, and he thought he saw belief in her eyes. But she was still upset and scared for her son, of course, and those emotions quickly won out over any sympathy she might be feeling.

"You're wasting time," she snapped. "That man, Hudson or whatever his name is, he and the rest of the gang still have Charlie. They'll kill him if you don't give them what they want . . . and you don't have it."

"I don't have the money," Seth agreed. "That's true. But I can give Hudson something else he wants — my life."

"He'll kill you."

"Even if I had the loot to give him, he'd do that because I double-crossed him." Seth's voice hardened. "Or at least he'll try to."

"He'll kill Charlie, too."

Seth shook his head and said, "No.

Wouldn't be any point in it. Once he's got his hands on me, he'll let the boy go."

"I don't believe it. Charlie could tell the law where they're hiding. Hudson wouldn't take that chance."

"They'll light a shuck as soon as I'm dead and leave this part of the country behind. They won't need their hideout anymore, so killing Charlie wouldn't serve any purpose."

Delta's forehead creased in another frown. She said, "You talk about them killing you like it doesn't mean anything."

"Compared to Charlie's life and your happiness, it doesn't." Seth's clasped hands clenched tighter together. "But once Charlie's clear, I don't intend to go down without a fight. I'll take Hudson with me if I can, and any of the others I can get in my sights."

"Your gunsights."

"That's right." Seth stood up then and walked over to a cabinet. He opened it, reached inside, and took out a coiled shell belt with a pair of holsters attached to it. Snugged down in those holsters were matching walnut-butted Colt revolvers. Seth ran his fingers over the smooth wood of one gun butt, and Lord help him, he thought, it felt good.

Delta stood up. Her clothes crinkled a little now that they had dried some. She took a step toward him and lifted a hand.

"They'll kill you," she whispered.

"More than likely. The odds are against me. But not until I've seen Charlie safely on his way back to you."

"I don't . . . I don't want. . . ."

"Sometimes there are no good answers, Delta," Seth said as he swung the gunbelt around his hips and buckled it. "I was foolish to think that I could change. All I can do now is try to keep things from getting worse."

"But you did change. I saw the truth in you. I saw the man you . . . you became. A good man."

"A good man never would have done the things I did." He slid the right-hand gun from leather, checked the loads, and then pouched the iron again so he could repeat the process with the left-hand gun.

"You need to get some help. Find the deacons. They'll go with you —"

"I can't do that," he said sharply as he holstered the second Colt. "They're good men, but they're not lawmen or gunfighters. If I asked them for help, they'd give it to me — and then they'd just wind up getting killed. Besides, if Hudson sees me coming with a posse, he actually might hurt Charlie because he'd think I was double-crossing him again." Seth shook his head. "No, I have to do exactly what he told me to do."

"You mean give up your life —"

"Some things are worth it," he told her.

Then, before she could try to stop him, he swung around and stalked to the door. He grabbed his hat and slicker from their nails and put them on as he stepped out onto the porch. He would take Felix Dugan's horse instead of saddling his own, he decided. It was a good mount, and that way Delta couldn't follow him. He wanted her to stay far away from Hudson and the rest of the gang.

"Seth, wait!" she cried behind him.

He paused at the edge of the porch. The rain was coming down so hard now he could barely see the church, even though it was close by. He turned and she came into his arms and lifted her mouth to his. The kiss took him by surprise, since she had been so angry with him only a few minutes earlier, but he responded and his arms went around her.

"Bring my son back to me," she whispered when she took her lips away from his.

"I'll send Charlie —"

"No. *You* bring my son back to me. I want both of you back."

He couldn't promise that. But he could kiss her again, hard and urgent, so he did that before he pulled away, stepped out into the rain, and jerked the horse's reins loose from the hitching post where they were tied. He swung up into the saddle and rode away without looking back, but he knew Delta was there on the porch anyway, watching him as he disappeared into the deluge.

CHAPTER THIRTY-SEVEN

One of the outlaws who had been keeping an eye on Evelyn Channing in the cave accompanied Tully back up onto the bluff to resume standing guard up there. The man Chance had shot through the shoulder, whose name was Shaw, stayed below so the other outlaw, Deke, could clean and bandage the wound. Shaw spent a lot of time glaring at Chance.

"I reckon that fella would like to return the favor and put a bullet in you," Ace said quietly to his brother as they sat on crates and leaned against the wall of the cave. A few feet away, Porter sat likewise with Evelyn, holding her hand.

"I just wish my aim had been a mite better," Chance said. "We might have been able to get away from the other one."

"But then Miss Channing would still be a prisoner here."

"She *is* still a prisoner here," Chance

pointed out.

"Yes, but she would have been on her own," Ace said. "Now she's got us to help her when the time comes."

"To make a break, you mean?"

"Yeah, and it needs to be soon." Ace's voice took on a grim edge. "What do you think's going to happen when Hudson gets back with the rest of the gang?"

"He won't be happy to see us," Chance said.

Outside, the rain poured down harder and harder. It sounded like a rushing river. More than likely, the rivers around here *were* rushing right about now, thought Ace. At the rate the rain was coming down now, flash flooding was inevitable, and it would probably be widespread. That was going to be dangerous.

On the other hand, it might help slow down the pursuit if he and the others were able to get away from the outlaws.

Their hands weren't tied. Deke and Shaw were a little too over-confident, Ace mused. If he and Chance could get their hands on some guns. . . .

Porter suddenly stood up and walked toward the two owlhoots, who were sitting on the other side of the fire drinking coffee. Deke set his cup down and put that hand on the butt of his gun.

"Hold it right there, mister," he warned Porter. "What do you think you're doing?"

"I want to offer you men a proposition," Porter declared.

Shaw let out an ugly laugh and said, "I don't think you've got anything to bargain with."

"Actually, I do," Porter insisted.

Evelyn said, "William, no. Please, it won't do any good."

He looked back at her, smiled, and said, "We'll see." Then he turned to the outlaws again and went on, "You men are bandits."

Deke chuckled and said, "I reckon you could say that."

"You've robbed banks in the past?"

"Sure. Won't hurt anything to admit that."

Because they figure we'll all soon be dead anyway, Ace thought.

"It just so happens I work at a bank in Austin," Porter went on. "So I propose an arrangement. You let Miss Channing go, and I'll help you gentlemen loot every penny in the vault."

Deke and Shaw stared at him for a moment before Shaw said, "You'd help us rob a bank in Austin?"

"That's right. Strictly *quid pro quo.* Something for something. My help in return for

Miss Channing's safety."

Deke thumbed his hat back and said, "There are two things wrong with that idea, amigo. Our boss is sweet on the lady, and he ain't a man you'd want to cross. If we was to let her go, he'd likely kill us. And the second thing is, Austin's a big town. The chances of ridin' in there, robbin' a bank, and gettin' away with it are too blasted slim, even if it was an inside job like you're talkin' about."

"Then perhaps I could steal the money and turn it over to you. I'd give you my word —"

Deke shook his head and snapped, "Go back over there and sit down. You're wastin' your time." He leaned forward to pick up the coffee cup he had set down.

As the outlaw did that, Porter did something that none of them expected, not even Ace and Chance.

He kicked the coffee pot off the rock where it was sitting near the edge of the fire, keeping warm, and sent it right into Deke's face.

Deke howled as the heated metal burned his skin. He jerked back and toppled off the crate where he'd been sitting. Beside him, Shaw cursed and clawed at the gun on his hip. His left shoulder was bandaged and that arm hung in a crude sling, but his gun hand still worked just fine.

However, Ace and Chance lunged forward from their crates as soon as Porter made his desperate move. Shaw had barely cleared leather when Ace threw himself across the fire in a diving tackle. Shaw was half-standing as Ace caught him around the waist and drove him backward. When they landed, the back of Shaw's head slammed against the rocky floor of the cave. He went limp.

Chance went after Deke, hurtling past Porter. Deke was still yelling in pain from his burned face, but he had his gun out and swung it up. Chance grabbed the barrel and thrust it aside just as Deke pulled the trigger. The bullet thudded into the cave's back wall.

Chance swung a hard right to Deke's jaw. The blow landed cleanly with all of Chance's lithe strength behind it. Deke's head jerked to the side, and he folded up as limply as Shaw had.

Ace and Chance scooped up the outlaws' guns while Porter ran back over to Evelyn to make sure she was all right. She embraced him and exclaimed, "Oh, William! That was so brave!"

"Foolhardy and desperate, you mean, my

dear," he said. "But there was nothing else I could do."

"The two up on the bluff will have heard that shot," Ace said to Chance. "We'd better grab our guns while we can."

They hurried over to where the outlaws had piled their gunbelts and quickly buckled on the weapons.

Chance said, "Maybe it's raining so hard they didn't hear that gun go off —"

The sharp crack of a rifle shot destroyed that hope. The bullet whipped through the air between the Jensen brothers.

"Will, get down!" Ace shouted to Porter, who grabbed Evelyn and dived to the ground, taking her with him. They scrambled on hands and knees behind some of the supply crates.

Ace and Chance split up, heading for different sides of the cave as fast as they could move. More shots rang out. The brothers returned the fire on the run. They couldn't see the rifleman but knew he had to be close to the cave mouth.

Chance found cover among the half-dozen horses in the rope corral, while Ace made himself as small as he could behind a little shoulder of rock. Ace had hoped they could get out of here before the other two outlaws closed off the cave, so they could fight in the open, but that wasn't going to happen. They were pinned down in here, and it wouldn't be difficult for Tully and the other man to keep them trapped until Hudson and the rest of the gang returned.

When that happened, Hudson would have even more reason for wanting the Jensens and William Porter dead. . . .

"Chance!" Ace called to his brother. "We can't stay here. We've got to make a break for it."

"How?" Chance asked. "They've got us bottled up."

"Cover me. I'm coming over where you are."

Chance opened fire with his own Colt and the gun he had picked up. As he blasted shot after shot toward the entrance, Ace sprinted across the cave toward the corral. A couple of bullets smacked into the ground near his feet and two more whined past his head, but he made the corral without getting hit and ducked under the rope.

All the shooting had made the horses skittish. Ace knew it wouldn't take much to make them bolt toward the opening. In fact, he was counting on it.

"We'll stampede them out of here and be hanging on the sides of a couple of them, the way the Indians do," he explained his plan to Chance. "Once we get outside, we'll take our chances with the other two."

"Reckon there's not much else we can do," Chance agreed. "Better tell Will what we're up to, though, so he and Evelyn won't think we're running out on them."

Ace knew the men outside couldn't hear them in that steady downpour, but he kept his voice down as much as he could anyway as he called over to Porter and Evelyn and quickly explained the plan.

"Do I need to come with you?" Porter asked.

"No, it'll be better if you stay there and look after Miss Channing," Ace said. He knew that Porter was a decent rider but didn't think the would-be writer was up to the sort of thing he and Chance were going to attempt.

"Good luck!" Porter called.

"We'll need it," Chance said under his breath.

There was no time to saddle the horses. The brothers swung up bareback on their usual mounts and jabbed their boot heels into the animals' flanks. The horses lunged against the others, and that was all it took to send all of them pressing against the ropes until the barrier gave way. Like a wave, the spooked horses dashed toward the open air.

Ace and Chance slipped down on the sides of their mounts, clinging to the horses with one hand and one foot. It was a dangerous ride. If they fell off, they stood a good chance of being trampled.

As they burst out of the cave, the horses scattered. That gave Ace and Chance room to drop off. They rolled and came up with their guns ready. The rain was coming down so hard it was difficult to see, but then muzzle flame spurted through the gloom from near the cave mouth. Ace and Chance returned the fire and heard a man yell in pain. At least one of them had scored a hit.

Another rifle crack sounded and Chance's left leg went out from under him. Ace leaped to his brother's side and knelt there as he slammed a couple of shots toward the second rifleman. He triggered again, but the hammer fell on an empty cylinder. The other gun he had picked up was already empty.

A menacing shape loomed out of the downpour. The outlaw called Tully stood there in his slicker, rain running off his hat brim like a river as he pointed a Winchester at them.

"Blast it, this is no weather for foolin' around," he snapped, raising his voice to be heard over the rain. "I think you killed Packy. I'm tired of this, and I know now you were just lookin' for that gal. The boss'll have to be satisfied with that — and your carcasses."

The rifle barrel came up a little as the outlaw brought the weapon to his shoulder. Ace knew he was going to kill both of them and was ready to try a last-ditch leap that probably wouldn't get him anything except a bullet in the face — when another shot roared and Tully was driven back by the bullet that hit him. He didn't fall, though, until two more shots blasted from somewhere behind Ace and Chance.

Ace had no idea who had come to their rescue. He glanced down at Chance, who was conscious and holding his wounded leg, then turned his head to look behind them.

A tall, dark figure strode out of the curtains of rain. The stranger wore a poncho of some sort over black clothes and had a black hat pulled low over his face. The light wasn't good, but Ace was able to make out rough-hewn features and a neatly trimmed mustache. The man held a Winchester pointed in the general direction of the Jensen boys.

"I know that was Tully Moran, a wanted outlaw," the stranger said in a deep, powerful voice, "but I don't know who you two young gentlemen are. I'd appreciate it if you wouldn't move too quickly until I'm sure what the situation is here."

"Mister," Chance said through teeth gritted against the pain of his wound, "I'm not gonna be going anywhere very fast with a bullet hole in my leg."

"We were prisoners of that fella and the gang he is with," Ace explained. "There are a couple more inside the cave."

"More prisoners or more outlaws?" the stranger asked.

"Both," Ace said. "They had a friend of ours and a young woman, and there are two owlhoots we knocked out while we were trying to get away."

"We'd better check on that, then, before those outlaws regain consciousness." The dark stranger finally lowered his rifle. "I can trust you, I take it?"

"Mister, we're so grateful to you right now you don't have a thing to worry about," Ace assured him. "Who are you, and how'd you happen to show up just now?"

"I've been doing a little outlaw-hunting of my own," the man said as he started past Ace and Chance. "And as for who I am — the name's Luke Jensen."

CHAPTER THIRTY-EIGHT

As Seth looked through the rain-shrouded hills at the looming bulk of Enchanted Rock, he thought how primitive this land appeared in these conditions, like a prehistoric wilderness filled with savage dangers.

And that was right, he told himself. Because somewhere out there, waiting to kill him, was Oliver Hudson.

The trail was awash with water. Every little gully was full and running swiftly, and sheets of water lay over the fields and the road. Mud sucked at the hooves of Felix Dugan's horse. The rain continued to fall, pounding against Seth like millions of tiny fists.

Whatever happened to him today, he deserved it, he told himself. But Charlie and Delta didn't. Charlie's life and Delta's happiness were at risk because of him, and knowing that gnawed at his guts like a hungry buzzard.

Four men on horseback suddenly appeared in the sodden gloom up ahead, urging their mounts out of a stand of bare-limbed trees next to the road. Seth would have spotted them before now if it hadn't been raining so hard, but he couldn't miss them as they blocked his path. His hands wanted to reach for the guns under his slicker, but he reined in the impulse. He couldn't just start shooting without knowing what he faced.

He didn't stop until he was close enough to see their faces under their hat brims. The rugged, unshaven features were familiar. None of them belonged to Oliver Hudson, however.

One of the men urged his horse forward a step and called out over the rain, "Hold it right there, Sam! Keep your hands where we can see 'em."

"Don't worry, Cameron," Seth told the outlaw. "I don't plan to start the ball. And the name's Seth Barrett now."

That brought a short laugh from the man, who went on, "You're Sam Brant and you always will be. Callin' yourself something else don't change a blasted thing."

Unfortunately, Cameron was probably right about that, thought Seth. His dreams of a new life were over, shattered by the inevitability of the past.

"Where's the boy?" Seth asked harshly.

"The boss has him. The kid's all right. He ain't been hurt. All you got to do to save him is turn over the loot you stole from us."

A bleak smile touched Seth's face as he said, "I guess I forgot there was supposed to be honor among thieves."

"I reckon you did," Cameron said. "Now shuck your irons and let's go. We'll take you to the boss."

Slowly, Seth shook his head.

"I'm not giving up my guns."

The four outlaws stiffened. Seth could tell that they were getting ready to draw on him.

"I wouldn't," he snapped.

"Four of us and one of you," Cameron said. "I know you're good with a gun, Sam, but you can't take all four of us and you know it."

"And if you kill me, Hudson will never get his hands on that money. I know *that,* too."

The argument went home. Cameron scowled in frustration.

"Hudson said we was to take your guns. He don't take it kindly when folks don't do what he tells 'em."

"He'll like it even less if all this turns out to be for nothing, won't he?" Seth said.

"That's what will happen if you force me to fight."

Cameron turned his head and exchanged glances with the other men. Then he looked at Seth again and said, "All right. Keep your irons." He drew a Winchester from the saddle sheath on his horse and worked the lever. "But if you try anything I'll kill you anyway, and devil take the hindmost."

Seth shrugged and walked his horse forward. The outlaws parted and let him through, then fell in around him.

"Lead the way," he told Cameron. "I want to get this over with as much as you boys do."

Under different circumstances, Ace would have been shocked that the man who had just saved him and Chance had the same last name, but right now there was no time for that.

Instead he helped Chance to his feet as Luke Jensen strode toward the cave mouth.

"Can you walk?" Ace asked his brother.

"Yeah, it'll hurt like blazes, but I can get around. We'd better try to catch up. If Will's gotten his hands on a gun, he's liable to get nervous in there."

That was a good point, thought Ace. He didn't want Porter to take Luke for one of the outlaws and try to shoot him.

Besides, as grim and hard-bitten as Luke Jensen looked, if Porter took a shot at him, it would probably be the young writer who got ventilated.

Ace looped an arm around Chance's waist. They went after Luke, Chance hobbling considerably as they did so. Ace called, "Wait a minute, Mr. Jensen."

Luke paused and looked back over his shoulder.

"I thought you said there are two more outlaws in there."

"There are," Ace said. "But it probably wouldn't be a good idea to spook our friend Will."

Luke leaned his head toward the cave and said, "Better let him know to hold his fire, then."

Ace nodded and called, "Will! Hey, Will, don't shoot! We're all friends coming in."

Luke grunted, and as the three of them started forward again he said, "I don't recall telling you boys we were friends. All I know about you is that I don't recognize your faces from any reward dodgers I've seen."

"That's because we're not wanted anywhere," Ace said.

"That we know of," Chance added. He grimaced with each step he took.

"What are your names?"

"I'm Ace, and this is my brother Chance." Ace paused, then added, "Our last name is Jensen."

Luke stopped and looked over at the brothers as he raised one eyebrow skeptically.

"Really?"

"Yes, sir," Ace said. "It's not that uncommon a name."

"We even met the famous Smoke Jensen a while back," Chance put in.

Luke stared at them for a moment longer, then abruptly he laughed.

"All right, whatever you say, boys," he told them. "Let's go see about those other two owlhoots."

As they walked into the cave, Ace saw that Deke and Shaw had regained consciousness, but Porter and Evelyn stood about fifteen feet from them, shakily pointing guns at them.

"Chance, you're wounded!" Porter exclaimed.

"I'll be all right," Chance told him.

Luke looked at the two outlaws and said, "Deke Connolly and Nate Shaw. You two aren't worth much, but it all adds up, I suppose."

Shaw curled his lip and said, "You talk

like a stinkin' bounty hunter, mister."

"Keep a civil tongue in your head or I'll kick your teeth down your throat," Luke said. "Ace . . ." He rolled his eyes, no doubt an indication of what he thought about the names the Jensen boys went by. "Help your brother sit down so the young lady can tend to his wound. Then you and Mister . . . ?"

"Porter, sir. William Sydney Porter."

"You and Porter can tie up these two while I cover them. And if they try anything, you'd better get out of the way in a hurry, because there *will* be gunfire. While you're doing that, you can tell me what's going on here."

The next few minutes were busy ones. Evelyn used a knife she found to cut away the trouser leg around Chance's wound while Ace and Porter tied up the two outlaws. Luke Jensen stood there, still dripping water from his poncho and hat and kept an eye on everybody.

When Evelyn had cleaned away as much of the mud as she could from the deep bullet graze in Chance's thigh, Luke reached under his poncho with his left hand and brought out a small silver flask. He tossed it to Evelyn and said, "Pour some of that on the wound, then bind it up. And that's the best bourbon money can buy, young man, so I hope you appreciate the sacrifice."

"Oh, I reckon I — Ouch!" Chance said as the fiery liquor bit into his flesh.

The heat from the fire was starting to dry all of them a little by the time Deke and Shaw were trussed up securely and Chance's leg was bandaged with strips of cloth discreetly sliced from Evelyn's rather bedraggled petticoat. That was the cleanest dressing they were going to find around here.

"Now I suppose I should get my horse and round up some of the mounts you stampeded out of here," Luke said. "Then we can all get started for Fredericksburg. That's the nearest town, isn't it?"

"That's right," Ace said.

Evelyn gnawed her bottom lip for a second, then said, "We can't leave."

Luke looked at her and said, "Oh? Why not?"

"Because I heard them talking . . ." She looked at Ace, Chance, and Porter. "Before the three of you were captured, I mean. When I was a prisoner here by myself. I heard Oliver giving orders and . . . and boasting about what they were going to do."

"You mean Oliver Hudson?" Luke asked.

Evelyn nodded and said, "That's right. He's the leader of this gang of outlaws."

"He is *now*," Luke said. "He didn't used to be."

"I know. That's part of what I heard." Evelyn took a deep breath. "He told the others they were going to kidnap a small boy, and that once they did that, someone named Sam would do anything they told him. I think Oliver means to kill this man Sam, whoever he is."

"I wouldn't doubt it a bit," Luke said. "And you're right, miss. Under the circumstances, we can't leave. Not with a boy's life at stake."

Ace frowned and said, "Mr. Jensen, you seem to have a pretty good idea who all these people are and what's going on here."

"That's right. I've been on Sam Brant's trail for quite a while." Luke lifted the Winchester in his hands. "And I don't reckon I'm leaving the Hill Country without him."

CHAPTER THIRTY-NINE

A short time later, Ace crouched behind a large rock on top of the bluff next to Luke Jensen. They couldn't see much as they peered out over the rain-swept landscape, but Ace thought they would be able to spot any riders approaching the cave.

Chance, Porter, and Evelyn were with the horses, back in the trees behind Ace and Luke. The two prisoners were with them, too, gagged now as well as tied securely, so they couldn't call out a warning to their fellow owlhoots. Ace and Luke had carried the two dead men up here as well, so when Hudson and the rest of the gang got back to the cave, they would find the hideout apparently deserted.

As long as Hudson was holding the little boy hostage, they wouldn't be able to make a move against the gang. Luke had explained that they would try to come up with some way to get the boy away from his captors, but they couldn't figure out how to do that until the outlaws got back.

As they waited tensely, Luke surprised Ace by saying, "So you and your brother have met the famous gunfighter Smoke Jensen, eh?"

"That's right. Sure surprised me when we did, too. I'd read about him in dime novels, but I never expected to run into him in real life. As it turns out, he's a fine hombre, too. He gave us a hand in a little scrape we got into up in Wyoming. It was a real pleasure meeting him."

Luke chuckled and said, "I'll have to tell him that next time I see him."

"You know him, too?" Ace asked as he looked over at the older man.

"You could say that. He's my little brother."

Ace's eyes widened.

"Really? And now we've run into you. What are the odds of that?"

Luke said, "For all the wide-open spaces, the frontier's not as big as you might think it is, especially for fellas who, let's say, have a habit of running into trouble. You and your brother do your share of that?"

"More than our share, I'd say," Ace replied. "We're not looking for it, but it seems to find us wherever we go."

Luke nodded solemnly and said, "Believe me, I know the feeling." He lifted his head. "Listen. I think I hear horses out there somewhere."

"Yeah," Ace said a moment later. "I do, too. They sound like they're coming closer."

Luke's eyes narrowed in thought as he said, "The gang kept guards up here all the time?"

"As far as I know. They only grabbed us earlier today."

"Then they'll probably expect some sort of all-clear signal," Luke said, nodding.

"Aren't they liable to catch on that something's wrong if you don't give them the right signal? Or see that you're not who you're supposed to be?"

"I'm counting on the weather to take care of both of those things. In this downpour, they won't be able to see all that well."

Ace supposed that made sense. He leaned forward a little, hands tightening on the Winchester he held, as they waited for the riders to come into sight.

That didn't take long. The men and horses blended together into large, almost formless masses as they approached the cave. They slowed and Luke breathed, "They're waiting for the signal."

He stood up, held his rifle above his head,

and swung it back and forth. The riders down below wouldn't be able to make out any more details about him than he could about them, but they ought to be able to see that movement, thought Ace.

The men on horseback started forward again and disappeared into the cave, so they must have been satisfied with the signal.

"Now what?" Ace asked. "They'll see that the place is empty and know something happened."

"And since he got the all-clear, the first thing Hudson will do is send somebody up here to find out what's going on. He'll be confused, but at this point he shouldn't think he's in any danger."

Ace hoped the older man was right. From the few things Luke had mentioned about his past while they were waiting up here, Ace knew he'd been a manhunter for a long time. By now Luke ought to know how an outlaw would think and react.

"Let's head for the trail," Luke suggested.

They hadn't gotten there when two men appeared, trudging up from below. Luke and Ace kept their heads down as the outlaws approached. One of the men called through the rain, "Hey, who's that? Deke? Tully? The boss wants to know what in blazes is goin' on. The prisoners are gone!"

Luke muttered something in return, but the men couldn't make it out over the downpour. They came closer, and the second man said, "What was that?"

Luke made his move then, leaping forward and sweeping his rifle up to smash the butt against the jaw of an outlaw. Ace tried the same thing, but the man who was his target reacted with quick instincts and twisted out of the way. He yelled and tried to bring up the rifle he was carrying.

Before he could do that, Luke rammed his rifle barrel into the man's midsection. It was a continuation of the same move that had laid out the first man, and as the second one doubled over in pain, Luke's knee came up and cracked against his jaw. He went down, too, out cold just like his companion.

"Sorry," Ace said.

"That's all right, kid. You're still learning. Just remember, there aren't many second chances in this business."

Ace didn't intend to go into the bounty hunting business, but he didn't figure there was any reason to point that out to Luke right now.

They dragged the two senseless men into the trees where Chance, Porter, and Evelyn were waiting. In a matter of minutes the two outlaws were tied and gagged like Deke and Shaw.

"Don't recognize these two right offhand," Luke said, "but when I have the time to go through my wanted posters I'll probably find them. This could add up nicely."

"What about the boy?" Evelyn asked.

Luke shook his head and said, "I couldn't tell if they had him or not. I believe there were about a dozen riders. How many are in the bunch?"

They had to look to Evelyn for that answer, since she was the only one who had seen the whole gang. She said, "I think there were a few more than that, but I'm not sure exactly how many. But I believe Oliver planned to send some of his men to carry a message to this Sam Brant."

"So Hudson's waiting for them to show up with Brant." Luke rubbed his chin and frowned. "He's got to be torn right now. He wants Brant, but he's bound to be upset about your disappearance, too, Miss Channing. Maybe he'll split his forces again and send some of his men to look for you. Come on, Ace. Let's get back to where we can keep an eye on the trail in case any of the others start up here."

They hurried back to the rocks where they had been hidden earlier. As Ace crouched there, he looked across the open area in front of the cave at the little creek running along the far side. Actually, it wasn't a little creek anymore, he thought. It was a raging torrent running bank-full. He could hear its rumbling even over the storm. And as long as the rain continued to fall, it wasn't going to go down anytime soon.

Ace was watching the swollen creek, so he wasn't aware that something else was happening until Luke said, "Riders coming."

Ace swung his attention to the figures on horseback approaching the cave. He counted five of them.

"You think that's . . . ?"

"I think that's the rest of Hudson's men," Luke said, "and they've brought Sam Brant with them."

Seth hadn't said anything else as he rode alongside the outlaw called Cameron. He didn't have any interest in carrying on a conversation with any of these men. His mind was too full of worry about Charlie's fate and what it would mean to Delta.

A wry thought nagged at his brain. Maybe he ought to tell them about the Lord and see if he could get them to repent their wicked ways.

But he supposed his preaching days were over, because what he wanted to do even more was skin out both smoke poles he carried and get to work. He remembered what it was like to hear the roar of shots, feel the guns bucking in his hands, and smell the sharp tang of powder smoke.

That beat praying any day, he thought bitterly.

He couldn't risk any shooting until he got Charlie away from Hudson, though. He could do that as long as he had the leverage of that stolen loot. Delta was the only one who knew he had spent it all on the church and other good works.

By faith are ye saved, not works, he reminded himself. That's what the Scriptures said. He wasn't sure it was true, though. He'd had faith, but it wasn't enough.

Some men just couldn't be saved.

They rode along a creek that was close to breaking out of its banks. Many of the fields and pastures were already flooded. When the creek overflowed it would just make things worse. This was going to be a great disaster before it was over, Seth thought, because today the heavens truly had opened up. He had never seen rain like this before.

Cold, wet, and miserable, the men started up a gentle slope. Seth caught his breath as he spotted the dark mouth of what appeared to be a large cave in the base of a rugged bluff rising ahead of them.

Cameron led the way. Seth hung back a little. He didn't mean to, but he knew that with each step his horse took, he was that much closer to death. No matter how strong he might be, nearly every man feared the end of his days. That end was approaching rapidly for Seth Barrett.

Then they were inside, and after the downpour in which they had been riding, it almost felt strange not to have the rain pounding against him anymore.

Gun-hung, hard-faced men were ranged around the fire. Seth spotted Oliver Hudson among them. Hudson was pacing back and forth angrily and didn't notice the new arrivals for a second or two. Then he stopped short, swung toward the men on horseback, and a gun swept up in his hand.

"By God, I ought to shoot you right here and now, Sam," he said. "You've got it coming for what you did."

"You pull that trigger and you'll never get your money, Oliver," Seth said coolly. He tried not to let Hudson see how desperately his eyes were searching for Charlie Kennedy.

There! The boy was sitting on one of the crates with an outlaw standing beside him keeping an eye on him. Charlie wasn't tied up, and he didn't appear to be hurt, just soaked and terrified. He sat there with the firelight reflecting from his wide, staring eyes.

"M-Mr. Barrett?" he croaked.

Hudson lowered the gun but didn't holster it. He said, "His name's not Barrett, kid. It's Sam Brant, and he's no preacher. He's an outlaw, just like us. Worse than us, because he stole from his partners. Didn't you, Sam?"

Seth ignored the question and said, "Let the boy go. You don't need him anymore. Put him on a horse and send him home."

Hudson let out a cold, humorless laugh. He said, "Send a boy out in a storm like that? You're loco, Sam. I wouldn't do that."

"I'll tell you where the money is, but only after Charlie's headed back to his mother."

Hudson shook his head.

"You *take* us to the money, and then the boy goes free. That's the only way this will work. Otherwise . . ."

Hudson half-turned. He lifted the revolver again and aimed it at Charlie as he thumbed back the hammer. Charlie whimpered and started to get up, but the man beside him grabbed his shoulder and shoved him back down on the crate.

"You kill him and you'll die half a second

later, Oliver," Seth said.

"Yes, I see you still have your guns."

Cameron said, "He wouldn't give 'em up, boss."

"It doesn't matter," Hudson said with a shake of his head. "Look around you, Sam. There are half a dozen guns pointed at you. I know you're fast, but you're not *that* fast. You make a move toward your guns, and you'll be riddled with lead before you can touch them."

Smiling faintly, Seth said, "And again, if that happens you don't get your loot, do you?"

Hudson's lips drew back from his teeth in a grimace. This was a standoff and he knew it. He tipped the gun barrel toward the roof of the cave and lowered the hammer.

"All right," he snapped. "I've got other problems to deal with right now. Tell me where the loot is."

Seth had been thinking about that during the ride here, so he had an answer ready.

"It's at the church," he said. "Buried under the floor where the pulpit stands."

Hudson stared at him for a moment, then threw back his head and laughed, a genuine laugh this time.

"You know, I believe you," he said. "All that time you stood there preaching, all holier than thou, you were really worshipping your real god, weren't you, Sam? You were thinking about all that money right under your feet."

Seth managed to smile. Let Hudson believe whatever he wanted to believe. As long as it kept Charlie alive, that was all that mattered.

"All right, I've told you. You can let the boy go now."

Hudson shook his head and said, "That's not the way it works, and you know it. I said you had to take us to it, but I'm willing to be reasonable. You and the kid don't have to go back out into the rain." He turned toward Cameron and went on, "Take five men and go get that loot. We'll wait for you here."

Cameron didn't look happy about the idea of going back out into the storm, but he nodded and said, "Sure, boss."

Seth started to object, but he changed his mind. Once Cameron and the others were gone, that would cut down the odds against him. They would still be ten to one, but right now Seth would take anything he could get.

Somehow, in the time that the others were gone, he had to find a way to get Charlie out of here. Then he would take his chances.

Cameron picked out the men who would go with him to the church. They mounted up and rode out of the cave. Cameron paused at the entrance, though, and called back, "I don't like the looks of that creek, boss. It's out of its banks and climbing. I'm not sure it can get this high, but it might."

Hudson nodded and said, "We'll keep an eye on it. If you get back and the place is flooded, you'll know we've moved up on the bluff." He frowned and turned to one of the other men. "Those gents I sent up there when we got here haven't come back. Ira, go see what's keeping them. Then we need to figure out where the others went with those prisoners."

"Could be they were worried about the creek getting in here and already went up top," Ira said. "But I'll take a couple of the boys and go have a look."

"Be careful," Hudson snapped. "I can't afford to lose any more men." He finally jammed his gun back in its holster. "Lord, it seems like everything's conspiring against me right now!"

Seth wished he could believe that was true. The rising floodwaters had given him a shred of hope at last. He would have a better chance to save Charlie if they were out in the open, even in this deluge.

For the first time since the storms had started, he found himself praying that the rain would continue and the water would keep rising. . . .

Maybe the Lord would hear one last prayer from a man beyond redemption.

CHAPTER FORTY

Luke wondered if he would ever be dry again. Logically, he knew he would — if he lived through this day, that is — but at the moment it didn't much feel like it.

He waited in the rocks with the kid called Ace. Surviving as long as he had in such a dangerous profession had made Luke a good judge of character, and he instinctively liked both Jensen boys. They were raw, sure. Ace was a little too serious, and Chance was a little too cocky. But they had the makings of something; Luke's gut told him that.

Something about them was oddly familiar, too. When he looked at them, he felt like he ought to know them. But he was certain that in all his wanderings during the past twenty years, he had never run into them before.

He put those thoughts out of his mind as he spotted three more men trudging up the trail to the top of the bluff. Luke nudged Ace to alert him to the outlaws. The young man nodded to show that he had seen them, too.

This time they didn't meet the outlaws or pretend to be the sentries. Instead they remained hidden in the rocks and allowed the three men to go past them. They were about to step out and get the drop on the men when one of the outlaws looked back and yelled, "Holy cow!" He pointed across the open area in front of the cave.

Luke looked in the same direction and saw a wall of water come crashing around a bend in the creek upstream. It was a good ten feet high, and Luke knew it must have rolled for miles downstream, picking up speed as it flowed from the hills to the northwest.

When the water hit the open area, it began to spread out, but it was still deep and swift. Shouts came from below. The men in the cave must have seen the flood closing in. The three outlaws who had come up onto the bluff started back toward the trail. One of them exclaimed, "We gotta help the rest of the boys get those horses out!"

Luke leaped from concealment and smashed the butt of his rifle against the back of an outlaw's head. He and Ace had a chance to whittle down the odds against them, and Luke was going to take it. As the man he had struck collapsed like a puppet with its strings cut, Luke pivoted and lashed out again, laying the rifle's stock against the side of another man's head. As that man collapsed, too, Luke watched from the corner of his eye while Ace knocked out the third man with a sure stroke of his rifle.

"That's more like it," Luke said, and for a second Ace grinned at the praise. Then they were both serious again as Luke went on, "Let's drag them into the rocks where the others won't spot them when they come up here."

"You think they're going to abandon the cave?" Ace asked.

"That flood's not going to give them any choice," Luke said.

As Seth watched the water rushing toward the cave, he remembered what the Good Book said about floods: the Lord had promised Noah that never again would there be a flood like the one that had almost destroyed the world in the Book of Genesis. The rainbow was a symbol of that promise.

It was starting to look like this one might come close, though.

"Get the horses out of here!" Oliver Hudson shouted at his men. "Take them up on the bluff where they'll be safe!"

The outlaws rushed over to the rope corral and began throwing saddles on the horses that weren't already saddled. Even Hudson was distracted by the frenzied preparations to flee the cave before it filled with water.

Seth knew he might not ever have a better chance to make his move.

He palmed out one of the Colts as he leaped toward the man guarding Charlie. The outlaw saw him coming, yelped in alarm, and tried to claw out his own gun. He was too late. The barrel of Seth's revolver smashed against his head and sent him sprawling.

Hudson twisted around and ripped out a furious curse as Seth looped his left arm around Charlie and picked him up. Hudson's gun came out with blinding speed and hammered a shot at them.

Seth felt the wind-rip of the slug's passage next to his ear as he dashed toward Felix Dugan's horse. The animal was strong enough to carry both him and Charlie. He twisted and threw a shot back at Hudson, coming close enough to make the outlaw dive for cover behind some of the crates. Hudson fired again as Seth practically threw Charlie onto the big black horse. The bullet burned across the animal's rump, made him whinny shrilly in pain and rear up.

"Hang on, Charlie!" Seth shouted. He thumbed another shot at Hudson and saw the bullet chew splinters from the crate where his old enemy had taken cover. Hudson had to duck again.

Seth used that split-second respite to leap onto the horse behind Charlie and slam his heels against the horse's flanks. The black horse bolted toward the rain-filled entrance.

Emerging into the deluge was like riding under a waterfall. Seth had his hands full controlling the horse and hanging on to Charlie. He sent the horse lunging through six-inch-deep water toward the foot of the trail leading to the top of the bluff.

They started to climb. The trail was a slick, muddy mess, and it took a firm hand on the reins to keep the horse moving. Seth didn't look back. He knew Hudson and the rest of the gang were probably riding out of the cave by now, and he had no doubt they would pursue him. He had to give them the slip in this terrible storm.

Hudson had sent men up here to check on the sentries, Seth recalled. That meant he might run into them. He had his right arm around Charlie, and that was the hand he'd filled with a Colt. He was using his left hand on the reins.

"Grab hold of the horse's mane, Charlie!" Seth told the boy as they approached the top of the bluff. "Hang on tight! I'm liable to need both hands here in a minute!"

The horse lunged the rest of the way up the trail and came out on the level again. Seth spotted a flicker of movement in some rocks off to his right and was about to swing the gun in that direction and fire when he saw a man in a black hat and poncho stand up and wave at him.

"Head for the trees!" the man shouted. "We're friends! We'll hold off that bunch!"

Seth realized he had never seen the man before. He wasn't one of Hudson's gang. Seth had no idea who he was, but right now the fact that he wasn't a murderous outlaw was enough to make Seth trust him.

"Hold on, Charlie," he said again as he sent the horse galloping across the bluff toward a stand of live oaks.

A slender man with a mustache stepped out of the trees and waved encouragement. Seth raced past him and then drew rein as he entered the thicket. Another young man with a bandaged leg was standing with his shoulder propped against a tree trunk, holding a rifle. He grinned and called, "Take the boy and get out of here, mister."

There was a young woman here, too, a

pretty blonde. She held a pistol but didn't look like she knew how to use it. Seth didn't know how many men were hidden in the rocks, but there couldn't be more than one or two. These strangers were going to be outnumbered by Hudson's men, a gang of hardened, cold-blooded killers. They wouldn't be able to hold off the outlaws for long.

Seth leaned forward and said in the boy's ear, "Charlie, do you know your way home from here?"

"I . . . I think so."

"I hate to send you on by yourself, but I need to stay here and help these folks."

Charlie looked around at him, ashen with fear.

"I can't do that by myself, Preacher!"

"Sure you can," Seth assured him. "Just stay away from any running water. You can make it if you're careful."

"I . . . I don't know . . ."

"Your ma's waiting for you, Charlie," Seth said. "I know her. She's praying for you right now. And her prayers are going to keep you safe."

"Well . . . if you're sure . . ."

"I've never been more sure of anything in my life," Seth told him. Suddenly, he gave Charlie a fierce hug and thought about what it would have been like to have a son like this. He would never know, but this moment was as close as he would ever get so he'd have to be satisfied with it.

That thought made an unexpected feeling of peace wash through him. He kissed the top of Charlie's head and then slipped down from the horse. As he drew his second gun, he said, "Go on, Charlie. Go home."

The boy gave him a shaky nod, then kicked the horse's sides and sent it into a run. Seth watched them disappear into the storm, then turned to the strangers.

"You're Sam, I reckon?" the young man with the wounded leg said.

"I used to be. My name's Seth Barrett now."

Sam Brant was already dead. If he died here today, it would be as Seth Barrett, a man of God.

"Whatever you say, mister," the young man replied with a reckless grin. "I'm Chance Jensen. This is Will Porter and Miss Channing. My brother Ace is over there in those rocks, and so is our friend Luke."

"You know you're in for a fight," Seth said. "There are a dozen outlaws who'll come boiling up that trail any minute now."

"Let 'em come," Chance said. "We'll give them a hot lead welcome."

■ ■ ■ ■

"That was Sam Brant," Luke told Ace as they crouched behind the rocks with their rifles ready. "I recognized him from all the wanted posters I've seen of him."

"Then he's an outlaw, too. But you let him go."

Luke shrugged and said, "He had the kid with him, and from the sound of what Miss Channing told us, the boy means something to him. Otherwise Hudson wouldn't have kidnapped him and tried to use him as a hostage. We can hash that out later. I *know* Hudson and the rest of that bunch are killers. I plan to proceed accordingly."

"You mean we stop them from going after Brant and the boy."

"That's what I mean," Luke said. "And here they come now!"

The first riders appeared at the top of the trail. Luke and Ace opened fire. Accurate shooting was difficult in this downpour, but they sprayed enough lead across the trail that one of the outlaws pitched from his saddle. The others retreated, firing wildly at the rocks. Luke and Ace had to duck as slugs spanged off the boulders and ricocheted around them.

"We've got them trapped!" Ace said in the lull that followed.

"Don't you believe it," Luke told him. "Hudson's no fool. He'll find a way to flank us. Then they'll catch us in a crossfire and overrun us by sheer force of numbers."

"Sounds like we're in worse shape than I thought we were," Ace said with a frown.

"We would be if we stayed here. What we're doing, though, is giving Brant enough time to get away with that boy. Then we'll pull back and get out of here."

"Those outlaws are liable to come after us."

"If they want a running fight in weather like this, we'll oblige them," Luke said. He looked back over his shoulder. Even through the rain, he was able to see a huge, dark hump looming about a mile away. "I've even got an idea where we can make our stand."

CHAPTER FORTY-ONE

"Ever see rain like this before?" Matt asked as he and Smoke rode toward Enchanted Rock from the north.

Smoke shook his head, which made water spray around him from the brim of his hat.

"I'm not sure I have," he said, raising his voice so his brother could hear him over the storm's racket. "Sort of like riding through a river, isn't it?"

"We might as well head back to the ranch headquarters. We're not gonna be able to find anybody in weather like this!"

Smoke hated to admit defeat, but he had a hunch Matt was right. They had spent the previous day out here and hours today, and all they had done was gotten wet. They hadn't found any sign of Chet Fielding.

"This is no way to spend Christmas Eve," Matt went on.

"It won't be much of a Christmas for Mrs. Fielding if we don't find her husband,"

Smoke pointed out.

Matt looked a little crestfallen as he said, "Yeah, I know. I don't mind staying out here as long as you want, Smoke."

Smoke thought it over and then said, "We'll look a while longer."

There was stubborn, and then there was downright mule-headed, he thought. But he was going to err on the side of persistence.

After a while he pulled out his rifle, aimed it at the sky, and fired three shots, spaced out regularly one after the other. Out of habit, he replaced the rounds he had fired, and he was sliding the Winchester back in its sheath when he suddenly heard something.

The reports were faint and muffled by the rain, but they were unmistakable. Matt stiffened in his saddle just like Smoke did and exclaimed, "Those were shots, Smoke!"

"Yeah, and it sounded like they were responding to the ones I fired," Smoke agreed. He heeled his horse into motion. "Come on!"

They rode toward the huge rock, urging their mounts to a faster pace that sent drops flying as the horses splashed through standing water. After they had covered several hundred yards, Smoke reined in, pulled out the Winchester, and once again let off three rounds.

The answering shots were louder this time.

"That way!" Matt said, pointing. They rode toward a thick stand of live oaks.

The next time they heard something, it was a shout. A man limped into view, propping himself up by using the rifle he held as a crutch. He steadied himself, took off a black hat with a drooping brim, and waved it over his head.

Smoke and Matt rode up to the man, who wore a big grin on his freckled face. Smoke could see now that the man had hurt his leg somehow. Broken branches were bound to it as crude splints.

"Lord a' mercy, I'm glad to see you fellas!" the man said. "Didn't know whether I was gonna drown out here or starve to death first!"

"Chet Fielding?" Smoke asked. The man was stocky and ruggedly built, a typical Texas pioneer cattleman.

"That's right," he said. "Who might you be?"

"Smoke Jensen," Smoke said. "This is my brother Matt."

"Smoke — ! Land's sake, I didn't expect to see you, Mr. Jensen, but like I said, I'm mighty glad to. Reckon you came down to see about buyin' that ol' bull o' mine." Fielding waved the hand he wasn't using to brace himself on the rifle. "He's around somewhere. I followed him down here, don't know how come the wanderlust to get hold of him like it must've, but I was gonna haze him back closer to home when my horse dang near stepped on a rattler and spooked so bad he threw me off."

"A rattlesnake?" Matt said. "At this time of year?"

"There are a few around," Fielding said. "The ground's so wet, the water must be runnin' 'em out of their dens where they'd normally be holed up for the winter. Anyway, I busted my leg when I fell. Fixed it up best I could, but I knew I couldn't walk all the way back to the ranch on it. Dang horse ran off and I ain't seen hide nor hair of him since. I figured somebody'd come lookin' for me sooner or later, though, if the whole country didn't wash away, so I been waitin' and stayin' out of the rain as best I could."

"We figured you might need a mount, so we brought an extra with us," Smoke said. "We've got a few supplies left, too, if you're hungry."

"Gimme a knife and fork and that pesky ol' Diablo Rojo bull, and I'll show you how hungry I am!" Fielding said. Then he waved his hand again and went on, "Naw, I'm just joshin'. I'm too fond of the old boy to ever eat him. But I'm a mite peeved with him for gettin' me in this predicament."

Smoke started to swing down from his horse but paused as more shots blasted through the air. They weren't that close, but they weren't evenly spaced signal shots, either. In fact, it was an explosion of gunshots that sounded like a dozen or more weapons going off.

Smoke knew the sound of a desperate battle when he heard one, and so did Matt. They looked at each other. Matt said, "Am I crazy, or does it sound like all hell's breaking loose on top of that big rock?"

"That's what it sounds like, all right," Smoke agreed. "You know anything about that, Mr. Fielding?"

"Not a blasted thing," the rancher said, "but it sure sounds to me like somebody needs help."

"I was just thinking the same thing . . ." Smoke said.

"Well, don't hang around here!" Fielding exclaimed. He waved a hand toward Enchanted Rock. "I can tell you boys want to take cards in that game. I can wait a while longer to get rescued!"

Smoke and Matt nodded to each other,

then galloped toward the massive rock formation. With that much powder being burned close by, they had to see what it was all about.

Jensens just couldn't do anything else.

Luke had been right about Oliver Hudson being smart enough to find some other way to get at them. Only a few minutes had gone by in the standoff when bullets began zipping into the rocks from a different direction. Some of Hudson's gang had climbed up the bluff where horses couldn't go, but men could.

"Reckon we'd better get out of here," Luke had said as he ducked a slug that whipped over his head. He cupped a hand to his mouth and shouted through the rain to the trio in the live oaks, "Give us some cover!"

Chance, Porter, and Evelyn opened up with their guns, throwing as much lead as they could at the outlaws. Luke and Ace burst out of the rocks and sprinted toward the trees. They really didn't have that much ground to cover, but the dash for timber seemed a lot longer than it actually was with all that lead flying around.

Luke thought he spotted more muzzle flashes than he should have, and when he and Ace reached the trees he saw the reason why. Sam Brant was still there, joining in the fight with the others.

Luke ducked behind the tree, pressed his back against the trunk, and called, "Where's the boy, Brant?"

"I sent him home to his ma!" the outlaw replied as he fired one of his Colts toward the edge of the bluff. "Do I know you?"

"No, but I know you!" Luke said. He turned, thrust his rifle past the tree trunk, and cranked off three more rounds. "We'd better get out of here while we still can."

"Sounds like a good idea to me," Chance agreed, "but we're short one horse now."

"Evelyn can ride with me," Porter said. "My horse can carry double."

"I hope you're right, mister," Luke said, "because we don't have any time to waste. Let's go!"

Luke and Ace kept up the covering fire while the others got mounted. Then they swung up into the saddles, and they all took off at a gallop toward Enchanted Rock.

"That's mighty big to go around!" Ace called to Luke.

"We're not going around it! We're going up it!"

"Good idea!" Brant said. "I've been up

there! We can stand off an army from the top!"

From a distance, Enchanted Rock looked like a smooth dome, but as they drew closer to it, Luke saw that it was anything but. The massive hump-backed rock was littered with boulders, dotted with brush, and split by fissures. The cracks in the rock weren't deep in most places, but they were big enough to break a horse's leg and had to be avoided.

Rifle shots cracked behind the riders as they started up the slope. Bullets whined off the rocks. Luke and Ace fell back a little behind the others and twisted in their saddles to return the fire. They weren't going to hit anything from the backs of struggling horses, but maybe their shots would make the outlaws leery and cause them to hang back for a few more seconds.

Luke halfway expected their horses to collapse underneath them from the strain of climbing the rock. Somehow all the animals made it to the top with their riders.

"Here!" Brant cried. "This is as far as we can go. If we start down the far side, they'll have the high ground and be able to pick us off!"

Luke agreed. He dismounted and handed his reins to Will Porter.

"You and the lady will have to hold the

horses," he said. "Can you do that?"

"We can," Porter said. "Can't we, Evelyn?"

"Will, you wouldn't be in the middle of this mess if it weren't for me!" she said as he helped her down. "Can you ever forgive me for being so stupid?"

"There's nothing to forgive," Porter told her. "We all make mistakes about people." He looked at Luke. "We'll hold the horses, sir, don't worry."

Luke just grunted.

A little ridge of rock near the top was the only cover up here. Luke motioned Ace, Chance, and Brant over to it. The four men knelt there and reloaded their guns.

"You seem to know this part of the country, Brant," Luke said to the outlaw. "Do you think Hudson will split his forces and send some of them around behind us?"

"I don't think he can," Brant replied. "There's a creek that runs along the base of the rock in places, and it's bound to be flooded by now. I'm not sure they can get behind us with all that high water in the way."

Luke grinned tightly.

"Looks like it's gonna be a head-on fight then," he said. "A fight to the finish, more than likely."

Brant looked over at him and said, "I reckon you know me from wanted posters."

"That's right."

"You're a lawman?"

"Not exactly."

"A bounty hunter, then."

Luke shrugged.

"I don't care," Brant said. "If Charlie got back to his mother all right, that's all that matters."

"Made friends with some of the folks around here, have you?" Luke asked.

"It's a long story."

"Maybe I'll get to hear it when this is all over. Right now —" Luke brought the Winchester to his shoulder. "Here they come!"

Hudson was canny, Luke saw as he opened fire at the muzzle flashes coming from below. Instead of a foolhardy charge up the rock on horseback, the outlaws had dismounted and were using every bit of cover they could find as they advanced. They took turns dashing from boulder to boulder, from gully to clump of brush, and the ones who weren't moving kept up a steady fire toward the defenders at the top of the slope. So many bullets buzzed through the air that it sounded like someone had disturbed a hornet's nest. They

435

wouldn't be able to hold off the outlaws for long, Luke realized. When Hudson and his men reached the top, it would be a close-quarters shootout as the defenders were overrun . . . a shootout that Luke and his companions would almost certainly lose since they were outnumbered more than two to one.

The battle seemed to last a lot longer than it really did. Blood dripped from a bullet crease on Brant's cheek, and the bandage around Chance's leg was red with blood where the wound had broken open again, but other than that the four men were still unscathed. That wouldn't hold true for much longer, because the outlaws were almost right in their laps by now. One more barrage of covering fire, one more rush, and it would all be over. . . .

Luke wasn't aware that it had stopped raining until a gap suddenly appeared in the clouds overhead. Brilliant rays of sunshine slanted down and illuminated the top of Enchanted Rock. For a moment the battle paused as men squinted and let their eyes adjust to the unexpected light.

Then Hudson bellowed, "Wipe 'em out!" and guns began to roar again.

Seth didn't know what prompted him to

turn his head and look over his shoulder at that particular moment. Divine guidance, maybe. But he saw the two tall, stalwart figures striding out of the light. For a second he would have sworn he saw wings behind them, and he couldn't help but think that somehow a pair of guardian angels had found their way to the top of Enchanted Rock.

But those weren't wings. They were slickers that had been thrown back to give the two men better access to their guns, and those revolvers leaped into their hands and began to roar. He heard Luke Jensen exclaim, "How in the world — !" then Luke was up on his feet, as were Ace and Chance, and Seth joined them, the Colts roaring and leaping in his hands, and a storm of lead unlike any ever unleashed in this part of the country swept the rocks clean of evil.

Charging outlaws suddenly spun off their feet as bullets ripped through them. Others doubled over as lead punched into their guts. They fell and rolled back down the slope.

Seth found himself facing Oliver Hudson. The leader of the gang was already bloody where he had taken some hits, but he stalked inexorably toward Seth, roaring blasphemies as he triggered his guns. Seth felt the hammer-blow of a slug rock him back, but he stayed on his feet. He knew that within moments he would die, knew that his soul would plummet to the depths of the fiery pit where it belonged, but at least he would take Hudson to hell with him. Both of Seth's Colts blasted as another bullet hit him, but even as he toppled back into the waiting darkness he saw Hudson's face turn into a smear of red as the bullets bored through his diseased brain.

Seth looked up into the sun shining in his face but didn't see the brightness of the Lord's promise, didn't see the rainbow arcing across the sky as the clouds began to clear.

He saw the faces of Delta and Charlie, and that was enough to take with him as he began his descent into eternal damnation.

Let the Devil do his worst.

Seth Barrett was at peace.

CHAPTER FORTY-TWO

"He's alive," Evelyn Channing said as she looked up at the men standing anxiously around her. "But I don't know how long he'll stay that way. He was wounded several times." She paused for a second. "Do any of you have any experience at dealing with bullet wounds?"

Smoke, Matt, and Luke Jensen all nodded. So did Ace and Chance Jensen.

"Matt, give me a hand," Smoke said. "Let's get to work."

"I'll check that bunch, make sure none of them are in any shape to cause more trouble," Luke said. He looked at his brothers and shook his head. "If this doesn't beat all. You two, showing up out of nowhere on top of a big rock in the middle of Texas, just in time to help us wipe out those outlaws."

"Jensens are drawn to trouble like iron to a lodestone," Smoke said with a smile. He nodded to Ace and Chance. "Including you two. I remember you from that dust-up in Wyoming a while back. But I sure didn't expect to run into any of you when Matt and I started up that slope."

It had taken only that flash of recognition for the two of them to know which side they were on in this fight, though, Smoke reflected as he started patching up the wounded man as best he could with Matt's help. He didn't know who the hombre was, but if he was fighting side by side with Luke, Ace, and Chance, that was good enough for Smoke and Matt.

Half an hour later, they had the man's wounds roughly bandaged and the bleeding slowed down. The outlaws who were still alive were tied securely and wouldn't be going anywhere until Luke brought lawmen out here from Fredericksburg to collect them.

"We'll put this fella on a horse and see if we can't get some real help for him," Smoke said as he straightened from his task. "He needs some dry clothes and a warm bed."

"I saw a church a few miles from here," Luke said. "Reckon he can make it that far?"

"He'll have to," Smoke said.

They gathered their horses and set off, with Luke leading the procession. As they rode down from the top of Enchanted Rock,

Smoke looked out over the miles and miles of countryside spread around them. It was a spectacular vista, although a soggy one at the moment because of all the standing water that shone in the late afternoon light. The Hill Country would be weeks in drying out, but the storms finally appeared to be over. There was more blue sky overhead now than clouds.

"Christmas Eve," Matt said as he looked up, too. "Don't know that I'd call it a miracle, but after all that rain it sort of feels like one."

Smoke looked at the wounded man, who was still unconscious, as he rode in front of Ace, who held him carefully upright on the horse.

"If there's going to be a Christmas Eve miracle, that's the fella who needs it," Smoke said.

As they approached the church, Luke saw a lot of horses and wagons outside the building, as well as people milling around. The nearby creek was out of its banks, but a wall of sandbags had stopped the water from reaching the church.

He also spotted four men sitting on the muddy ground with their hands evidently tied behind their backs. Several men stood

441

nearby, holding shotguns.

A woman burst out of the crowd and ran toward them, crying, "Seth! Seth!" A boy chugged along behind her, his short legs pumping. As the woman came alongside Ace's horse, she clutched at Sam Brant's leg and asked with tears running down her face, "Is he alive?"

"Yes, ma'am," Ace said, "but he sure needs help."

"Get him down and take him in the parsonage," one of the local men said. "We'll fetch a doctor."

The Jensens, Will Porter, and Evelyn Channing remained on horseback as gentle hands carefully lowered Brant and carried him into the little house behind the church. The woman went with them, still crying as she held Brant's limp hand, but the boy stayed behind.

"Son," Luke said to him, "who is that?"

"Why, that's Mr. Seth Barrett, the preacher," the boy said. "He's our pastor here. And he's my ma's friend. Mine, too. He saved my life from those outlaws."

Luke grunted, said, "Good man, is he?"

"Mr. Barrett? Why, I reckon he's just about the best man in the whole Hill Country!"

Smoke looked over at Luke, smiled faintly,

and cocked an eyebrow. Luke just grimaced.

He caught the eye of one of the locals, nodded to the four prisoners, and asked, "What about them?"

"They were inside the church, tryin' to tear up the floor under the pulpit, when some of us got here to check on the creek. We got the drop on 'em and tried to make them tell us what in the world they were doin', but so far they won't talk."

"I reckon they will once they're locked up," Luke said. He had already recognized the men as more members of Oliver Hudson's gang. Sam Brant's gang, once. But no more. Because evidently Sam Brant was now Seth Barrett, pastor of the Enchanted Rock Baptist Church.

If Barrett lived, Luke knew he was going to have a decision to make.

Instead of the leering face of the Devil or one of his imps, which was what Seth expected, he saw another angel when he woke up.

Or rather, Delta Kennedy, but that was the same thing as far as Seth was concerned. Her eyes were red from crying, but she wore a smile and her hands were strong and warm as they gripped his hand. He drew comfort from that.

"I'm not . . . dead . . . ?" he whispered.

"No, and you're not going to be," she told him. "Not for a long time yet. You're going to be right here with me and Charlie."

Seth sighed and closed his eyes. He had never felt better in his life.

Later, when he heard music playing, he asked Delta where it was coming from.

"The church, of course," she told him. "Everyone's decided to hold a Christmas Eve prayer service. To give thanks to the Lord for getting us through that terrible storm and for bringing you and Charlie back to us. And to pray for you to recover and grow strong again."

"That's what I intend to do," Seth said. Worry still nagged at him, though. "Those men you told me about, the ones who brought me here . . ."

"Some of them are still here. The ones called Smoke and Matt said they had to go help a friend of theirs, a man named Fielding. But Luke and Ace and Chance are still here. I think Ace and Chance are over at the church, but Luke is waiting in the front room. He said he wanted to talk to you when you were strong enough."

Seth nodded. He was starting to feel a little hollow inside. For a while he had allowed himself to hope, but it looked like that dream was about to be snatched away from him again.

"You can bring him in here," he told Delta. "Wait, though . . . everything I told you earlier today . . ."

She looked at him and said, "You didn't tell me anything except that you would bring my son back to me. And you did, Seth. None of the rest of it matters."

"Yes, it does. All the things I've done —"

"That's right." She gripped his hand again. "All the things Seth Barrett has done since he became part of our lives. Those are the only things any of us around here care about."

He swallowed hard. He understood what she was trying to say. She was holding out forgiveness to him, and all he had to do was take it. He wanted to, more than he had ever wanted anything.

But Luke Jensen would be a different story.

"Tell Mr. Jensen I'll talk to him," Seth husked. "And when you go out . . . could you leave the door open, so I can hear the music better?"

"Of course. I'll open the front door, too."

Seth lay there, looking at the ceiling in the warm yellow light from the lamp on the

445

table beside the bed. The music got louder as Delta opened the doors as she had promised. Hark, the Herald Angels Sing, he thought. Beautiful.

He heard a soft footstep and looked away from the ceiling to see Luke Jensen standing beside the bed, holding his hat. Luke said, "I'm glad you're feeling better, Mr. Barrett."

Seth licked his lips and said, "You know —"

"I know there's a reward for the outlaws your deacons captured," Luke broke in. "I'm going to see to it that they collect. But all of them have already said that they're giving the money to the church." Luke smiled a little. "I'm sure you can use it to repair the damage those owlhoots did, with plenty left over to help out any of your congregation that need it."

"Yes . . . Yes, I could do that . . . if I was —"

"If you were a man of God named Seth Barrett? It's a good thing that's who you are. You see, a fine young man named Charlie told me all about you, Mr. Barrett. He said you were the best man in the Hill Country, and the more I learn about you, the more inclined I am to believe that. Charlie also said you were friends with him and his mother. I think once you're back on your feet, you ought to see about being even more than that. That boy could use a father, Seth."

"Yes," Seth whispered. "I . . . I think he could, too."

"I just wanted to check on you, see how you're doing," Luke went on. "I'll be honest with you, I'm not much of a church-goer. Haven't set foot in one more than a dozen times in as many years. But I think I'll walk on over and join the prayer service for a while. My new friends Ace and Chance are there, and Mr. Porter and Miss Channing." Luke chuckled and shook his head. "What are the odds of running into some Jensens who aren't even related to me, right in the middle of all that trouble? Well, no more than the odds of my brothers showing up like that to tip the scale in our favor, I suppose." He put his hat on and tipped it at a jaunty angle. "Jensens have a way of doing that, I guess."

With that, he lifted a hand in farewell and left the room. Delta came back in, pulled a chair over by the bed, and sat down so that she could take hold of Seth's hand again. He rested his head on the pillow and looked at her. The hymn in the church had ended and another song was playing, but not on the piano this time. Someone had brought out a guitar, and the sweet notes of "Silent Night" drifted through the darkness as the congregation sang softly.

"I . . . I don't deserve this," he said.

"None of us deserve the Lord's grace," Delta said, "but He gives it to us anyway." She leaned forward and brushed her lips over his forehead. "Merry Christmas, Seth."

He squeezed her hand, listened to the music, and drifted off to sleep, secure in the knowledge that she would be there when he awoke.

EPILOGUE

Fredericksburg, 1975

"That's a good story," the oldest of Helen's grandsons said. At twelve, he already had some of the cockiness of his rapidly approaching teenage years. "But it's crazy."

Helen frowned and asked, "What's crazy about it?"

"Okay, you've told us stories before about all those gunfighting Jensens, and it was farfetched enough when you said Smoke thought his brother Luke was killed in the Civil War and was dead for all those years, but really he was a bounty hunter and used another name until he and Smoke met up. And then that business about Luke having twin sons he didn't even know about —"

"That's the way it happened," Helen said sternly. "It's all documented. I'm not making it up."

"And nobody even *heard* of Matt starting out," the boy pressed on. He threw his

449

hands in the air in exasperation. "And what about Billy and Bobby?"

"They came later," Helen said calmly, "after Smoke and Sally had children of their own. We just haven't gotten to them yet."

The boy shook his head and was about to argue some more, but his younger sister swatted him on the arm and scolded, "Just hush, Ben. I want to hear about how Will Porter married Miss Channing and they lived happily ever after."

Helen sighed and shook her head.

"I hate to say it, but that's not the way it worked out. They never got married. Mr. Porter's undying love for her . . . well, maybe it wasn't quite as undying as he claimed. He *did* become a writer, though. Have you heard of O. Henry?"

"The candy bar?" one of the little girls asked.

"No, that was the name Mr. Porter used for the stories he wrote. He became very famous. He even wrote a story about a famous outlaw called the Cisco Kid." Helen nodded. "I like to think he was inspired some by the adventure he had with the Jensens."

"What about Ace and Chance?" one of the boys asked. "Did they ever find out that Luke was their father?"

Ben, the twelve-year-old, muttered something, but Helen ignored him.

"Of course they did, but not until a good while later. They had all sorts of adventures first. I can tell you about them . . . but not today. I think dinner's ready, and afterwards we're going to sing Christmas carols and open one present apiece." She held up a finger. "But just one. We'll open the rest in the morning . . . after Santa's been here."

"Santa Claus," Ben said. "That's about as believable as —"

The stern look that Helen directed at him made him stop talking.

"What about Preacher?" the youngest boy said as they all made their way to the dining room. "You didn't say anything about Preacher, and he's my favorite."

"Well, he wasn't there for that adventure," Helen answered. "He couldn't be everywhere you know. He's not like Santa Claus . . . although I've heard it said that he *looked* a little like Santa."

"Yeah, if Santa was dirty and wore buckskins," Ben said.

"That's just about enough out of you, young man."

"There are more stories about him, though, aren't there?" the youngest one persisted.

"Oh, my, yes. Lots and lots more stories about all of them." Helen smiled to herself, knowing that she would never live long enough to tell all the exciting tales there were about the brave men and women of the Old West named Jensen.

But there would always be someone to carry on.

ABOUT THE AUTHOR

William W. Johnstone is the *USA Today* and *New York Times* bestselling author of over 300 books, including *Preacher, The Last Mountain Man, Luke Jensen Bounty Hunter, Flintlock, Savage Texas, Matt Jensen, The Last Mountain Man; The Family Jensen, Sidewinders,* and *Shawn O'Brien Town Tamer.* His thrillers include *Phoenix Rising, Home Invasion, The Blood of Patriots, The Bleeding Edge, Suicide Mission, Stand Your Ground,* and *Tyranny.* Visit his website at www.williamjohnstone.net or by email at dogcia2006@aol.com.

Being the all-around assistant, typist, researcher, and fact checker to one of the most popular western authors of all time, **J. A. Johnstone** learned from the master, Uncle William W. Johnstone.

He began tutoring J.A. at an early age.

After-school hours were often spent retyping manuscripts or researching his massive American Western history library as well as the more modern wars and conflicts. J.A. worked hard — and learned.

"Every day with Bill was an adventure story in itself. Bill taught me all he could about the art of storytelling. *'Keep the historical facts accurate,'* he would say. *'Remember the readers, and as your grandfather once told me, I am telling you now: be the best J.A. Johnstone you can be.'* "